Find Dixie
all my best

Perfect?

Glen Ellen Alderton

Note: This is a work of fiction. Names, characters, places and incidents either are the product of the author's imagination or are used fictitiously, and any resemblance to actual persons, living or dead, business establishments, events or locales is entirely coincidental.

Published by Zailsky Associates
ISBN-10: 0615609562
ISBN-13: 978-0615609560 (Custom)

For David, who patiently read and reread the many drafts; Margo for all her editorial advice; Ellen for practical suggestions; and members of "Press and Authors" and "Creative Writers" who offered input as well as the many friends who provided encouragement.

CHAPTER 1

Pat's hand reached for her phone to push the automatic dial for Paul's office. Then, she drew it back and sat wondering—about him, about herself. Something had gone wrong, and yet when she had married him it seemed as though he was the person she had been waiting for all her life, cliché or not. Paul, with his lopsided grin, the man who murmured endearments in soft French—a kind, gentle soul who found numerous ways to please her. But of all the things he did for her, it was the poetry that was the greatest surprise. She had been astonished when she found a scrap of paper with a few lines scratched on it. "Where's this from?" she asked with avid curiosity.

Almost embarrassed, he answered. "It's just something I was playing with."

"You write poetry?"

"I dabble," he said shyly, avoiding direct eye contact.

"But this is good, Paul. It really is. Have you ever published?"

"College...a regional contest once. My English professor entered one."

"Do you have any more poems here? May I see?" she asked eagerly, thrilled at this talent her new husband possessed, as well as his uncharacteristically demure manner.

"You really want to?" Paul, usually so unruffled, seemed surprised.

"Of course. What you've written about the woman's face in the moonlight. It's beautiful."

"That's you," he said softly. "At night, when you're asleep and the moon creeps in, I've spent hours gazing at you."

Pat looked at him, unable to say anything, her breath catching at this unanticipated revelation. Holding out her arms, she pulled him to her. "No one has ever said anything like that to me."

"I've never written anything like that before. I never had a reason to."

"Thank you." She reached up and kissed him, her large brown eyes misting, but the thought that someone had written a poem about her continued to govern Pat's subconscious.

Later, she reminded Paul again that she wanted to see his other poems and finally, pulling open the bottom drawer of his desk and searching for a moment, he produced an old notebook that he handed to her. Pat sunk down into the battered blue easy chair in their little study, a homey souvenir from her beloved GG, the great grandmother for whom she'd been named—Mary Patton Lind. This was almost all that she had brought from her studio apartment when she married Paul just months before.

Holding the modest little book for a moment, she wondered at its content. It was just a spiral pad for school assignments, tattered and marred, faded beige in color. It was the sort of thing she'd used for her many classes and not what she would have expected to hold his poetry. No slender leather volume embossed with gold or silver, begging to be opened to reveal a lyrical treasure. Yet, that was what she now expected to find.

Pat was in awe of poetry. She always had been, although she'd never really thought about real people being poets. If asked to describe one, she probably would have visualized an aesthetic-looking individual sitting under an appropriately romantic weeping willow gazing out at the surrounding beauties of nature perhaps through a soft mist. Or instead, an intense, tortured being with haunted eyes hunched over a candle-lit desk late at night, frantically scrolling away with a quill pen. Paul, although attractive, was just too healthy to appear like the pallid, vinegar-drinking Victorian romantics and his beautiful green eyes were far from haunted. Quill pens were also out—another sentimental notion of the past. No, computers were more his métier or at least a trusty #2 pencil. Nor would he have been caught dead with long hair, a voluminous velvet cape, or the other theatrical trappings that she envisioned a poet wearing.

That thought was quickly reinforced as she opened the notebook and saw the hand-scrawled verses with notes scribbled in the margins and words crossed out and reworked repeatedly. Instead, she now saw him, the real Paul, chewing on that pencil, struggling to find the appropriate word or phrase. No, Paul wouldn't chew on a pencil, not even as a tiny schoolboy; he was too self-possessed. He would, though, have been suitably pensive. Her husband was a very thoughtful man, which had no doubt contributed to his professional success.

Paul had turned away and walked over to the window to stand and watch traffic on the side street below. Outwardly calm, he realized how much he feared her reaction, almost as much as he wanted it. He'd never shown the book to anyone before. Meanwhile, Pat sat quietly, reading and re-reading his penciled verses. When she finally finished, she looked up and stared at him contemplatively, not yet able to form the words. Eventually he turned from the window and stared back at her, still inwardly tense, saying nothing. At last she spoke, "They're beautiful... especially that one about the wolf caged in the zoo, pacing, haunted. But they're so sad, and so many deal with death. The one you were writing about me, that's different."

A radiant smile crossed her husband's face, lighting up his expressive eyes. "Things are different since I met you," he said simply. "Those were written a long time ago. I haven't done any for years."

"You must have been very unhappy then," she replied, half inquiring. There was so much she still didn't know about this man she'd wed—a man she had met less than a year before.

"Possibly. I don't know. They just were things I was thinking then—adolescence. Kids are always emotional," he said, striving to be nonchalant. "I told you I haven't written anything for a long time. I guess I didn't need to."

"And you do now?"

"Maybe," he smiled, pleased and relieved at her

reaction. To him, part of his new bride's appeal was her nimble mind, which in contrast to her size, was far from small. "Maybe not. It was just a thought."

"You've got talent, real talent," Pat said earnestly.

"So I can starve in a garret?" Paul laughed, making an effort to dispel the seriousness of their conversation. Even though he hadn't written for years, poetry for him was a significant matter, but he couldn't tell her that, not yet. It had been his mental salvation in adolescence, a secret deeply guarded from his peers. They would have tormented him endlessly if they'd discovered his way to escape. When he finally managed to escape for real, he had filed this secret carefully away, able to find other outlets for his frustrations and problems. "They're words, sweetheart, just words."

"The ones you were writing for me were truly beautiful. Thank you."

"You're beautiful. I love you. I was just trying to think of another way to say it." And maybe that's why he had started writing again, he suddenly realized. Not seeking escape this time but having to address another emotion, one he had feared he would never experience.

"I wish I had a beautiful way to say that to you."

"Oh you do, you definitely do. You say it the most beautiful way a person can." He came over and leaned down to tenderly squeeze her tiny hand before momentarily pressing it to his lips. "Your kind, eloquent eyes tell me when you look at me and your gentle hands when you touch me. I know it when you kiss me and hold me. Your whole body tells me, sugar."

"Good," Pat replied satisfied. "You do the same for me, but I still wish I had the words or something better."

"They're not needed, but maybe someday you will. For now, I like the ways you tell me."

Pat thought about what her husband had said and also, about the fact that during times when she was asleep, completely exposed and totally vulnerable, that Paul would lie there quietly and look at her. "I still can't believe you watch me as I sleep."

"You look at me when I'm unaware, don't you? I thought that was part of being married, that we watched, observed, got to know each other—that that was part of cherishing, not voyeurism. Besides, aren't I supposed to be there as your protector, at least symbolically."

"I hadn't really considered that," she replied, but she realized that of course he was right. Even though there were mere months between them in age, he seemed so much older at times. Yet at others, it was his boyish enthusiasm that was so appealing.

It was therefore with no surprise that Pat awoke early one morning a few weeks later and saw that Paul was already awake. He was resting on his side, staring at her, a solemn, contemplative, almost distant expression on his strong, lean face. She started to smile, but when he didn't respond, she was baffled and she felt her smile slip away.

Stretching out her arms, she moved toward him to reassure herself, almost wondering if he would let her touch him. He rolled over into her welcoming grasp but the quiet, detached look remained on his face. Then rising above her, he gazed down for a moment and she stared back uncertainly. There was clearly sexual tension between the two of them but he made no effort to kiss or caress her even though she could feel that his body was hardening. All of a sudden, swiftly, almost brutally, he entered her and started making savage, demanding love. Love, she thought shocked, is this love? Still, she was responding, surprised at the stark harshness but excited by the act. It wasn't violent, but it wasn't the wooing or gentle seduction she'd learned to expect from her husband. No, this wasn't the man who had proved to be such an innovative and sensitive lover.

Then suddenly, Paul, this fiercely aggressive Paul, stopped. He surveyed her again intently almost analytically— his eyes puzzled—before once more thrusting deeply into her until at last she felt her orgasm began. Immediately, he joined her and then his physical release effected, rolled off.

Again, Pat started to reach for him to snuggle as they always did, but to her surprise, he sat up abruptly, his long, muscular legs dangling over the side of the bed. Silently, he remained there a moment, staring at the adjacent blank wall as though there were something fascinating to behold. Then without a word, he got up and walked into the bathroom. Shutting the door, he started a shower and she lay back on the bed utterly astounded. She didn't know what to say—something quite uncharacteristic on her part.

What had just occurred? What could be the matter? Never had anything like this happened during the time they had known each other—granted, that time was short, and only the few months as newlyweds. Her husband was one of the most considerate men she'd ever met. Lovemaking with him had been sweet and satisfying but never anything like this. Teasing and laughing had been their pattern with that added comfort of cuddling afterwards. Yet just now it was as though a perfect stranger had been in their bed and had taken her indifferently, with great callousness.

Pat started to say something when Paul came out of the bathroom, but he brushed by her, the vacant look remaining on his face. Shutting her mouth in amazement, Pat watched as he walked to his closet, pulled out some clothes, and then walked back into the bathroom to dress. It was as though he were totally alone. Within minutes, he had left the room and she heard him go downstairs, open the front door and leave. The silence of his departure upset her even further. Bemused, Pat got up and began to prepare for her day.

It was a long and disturbed day. On the subway into work, she was oblivious to the jostling and swaying of the packed car, usually an irritation during her morning commute. She didn't even notice one of her fellow workers who rushed up to join her once they'd detrained, chiding humorously, "Honest to God, Pat. I tried to get your attention a half dozen times. Where were you? Cloud Nine?"

"I should be so lucky," she murmured tersely without any of her usual cheerful chatter. After another aborted attempt at conversation, her companion became silent and the two made their way to the top floor of the new building of the Department of Agriculture. Calling the building 'new' was a misnomer for the well-preserved edifice constructed in the 1930s. It had been the largest Federal office building—a title lost the following decade when the Pentagon was built. Although less opulent than its neighbor, Old Ag, it still reflected a period when even government cubicles were expected to have crafted woodwork and bathrooms boasted marble floors—all of which Pat ordinarily appreciated. This morning, she might as well be entering one of the cheaply partitioned crannies into which most of her bureaucratic counterparts were located. Parting at their respective doors, her friend looked at her puzzled as Pat entered her office without a remark.

The rest of the day at work Pat kept to herself, and more than once, wondered why she hadn't said something to Paul this morning. She hadn't been afraid she realized—not really, but it had all been so peculiar. She'd just been disoriented, almost mesmerized by the whole experience.

When she got home that night, the tiny red light was blinking on the answering machine. The message was short. It was Paul's voice, emotionless, "I'll be delayed so don't bother to wait up."

But Pat did of course as she sat in front of the TV not comprehending what she was watching nor knowing what she had eaten. When she finally bothered to look down to scrutinize the mystery meal, she saw it was a half-finished microwave dinner of fried chicken—nasty fare that ordinarily she never selected and certainly would never have purchased. She supposed it was something that Paul had tossed into the freezer predating their marriage. Clearly she hadn't been too observant when she pulled it out; excavating the freezer to get rid of outdated produce was definitely a new item for her 'to do' list. Then realizing that she had been dozing and that it was now after 11:00, Pat got up and made her way to the bedroom. There she tossed and turned for another hour before she finally fell asleep, at last escaping her agitated thoughts.

Sometime in the middle of the night, she again awoke and saw by the moonlight filtering through the partially open blinds that her husband was lying in bed, his long, lanky body turned to the wall. No poetic thoughts ran through her mind when she looked at him. He seemed very silent and she wondered if he were really asleep. This time she didn't reach out to him and just lay there, perplexed and uneasy, until she once more drifted back to sleep.

When the alarm went off, Pat rolled over to confront Paul, but he was gone. Stretching out her hand, she let her fingers run across his side of the bed, cold now with no sign that he had been present. There were no sounds from other parts of the house and once again the silence seemed unnerving, eerie compared to the comfortable hominess she was used to. Theirs was ordinarily a cheerful household despite harried mornings getting ready for work, usually on her part, since Paul always seemed to be prepared.

Shaking her head at such an odd reaction to finding herself alone, Pat got up and walked into the bathroom. A towel was damp, so was his toothbrush, the only indications that her habitually neat husband had used the room. Clearly Paul had risen and left again without saying anything. And with him had gone the pleasant chit chat, his happy whistling, last minute comments, and the hug or kiss they usually shared when leaving for work.

Gone too was the generally good start she had come to expect to her day, and this day dismally went much as the one before. She went to work, did her tasks efficiently but without enthusiasm, and was uncharacteristically quiet once again. Her officemates noticed, but she brushed off their questions by just responding she was feeling a bit out of sorts—which she was.

Throughout the long hours, she thought repeatedly of calling Paul, her fingers fidgeting to press the automatic dial, but something held her back. Just two days ago, she would have said she knew everything about her attractive husband. She had been the envy of her female friends after her whirlwind romance and marriage to the amusing, successful young lawyer. Now, she wasn't so sure.

CHAPTER 2

Pat met Paul one weekend early in December up in the mountains of Pennsylvania. She had gone to ski with a friend on a special, winter package at a hotel resort. It was her first attempt at the sport, despite a Minnesota background, and she'd been pleased to progress from the bunny slope to intermediate within a day. At the same time, she soon decided that cross country probably was more her style, especially when she looked at the more difficult runs. She'd always been a bit leery of heights. Still, it was a sport she thought she might continue to pursue.

That night, Pat felt she had returned to her childhood as she slid out on the resort's frozen pond in a pair of skates. The night was crisp and the ice mirror smooth. Holiday guests from the adjacent lodge glided in tandem with their partners to the music—a medley of popular Christmas tunes. Strings of multi-colored lights were hanging from the surrounding evergreens and it was a festive scene, reminding her of an illustration from a children's book. Pat's imagination had been working overtime again and she was sure with a change in dress, the skaters would have made suitable models for a Currier and Ives holiday card.

She was sprinting across the ice, twisting and twirling—remembering the nights she used to go to her Twin Cities school yard as a child and skate with her friends. Then she met Paul. Unfortunately, their meeting took place accompanied by a huge collision, knocking her topsy-turvy and sending her sliding across the ice most ungraciously on her butt. That definitely was not part of the hotel's image on how to meet an attractive member of the opposite sex, which was what the winter resort had been pushing in all its PR materials. Pat finally came to an abrupt halt and looked up, slightly dazed. Skidding to a stop, ice slivers scattering and twinkling in the Christmas lights, was a young man in a bright blue ski sweater. Well at least that part fit the romantic image.

Anxiously, in a soft, slightly southern drawl, he inquired, "Are you all right? I didn't even see you."

Mortified by the mishap, Pat tried to brush if off, "I'm fine. Really." But as she attempted to stand from the ice, she felt a sharp pain in her ankle. Solicitously, her rescuer—or perhaps the accident's perpetrator—helped her up and steering her on one skate, slowly propelled her back to the edge of the rink. There he left her on one of the benches while he went off to find her boots. Pat recalled that instead of thanks, her first words as she stood up were, "Clumsy oaf. There goes the skiing." Then realizing the attractive stranger probably thought she meant him, she flushed and apologized. "I'm the oaf, that is. I thought I was still a skating champ."

Laughing, he assured her that he might have been just as guilty of stumbling into her. "Were you a skating champ? I didn't get to see your routine before we ran into each other."

"Some routine but I guess I'm lucky," Pat conceded, resigned to the fact that the athletic portion of her holiday was over, not that so far there had been any other part. "I thought if I got hurt it would have been skiing but I grew up skating! I guess I just wasn't looking where I was going and was showing off. I'm sorry I bumped into you."

"No problem. I'm sorry you got hurt. Do you have friends out here? Someone to help you to the lodge?" the man asked, concerned.

Later, when she knew him, Pat teased that the only reason he'd stayed to help her was because he was worried about a law suit. "Hell," Paul had responded cheekily, "in a minute I would have had ten witnesses swearing that you were the one who knocked me over, an ambulance taking me away, and I'd have gotten half your salary for life."

"You've gotten it now," Pat had countered before bursting into laughter.

"But it's much more fun this way as your lawfully dearly beloved," he'd grinned.

A smile came to Pat's lips as she recalled the rest of

their first meeting. As Paul sat next to her she had told him about her weekend. "No, the friend I came with is a skier only and she wasn't interested in skating out here tonight. She's probably at the bar now, scoping out the scene." Oops, Pat thought, realizing she and her friend now sounded like man-hunters.

The man laughed again, a pleasant, genuine sound. "My friend's probably right there with her. But I hadn't been on skates for years, and I really don't enjoy hanging around bars all that much. Let me take you back to the resort. Maybe you should see a doctor."

"No, it's just a sprain. I've had lots," she admitted ruefully, sounding resigned. "I guess I'm not exactly a prize athlete any more, if I ever really was."

"Me neither," he said self-depreciatory. To her eyes though, he had the rangy good looks of someone who spends a lot of time outdoors—someone who fit the resort's publicity profile. He had to be almost six feet, lean with broad shoulders, and attractive in a rather craggy way. The nose was too prominent for him to be really handsome. It was slightly curved, kind of like one of those seen in pictures of desert sheiks. The lines of his face were strong too. His hair was a thick, straight dark brown and he had the most fantastic green eyes she had ever seen. He also had a lovely smile, revealing brilliant white teeth. It softened his face and made him look extremely young and sweet.

Pat noted all this at rink side, while he gently removed her skates and then placed her feet into her snow boots. His grip as he helped her up from the bench was firm and he was especially careful as he supported her weight while she slowly hobbled back to the hotel. "You're sure about not wanting to see a doctor?" he asked en route, clearly concerned as he observed her hesitant, painful progress.

"Positive," she declared, forcing herself to sound casual, to deny the throbbing pain. "If you can just get me up to my room, I'll order some ice and get in bed." The ankle really hurt. She'd been a fool to walk on it, but she didn't intend to wimp out now. Instead, she just leaned on him harder and clinched her teeth.

"Not exactly the best way to spend a holiday," he continued. "I truly am sorry."

"Hey, I told you it probably was my own fault. I shouldn't have pretended I was in the Olympics." When they reached the door of her room, she stuck out her hand, and thanked him politely. All she wanted to do now was collapse and lick her wounds. "Thanks again for your help. My girlfriend will be up in a little while so I should be okay from here on." At least she hoped that was the case, if Betty didn't drift into someone else's room. With Betty, one never knew. She was constantly on the prowl for men, which could make traveling with her quite an experience.

The next morning Pat awoke to discover that Betty still had not returned, unsurprisingly. Pat's night had been far from comfortable. The sprain was worse than she expected and she had been awakened several times by her throbbing feverish foot. Even ice packs proved useless. Fortunately she had brought aspirin and probably was in danger of losing her stomach lining, considering she'd been consuming them like popcorn. She was thinking about calling down for something stronger along with coffee, when there was a knock on the door.

Extricating herself from the twisted bedcovers, she grabbed her robe and hobbled painfully to the door. Unlocking and pulling it open a crack, she saw a waiter with an oval tray holding a small silver pitcher, cup and saucer, and a plate of croissants. Balanced amid the dishes were a crystal vase with three red roses and a minuscule package with a matching bow. "I didn't order this," Pat snapped, annoyed that she'd gotten up for someone else's error.

"This is room 222, isn't it?" the overly cheerful and pimpled youth inquired.

"Well, yes," she admitted rather ungraciously, still grumpy from having to limp across the room.

"Then this is where it belongs." Stepping jauntily into the room as if he was God's gift to women, the young man placed the tray on a small table by the bed. "Some guy said you'd hurt your foot and probably would need something to eat."

"Am I supposed to sign a bill?" she asked, thoroughly perplexed.

"Naw, he took care of everything—nice tip too." Then with a grin, the cocky young waiter winked and left.

Still annoyed at having to get up, but also mystified, Pat stared at the tray as she sunk back into her bed. Propping her foot back up on a pillow, she picked up the pitcher and took a sniff: hot chocolate. Carefully, she poured some into the china cup and took a sip. Rich and creamy, the chocolate was delicious, in fact she hadn't had any this good for years. Her mother used to serve exceptional cocoa like this when she and a gang of friends came in from sliding and skating on a cold winter day and suddenly Pat felt a different kind of warmth from the memory.

Then she reached for the package. After unwrapping it, she saw it was a small jewelry box. Nestled inside was a pair of gold earrings in the shape of tiny ice skates. They were accompanied by a card, which read: *My sincere apologies and best wishes for a speedy recovery, Paul M.* Flipping the card over, she saw that on the other side it was a business card for Paul W. Martin, Attorney-at-law. Lightly brushing the embossed lettering with her fingertips, she read the name of his firm, located in Washington, D.C.

This was certainly classy, Pat decided, but then he'd seemed a classy guy. Soft-spoken, polite, intelligent—no, she wasn't surprised that this Paul Martin was an attorney. She leaned over and smelled the roses, which gave off a sweet fragrance as though just picked. She could thank the man or she could ignore his offerings. No obligations on her part. She thought for a moment and then courtesy triumphed. Picking up the telephone, she asked to be connected to Mr. Martin's room. "I'm sorry," responded the operator, "Mr. Martin checked out this morning."

Well that definitely puts it in my court, Pat reflected. She knew who he was and where he worked, but he had no idea of who she was. Mr. Martin of Washington, D.C. She had never told him she was from there too. They never even exchanged names. Pat wondered if she should contact him when she got back to D.C.

Suddenly, the door to the room burst open and Betty bounced in, blonde hair tousled and face flushed, but looking none the worse for wear, although it was obvious that she had been having an active time. Pat was willing to bet there was someone waking up somewhere in the lodge, wondering where the pretty blonde he had picked up last night had disappeared to. Betty clearly was never going to grow up or at least progress beyond a teenager in heat.

"My God, where were you last night?" Betty exclaimed loudly. "I met the most gorgeous man and he had friends too!" Then suddenly noticing Pat's propped foot, she squealed, "Jesus, what happened to you?"

"I took a tumble at the skating ring and twisted my ankle."

"No skiing today?"

"No skiing period. I guess I'm just lucky this is our last day."

"I certainly can't say the same. God, I wish we'd just gotten here. Georgie is absolutely gorgeous but damn if he isn't from New York," Betty called over her shoulder as she swept into the bathroom.

"That's only a few hours by train," Pat replied, knowing full well that if he were like Betty's usual conquests he might as well be from the jungles of Brazil or the icy steppes of Siberia. This episode would be brief, hotly carnal, and over soon. Betty would remain in love until her next encounter, which would run the same course. Pat had once tried to talk to her friend about her roller-coaster love life, but it was clear that for Betty, life was meant to be lived for the moment. She was a throwback to the free love of the '60s and '70s. Even in looks, she reminded Pat of an ersatz Marilyn Monroe.

Still, Betty was fun, kind, and usually considerate, and as a result, they had become friends. She also was amazingly intelligent—a multi-degreed natural resources specialist respected for her work. Yet despite the impressive credentials, Betty sometimes lacked just basic common sense.

Pat and Betty had met at the Department's Health Club during Pat's first year in D.C., and they had developed an easy-going, casual friendship over the years despite their different outlooks on life. Still Pat was fairly certain that in a real pinch, Betty would be there to help. Moreover, her friend was an amusing luncheon companion, someone with whom to catch a film, and an occasional fellow traveler to places like New York or Orlando or even a skiing holiday in Pennsylvania, provided Betty was between men.

"That's true. New York is only a few hours. We'll just have to see how today goes," bubbled Betty, now stripped and ready for a shower, her voluminous hair confined in the flimsy plastic cap provided by the hotel. Peeking out of the bathroom door, she belatedly inquired with guilty chagrin, "Is there anything you need? My God, they even send up flowers. I didn't know this place was so ritzy."

Trying to decide whether or not to correct Betty's assumption, Pat chose not to. "Probably just a consolation prize to the wounded warriors. Are you going out on the slopes?"

"Of course," Betty said. "As soon as I get cleaned up and changed. I've got to meet Georgie in fifteen minutes and he's going to give me some lessons." What kind of lessons, Pat thought a bit meanly, wondering if the couple would even reach the slopes. She was still annoyed that her own stupid mishap would leave her holed up in the lodge for the rest of the trip.

"Georgie skis all the time. Are you sure you're going to be ok?" Betty dutifully added.

"No problem. I've got a couple of mysteries in my bag and I'm sure I can hobble down to the lobby later. I doubt that I'm the only walking wounded around here. I'll find someone to talk to and see if they have other activities available." Or, there's always room service, she reflected, wondering if indeed she was up to hobbling around. Good thing she had crammed the Elizabeth Peters and John Sandford in her backpack at the last moment—nothing like a little diverting suspense while safe in bed.

"You can say that again," Betty enthused, and then embarrassed, added, "at least about the wounded. They were bringing in someone from the slopes this morning when I was downstairs waiting for the elevator. From the look of him, he won't be doing any hobbling for several weeks. Anyhow, if you're sure you're ok..." Betty looked at her apprehensively and Pat had to smile again, knowing that it wasn't her state of health that was bothering her friend but rather the fact that Pat might need her attention.

"I'm positive. Enjoy Mr. Gorgeous, but I'll see you again today, right? And we'll be checked out of here first thing tomorrow? You're going to have to do all the driving back, I guess."

"No problem. I'll come back this afternoon to pack up...I..."

"You'll probably not be here tonight. I already figured that out, Betty," Pat said smiling. The fact her friend had even slept in their room two nights during their stay had been the real surprise.

"You're sure?"

"We're big girls, remember? Have fun." It was obvious that Betty intended to waste no time in getting back to Gorgeous George, and then Pat giggled to herself, remembering an autographed photo her grandma Mary Patton had once had of a wrestler with that same name—a bulky blustering man with a massive mop of curly blond hair. Her great grandmother had loved the early flamboyant stars of the theatrical sport. The old lady especially enjoyed watching George's valet spray the ring with perfume, and swore she'd voted for the man when he ran for president in the 1950s. Pat, as she got older, assumed her grandma was teasing, but with the elder Mary Patton, one never knew. Then again, a professional wrestler had done all right as a politician in her home state years later.

Anyhow, surely Betty's George didn't resemble

Gorgeous George—although Pat would have loved to see for herself! Betty, meanwhile, puzzled at Pat's continued bursts of giggles popped her head around the door, than stepped back into the bathroom, which was fine with Pat. Her own hands were busily toying with the tiny skates, which twinkled in the sunshine now pouring through the window. Paul W. Martin, wonder what the W stands for, she mused. William? Wyatt? Walter? And, would she contact him when she got back to D.C.? Now that was the big question!

Her mother had brought her up to be courteous, and supposedly mother knows best, so a call back would be the polite thing to do. Plus gold earrings and red roses in a real crystal vase—she had plunked it just to test it—that definitely showed class. The only nice jewelry Pat had ever received from men was a high school graduation bracelet from her dad and a chain from her brother on her twenty-first birthday. The men she met didn't usually give her jewelry, not that she was in the habit of accepting expensive gifts. But he was a lawyer, and lawyers were rich, weren't they? She had actually thought the breakfast and hot chocolate was the nicest part of his gift—both thoughtful and romantic. The man was attractive too, with his lean looks and smile that almost seemed waggish. She hadn't met that many intriguing men lately. But was she ready to meet someone new?

To be honest, her social life in D.C. hadn't been very exciting recently, although she had her girlfriends and a few guys she saw sporadically. Calling Mr. Martin was definitely something to consider.

Pat was still indecisive about what to do when she hobbled into work after the weekend. Of course there was the usual round of teasing from her co-workers about her injuries, especially when they discovered it was skating and not skiing that had done her in. Odd that skiing would have evoked sympathy, like earning a purple heart for the valorous wound, whereas landing on her rear end while skating was considered a joke.

"Way to go, Strom," said her friend Todd. "Did you

think you were the next Michelle Kwan? I thought all you Nordskis skated to school in that God-forsaken state you come from."

"Cool it or I'll get a spear out of the igloo and sic the sled dogs on you."

Todd snickered. With a name like Matsen, he should talk, but his Midwestern family had kept mushing until they ended up in Washington State. A fellow economist, he was someone Pat might have considered dating if they weren't working together in the same office. He apparently had had similar thoughts until snagged by Penelope, a pretty secretary two sections down. Yet, their friendship had strengthened once the question of a potential relationship had disappeared. Within the office, Todd was her closest confidante.

Still during the years they had been working together, Pat had wondered more than once if she had made an error in rejecting Todd's tentative advances when they first met as young interns. Tall and blond, he definitely was a Nordic hunk and his good humor was catching. Still, it would have been awkward if things had gone wrong, and Pat had just escaped another painful relationship.

Most of the men Pat had dated in the last few years she had met through a work contact or friends. This Paul W. Martin was an unknown, who had made a first good impression but still did she need to take a chance? She had already had one awful experience, not long after she moved to D.C. She had noticed the movie-star handsome co-rider on the subway when he inadvertently, or so she thought, pushed into her getting on at the Foggy Bottom stop. The man continued beyond her Smithsonian stop and over the next few weeks, they saw each other several times again on the train. A smile turned into a shared seat, then a few short conversations. Pat finally agreed to meet him for a drink after work one evening, where he matched her one drink with several, becoming louder and more aggressive as the night went on. She felt lucky to escape his clutches by sneaking out through the bar's back entrance and catching a cab home. It had been a nasty episode.

The next few times she had seen the man while riding to the office, he'd refused to leave her alone, saying obnoxious things on the subway and making it hard for her to get off at her stop. Although she was afraid she was overreacting, she worried she might have attracted a stalker. Fortunately she was able to change her work schedule and avoid bumping into him thereafter, but it had been an unnerving situation that left Pat stressed for weeks.

Paul W. Martin, Attorney-at-law, had seemed normal during their first meeting, but then so had her subway nemesis, as she had come to refer to him. While Pat was deciding what to do, she found herself wearing the tiny gold skates almost daily. On Friday, Pat made her decision. Picking up her phone, she dialed Paul Martin's law office. The answering secretary with the crisp voice one might expect from an important legal firm informed her that "Mr. Martin is not in and is not expected until next week. Do you wish to leave a message?"

"Just tell him that Pat Strom called to thank him for the flowers and gift and that her ankle is fine."

"Do you want to leave a number, Ms. Strom?"

"No, that's ok, thanks," Pat replied and she hung up. Well, she'd done the proper thing and thanked him. Mother would be proud. If Paul Martin had been there and they'd spoken, who knew what might have happened? But he wasn't, and that was the end of the story, as far as she was concerned.

It was therefore with utter amazement that she picked up her phone at home one night the next week and heard his voice. "You're certain the ankle's fine? I don't need to worry about any sleazy lawyers coming after me?" His slight southern accent was immediately identifiable.

"Paul? Mr. Martin? How did you find me?"

"After getting your message, I had my secretary call the resort and mention there'd been an accident the weekend before last and that my client wanted to contact a witness, who had been staying in your room. It's amazing how helpful a place like that can be when they're worried about a possible lawsuit."

"Is that kosher?" Pat asked laughing.

"No, and probably not ethical either," he chuckled in turn, "but it worked. Anyhow, I got a choice of one Betty Perry or a Mary P. Strom. I knew by then you weren't the blonde Betty in the room. She apparently made quite an impression on the desk clerk; but you didn't seem a Mary either. Pat?"

"Short for Mary Patton, my great grandmother—who was also short like me."

Amused, he countered, "Well, fortunately the clerk also remembered that it was the petite, not short, Ms. Strom who was limping. Anyhow, I was hoping you'd call but when you did, I didn't think you'd neglect to leave a phone number. I really didn't want to call every Strom within the greater D.C. area."

"How did you know I was from here in the first place?"

"I found out after I'd taken you to your room that night. Amazing what twenty bucks will do to encourage a desk clerk, although he wouldn't reveal more than where you and your friend were from."

"Ah...an innovative man."

"God helps him who helps himself, as my grandmother always said." Mine too, thought Pat. "How's the ankle really, or is there a lawsuit in my future?"

"I admitted I was probably at fault, counselor."

"Not wise to confess so readily. Obviously you do need legal advice but I'm glad." His voice was relaxed, pleasant. Then suddenly he cut to the chase, "May I see you sometime?"

She smiled to herself. "You'd like to?"

"Of course. You don't think I would have gone to all this effort otherwise? The flowers and breakfast, since I was sorry about the accident, but I certainly wouldn't have spent all this time trying to track you down."

Pat was pleasantly surprised at his candor. "You've convinced me. But nothing athletic, ok?"

"No ice hockey, mountain climbing, sky diving?"

"No dancing, long walks...at least not for the next month or so."

"Too bad, I like long walks but I get the picture...how about that?"

"That?" She asked, puzzled.

"A picture—dinner and a movie."

"That sounds nice."

"Good. Are you free this weekend?"

Do I play hard to get, Pat wondered and then she realized that she didn't want to. "This weekend would be fine," she answered. "Saturday?"

"Sounds good to me. I see from the information we got that you live in Rosslyn."

"Well, your secretary was certainly thorough." Pat wasn't sure if she was at ease with him knowing where she lived, even though she had just been about to suggest a theatre around the corner from her house.

"I told you. Resorts don't need lawsuits. So, how about 6:00 and we can have an early dinner and hit a film after, if that's all right with you." It was... and of course that was how it all started.

CHAPTER 3

Yes, Pat thought despondently, that was how it all started but throughout the excruciatingly long day at work, she continued to wonder where it would end. Not a clock watcher by nature, she found herself glancing at one every few minutes and being continually surprised that so little time could have passed. It was one of the longest and most painful days she had ever experienced, intensified by the exasperation she felt in not knowing what to do. She wasn't usually an indecisive individual, but she'd never found herself in a situation like this.

Early that evening, Pat got home from work, surprised that she had arrived. It must have been by magic since she had been oblivious to the metro. In fact, she'd been so lost in her thoughts that she'd almost missed her stop. There were no messages on the machine and Paul wasn't there.

Sitting down, she tried to decide what to do. Should she just go on as though nothing had happened? What else could she do? Rant and rave? To whom—Paul wasn't even around to hear her out. To her friends—but what could she tell them? That she woke up the other morning and there was a changeling in bed and she didn't know what had happened to her husband Paul?

Changeling? She was supposed to be the changeling in the family—a constant razz by her siblings over her diminutive size and dark coloring compared to their large, blond Scandinavian handsomeness. Yes, she'd been the recipient of Mary Patton's genetic contribution to the otherwise Nordic brood—that tiny, half English half Scottish interloper amid the giant Viking horde.

How wrong they'd been. It was Paul who fit this role of the changeling and that realization pained Pat. It wasn't as though he'd hurt her, physically, but emotionally? She felt battered and bruised.

Flinging her briefcase across the room, Pat ran up the

stairs, and slipped out of her suit. Grabbing the black and gold T-shirt, distinctive of the University of Wisconsin's Milwaukee campus, from her bureau drawer, she pulled it on and got into a pair of faded, old jeans. Comfort—that was what she needed. A quick glance in the mirror and she felt as though she had been transported back to her grad school days, another time when she was in a quandary about her life. But that was then... Paul was today... she hoped. But some important things had to be worked out.

"Go, Go Panthers," Pat murmured and whistling *On Wisconsin* with false bravado as she went down the stairs. Entering the kitchen, she opened the refrigerator. "Dinner for two, Madame, or one?" she asked herself. Hell, comfort was the order of the day. Perhaps spaghetti? She opened a container of left-over hamburger, sniffed, and decided if she cooked it long enough she should survive any *E.coli* or whatever else was the current culinary danger.

So many dangers nowadays, she mused. Had her parents had those worries? Certainly not terrorism or drugs or the crime rates D.C. faced now, but her mother had been a child during the beginning of the nuclear age. She probably had had nightmares about mushroom clouds and glowing in the dark. Those were the days when they made the little school kids duck under a desk and cover the backs of their necks with their hands. The theory, Pat supposed, was that that would protect them from the atomic blast. Pat had laughed when she heard that one. Her mother though hadn't been amused. No wonder Mom had always disapproved of all those hokey Japanese science fiction films about radioactive mutants and wouldn't even go to see the *Planet of the Apes* series.

Nora Strom would have also worried about catching polio. Hadn't one of her grammar school classmates died from it and another ended up in braces?

To Pat's generation, braces were used to straighten teeth or hold up trousers, particularly bright red ones like the suspenders she had once worn in a dance recital in middle school and which Paul occasionally sported even today. A bit of hidden frivolity beneath his well-tailored but usually staid and conservative suit coats, so appropriate for an escalating lawyer.

"The superman syndrome," he'd quipped when first she'd seen and commented upon the garish item one morning as he was dressing.

"Clown, you mean," she'd retorted, grabbing and snapping them at him, which had led to more horseplay and a happy romp in bed with him scolding her, although not too seriously, for making him send his now rumpled trousers back to the cleaners.

At present, nothing seemed too funny and it was obvious that Paul disguised more than red suspenders. Now, she could readily empathize with her mother's pessimism. Since yesterday, she felt like she was living in some alternate world herself. Life was always full of uncertainties—like meeting and marrying a stranger who turned out to be somewhat stranger than expected.

Well at least she could make a decision about dinner—spaghetti and calories be damned. She could take out her frustration by chopping vegetables to add and if Paul or whoever her husband was tonight deigned to show up, there'd be plenty to eat and if not, she could always freeze part for another night. At this point she would have liked to freeze the last two days—wrap them up neatly in aluminum foil, put them in the deep fridge and forget all about them like some of the putrid microwave dinners predating their marriage.

Starting the meat simmering, Pat returned to the fridge. Taking out the vidalias, celery, green pepper and fresh mushrooms—nonradioactive of course so she wouldn't turn into a mushroom person like one of the Japanese horror films, she carefully washed and spread them out before her on the wooden cutting board. As she started chopping, she began to cry. She was ready to blame it on the onions, when she looked down and realized that she hadn't even begun to peel them. Worse, her ordinarily aesthetically pleasing slices of celery and green pepper were now a minced heap indistinguishable from a pile of coleslaw. Putting down the knife, she placed her hands over her eyes and sobbed. She wasn't sure if it was from frustration or anger or misery—certainly she felt all three emotions at this point. Then suddenly, she realized she wasn't alone in the room. With reddened, blurred eyes, she looked up to see that Paul was standing next to her and staring down, a concerned look on his face. A fragrant bouquet of multi-colored carnations was in his hand.

Placing the flowers on the table next to her, he reached for her and slowly pulled her to her feet. Holding her trembling body gently, he patiently waited for her to stop crying, saying nothing but running his hand soothingly up and down her back. When she had stopped hiccupping and quieted, he released her, walked over to the stove and turned off the burners. Then he returned, holding out his hand. She took it and they started up the stairs, one of his arms around her and she leaning against his sturdy frame.

In the bedroom, he pulled her down on the bed, hugging her tenderly for a moment before he began slowly removing her clothes, kissing her and caressing her, being himself again, not the strange, frightening man who had shared her bed. When it was over, he whispered, "I love you," and continued to hold her protectively. She knew she should say something to him, but somehow, she couldn't.

CHAPTER 4

Days passed, than weeks, and it was as though the strange episode had never taken place. Pat almost began to wonder if it had. Paul was his usual, teasing self. Mostly quiet and fairly contained when in public, he could be capricious and downright silly when they were alone. He could also make anything seem an adventure and he would surprise her with little gifts and excursions or unexpected hidden qualities like the beautiful but melancholy poetry. Pat realized how much she loved him.

Life appeared back on track and they had even started a new hobby. It had come gradually as part of their slow furnishing of their town house. Just last month in fact, when in nearby Frederick, Maryland, on one of their weekend excursions to the still quaint towns surrounding greater D.C., they had spotted a wrought iron kitchen set. "Vintage ice-cream parlor," Paul described it, obviously delighted with the find. Complete with four chairs with heart-shaped backs, he claimed it was the exact same set his grandmother had had. This no doubt was the reason he'd paid an exorbitant amount, even though refinishing the set would take hours. "Hey," he'd excitedly told her, "how can that card table we've been using begin to compare with furniture like this!"

Cheerfully, he'd spent his only free day the next weekend removing layers of chipped paint. After all his hard work, he proudly presented the gleaming white set, which Pat agreed did turn out well. Her major contribution was recovering the seats in cherry red material, with mental thanks to her elder sister Joan for sewing lessons.

Now Pat was looking forward to their project this weekend. This time they were finishing their sparsely furnished living room, and the items were Pat's selection, although Paul had enthusiastically approved her choice—a pair of old wingback chairs that they'd picked up in Warrenton, Virginia, after a late summer picnic on Sky Line

Drive. Pat had been thrilled with this find—though getting them home had turned into a real adventure. They'd had to strap one of the chairs to Paul's Miata and Pat had hung out the car watching it, terrified it would come loose and bounce down busy Route 66 causing an accident. Paul, half amused, half annoyed, had admonished her, "Surely you know that of all people, I would never take the chance at having a lawsuit!" Pat had laughed in response although she'd kept her tense vigil. The next day they'd returned for the other chair in her larger car.

They'd talked of refurnishing the chairs since they brought them home, but somehow they'd never found the time. Pat was determined to have the house done before the holidays, and it was already early October. So Paul had gotten some library books on upholstery, sure that between the two of them they'd figure it out. "You have to foot the bill for a professional if we screw up," Pat threatened.

"My sworn obligation, Madame, and I will wager you your superlative veal scaloppini that we don't. I'll even spring for the wine."

"Deal," she agreed and now she moved over to nudge him. Paul ordinarily loved to sleep in on Saturdays if he didn't have to go to the office so she was surprised to find he was already awake, staring at the ceiling. Worse yet, as Paul rolled over and gave her a look devoid of emotion, she realized that her Paul, of just the night before, was gone again. Once more she was alone with this strange and frightening lover—so cold, impersonal and distant.

This other Paul scrutinized her with old, penetrating and weary eyes. He didn't bother to cajole and woo her. He merely took what he wanted, and although she complied, she wondered what he would do if she were to deny him. His savage passion was exciting but she felt spent, almost ravaged when they were done.

Then as previously, he stared at her, detached, seemingly without recognition, before abruptly leaving their bed. Within minutes, he was once more gone from the house without a word.

Pat lay there in shock and when she finally arose, she puttered around, wondering what she should do. They'd have to talk this time when he returned and was acting normally again. They'd just have to, but what would she do if he wouldn't? And what if this time, he continued to be this strange man rather than the sweet husband she loved and had thought she knew. Worse yet, what if he didn't return? To whom would she talk and what would she say? It wasn't something she wanted to share even with those nearest and dearest. The whole experience was unsettling— actually frightening.

That night Pat tensely waited for Paul, determined that she would find out what had happened, but he didn't return and the phone never rang. Ultimately, she fell asleep on the living room sofa. When she did awake, the dark and silence seemed foreboding and she wondered if she were still alone in the house. Quietly, she went upstairs seeking her husband. He wasn't there and for a moment, she was almost relieved. There was no indication that Paul had been back either, which suddenly made her feel frantic. She cursed her vacillating emotions. Pat knew she should call someone, but the question remained: whom? Paul was an orphan and had no siblings. And what could she say to her family or friends?

Pat thought of whom to call. Certainly not Betty, whose friendship had become tentative now that Pat no longer was a free agent. Momentarily she then considered Todd. He had been a real confidante before he'd met his own pretty Penny, shades of Pat and Todd's favorite cult classic, *The Adventures of Buckaroo Banzai Across the Eighth Dimension*. But, as her relationship with Paul had grown closer, she'd become hesitant to 'tell all' to anyone. Paul had so rapidly become special to her. Their bond became a secret she wanted to protect. And as she and Paul became intimate, there had been no reason to share personal thoughts with others. Her husband had become the only confidante she needed. She had thought that was what marriage was all about. But what happens when marriage itself is under siege, she wondered? Was that what her marriage had become: forced isolation and her own husband a terrifying menace rather than the loving protector she had believed him to be? Was she at danger in her own home?

No, she couldn't think like that. Paul was her husband, and obviously something was wrong with him. He could be lost, he could be hurt—she had to do something.

Pat wondered if she should call someone from Paul's office. He had moved to D.C. early the previous autumn to join the prestigious law firm of Beck and Stringfellow after leaving the military. Although he'd occasionally refer to college or Air Force friends, none seemed to live within the area, or at least Pat had not met any. Those people Paul did know locally were from work, but he didn't seem particularly close to any of them. While they had gone to some mandatory affairs, such as a dinner party at the home of his boss, no one struck her as being real friends.

Pat decided not to call anyone, at least not yet. She didn't want to involve others. She wasn't sure if this was this due to pride or fear that she'd have to reveal that her perfect mate was not as perfect as she had thought. If there'd been an accident, she could have called anyone. But she couldn't talk about something like this. Pat had never realized how private she was when it came to her love life.

Everything had happened so fast in their courtship. Although to begin with, Paul had been hesitant about becoming physical—so much so, that Pat began to wonder if perhaps she should be more aggressive, despite the fact it was not her style. Pat could feel the sexual attraction every time she was with him. She just wasn't sure what to do about it. Perhaps some of that strong Minnesota Lutheran background was still present in her subconscious.

The first few dates were fun—fabulous in fact, but strictly platonic. Pat was amazed at how comfortable she felt with this attractive young man. Paul was amusing, courteous, and interesting, plus he seemed to enjoy many of her favorite pastimes: reading, films, museums, good food, and once her ankle healed, taking the long walks. That of course was weather permitting, for it had been a typical D.C. winter.

Temperatures would be in the teens one day, approaching fifty degrees the next.

Those walks in fact had been as instrumental as anything in bringing them closer together. The two would talk incessantly as they slowly rambled from her small apartment in Rosslyn, across Key Bridge, and then through the side streets of Georgetown, which was one of Paul's favorite destinations. Pat teased him once about not choosing to live there, but to her astonishment, he'd answered almost curtly, "I can't afford it. At least not in the style I want," he'd added, softening his surprisingly gruff retort. As if to apologize, he then said with one of his beguiling smiles, "As soon as the weather improves, I'll get over this obsession with the area. Proximity, I guess. Then we can go to the National Arboretum for all the spring flowers, or to Great Falls and the C and O Canal. Maybe we can even hike the Appalachian Trail if you'd like."

"So you like mountains as well as tropical islands," she quipped.

"Why not, though it's hard to beat Hawaii. The Air Force did good by me when I got posted there!"

"Hmm," agreed Pat, still wondering why the posters hanging in his house were those tattered, faded ones of the Caribbean rather than views of Maui or Kauai.

Ultimately they began to meet her friends, when he finally accompanied her to a party at Todd's place. "Hey," whispered Todd when he'd gotten her alone. "No more Penny Priddy jokes from you about Penelope. He seems like a really nice guy, and he looks like Peter Weller except for the nose.

"And the coloring and the eyes," refuted Pat, although she'd always found the younger version Weller attractive, short of being armored as the mutilated changeling RoboCop. Another changeling—was there something in Pat's genetic makeup that made them attractive, she now wondered?

Still it was obvious that Paul fit right in and that he especially attracted the attention of other women. It wasn't only Betty who gathered around him, laughing and flirting. To everyone, he was polite, but it was soon apparent that Pat alone was the focus of his attention. Yet, it was more than a month after their first date before he even kissed her and that almost a chaste goodnight gesture. By then, Pat began to wonder if she had misinterpreted the relationship. Was Paul destined to be another one of her buddies rather than someone more meaningful?

Pat had hoped that he wouldn't join that small list of escorts she had acquired over her years in D.C. Those were for week-night dates, but Paul she wanted as her Saturday night material, so she couldn't help but be concerned about the lack of physical intimacy. Luckily, once he did take that big step, it was clear that the physical attraction was there for them both. So much so that within days, he asked Pat to come and spend the weekend in New York with him.

The weekend trip was a dream come true for Pat. Paul had surprised her with a room at the Waldorf, orchestra seats at two hit plays, and dinner at the Four Seasons. But all that faded in comparison to the nights. Paul turned out to be an eager lover, sweet and intense, but she couldn't help but tease him about his slow approach.

"Hey, I was fairly sure from the start. I just didn't want to scare you off and I wanted to be certain you were as interested as I was."

"And?"

"And...I think you've convinced me," he confided smugly as he pulled her to him.

But the real surprise of the weekend was the finale—his proposal. After taking things so slowly, Pat worried about the speed things were developing. "Don't you think we might be rushing into this?" she asked, taken aback by the shift from school-zone to Autobahn.

"When I make up my mind, I go for it. I wouldn't have asked you to go away with me if I hadn't already had this in mind."

"You don't have relationships with women unless you plan to propose?"

"I didn't say that, did I?" he answered with an easy smile.

"No, but..."

"We have been seeing each other constantly for a couple of months now. I've met your friends, you've met mine. We've gone places together, solved the world's crises, discovered each other's interests, had fun, and...," he leaned over and kissed her lightly, "now had good sex. What else is there?" Somehow Pat didn't have an appropriate answer but just looked at him. "I rest my case," he said gently. "Have you decided on a verdict?"

"I..."

"Incorporation?"

"Yes," she answered hardly believing she'd accepted so readily.

"Good. How about next week?"

"You're crazy!" Pat sputtered, truly shocked at the suggestion.

"No, I just don't believe in long engagements and for once, I'm between major work assignments and can take some vacation."

"But you haven't met my family or anything."

"I'm not marrying your family and I don't have any to show you. If you really feel I should, we could fly out to Saint Paul for a weekend but I was thinking it might be nicer to take a week or two, escape the end of this dismal winter, and head to the Caribbean. If I recall correctly, you didn't do too well in snow and ice the first time we met. Besides, the lot of a legal associate is fairly low. You'd better take advantage of my having some free time."

Pat burst out laughing, her face flushed and happy. "So being bored and having some vacation time coming up, you thought you might as well get married too!"

"*Très drôle, ma petite.* There are lots of lovely girls in the islands, but you're the one I want."

"I won't argue but I'm going to have to take you home some time."

"Fine, Minnesota when the snow melts if it ever does.

Isn't that the state that has two seasons? Winter and road repair?"

"And the state bird is a mosquito," Pat retorted pertly. "Easter is late this year. We'll go home for that, but I'm not sure if I can get a week or two off now. I have a presentation coming up."

"Try. It would really be lonely to have to go on a honeymoon by myself." Paul looked so sad when he said this that she burst out laughing again. Luckily, she was able to get her leave, after agreeing to burn the midnight oil for several days before and after.

Equally easily, Paul had persuaded her to spend an extra day in New York with him, delaying their return to D.C. until late Monday. This was because he had planned a trip early that morning to Tiffany's so they could select her ring. To be honest, Pat could have cared less about a ring at that point, she was so deliriously happy, but it was obviously important to her new fiancé.

Once back in D.C., she called home to announce the engagement. Her mother was thrilled by the news, having received weekly reports on Pat's dashing new romantic interest. But she was upset when she learned that there'd be no family wedding nor opportunity to meet Paul before Pat married him. "Really, Mom, I'll bring him home in April for the Easter holiday to meet everyone," Pat soothed diplomatically.

"But Pat, what if?"

"What, Mom? If you don't like him? You will, I know you will." But they both knew Pat was saying that she'd decided to marry her southern gentleman even if the family disapproved. "We don't have a lot of time off, Mom—just a week and I'll have to get ready to move too. No one's even going to the courthouse with us since we're flying to Jamaica right after. The only celebration will be an open house when we return, which is just going to be a big party. At Easter, there'll be time to get to know him. I'll introduce him to the whole family. You know how the clan gathers at the Gramps," she added. "It will be better that way," Pat cajoled gently. Her father agreed and Pat was grateful, aware that he'd comfort her mother who was torn between happiness for her daughter and fear of this unknown man to whom her daughter had pledged herself. Unknown, yes indeed, Paul was that.

With Paul of course, meeting his family was impossible. "I'm sorry I won't be able to show you my roots, sugar," he told her, "but there's really no one left from my childhood."

Both his parents were only children and his mother had died in childbirth with her second child when he was small— only aged four. The newborn brother had lived mere days. Then when Paul was starting high school, his father, a lawyer, was killed in a car wreck and he'd lost his grandparents while he was in college. Truly, he was alone when it came to relatives.

So, on the chosen day for their wedding, St. Patrick's Day to be precise, there would be only the two of them. This Paul said was only appropriate.

"Why? We're not Irish," Pat commented baffled.

"No, but don't forget Mary Patton the First. You always say she was Celtic."

"The language, Paul," Pat protested, "not Irish—more Scottish Gaelic."

"They're both Celts, aren't they? Besides, you're one of the little people," he laughed and she'd hit him in response. Never forcefully—horseplay only. She'd never want to hurt this lovely, sweet man—not that she expected she could. Equally, she had been just as positive that he'd never harm her.

As it turned out, D.C. had a heavy snow forecast for the night of March 16 and Pat was afraid everything would be closed the following day. Paul, more pragmatically, said they'd just go on the honeymoon first since he'd already paid for the resort and tickets. They could have the wedding when they got back. The important thing was catching a flight to Jamaica.

"And I thought you were the romantic," Pat wailed and broke into tears. "Crass, you're utterly crass."

"We'll marry under a palm tree then, darlin'," he said, trying to console her, surprised at her unexpected tears.

"Paul," she wailed even louder, making him feel bad for teasing her about such an important event. Fortunately, the snow amounted to only inches, the courthouse opened promptly at 8:30, and they were at the airport in plenty of time to catch their flight to Montego Bay. Pat was not sure if they would have gone if they hadn't been able to make that all important stop at the courthouse and Paul would never give her a straight answer.

The trip to Jamaica had dwarfed the New York weekend, which she thought never could be surpassed. It was also her first trip out of the United States with the exception of a few ventures across the Canadian border when she was a child, disappointed then to find everything seemingly indistinguishable from Minnesota. Heresy of course to Canadian acquaintances. But this tropical island, this really was a foreign country and Pat was captivated. Paul, slightly cynical, pointed out that staying in a luxury resort wasn't exactly being in a foreign country—one beach complex was much like another.

"Hey, Mr. World Traveler, maybe it's not for you, but if you want to look at it that way, then I'm going to count this excursion like visiting two countries! I've never been in a place like this either!" Pat declared stoutly, admiring their private bungalow overlooking the ocean. Complete with jacuzzi, its patio was enclosed by a tall cement wall painted a shocking pink and covered with a riot of tropical vegetation. The room was luxury itself, bright and airy and large enough for a dozen inhabitants rather than just the two of them.

"Oh, my poor little waif. Did you have to stand on the corners selling newspapers as a child in the cold blustery Minnesota winter?" Paul taunted teasingly.

"As a matter of fact, I had a job one winter delivering advertising supplements," Pat answered with great dignity. "My best friend's brother talked her and me into doing it together since he got a percentage for lining up new recruits. Then just after we started, she decided it was too much work. I was still in grammar school and I remember my brother, Lyle, with his infinite, superior wisdom as a high school senior, telling me what a fish I was."

"Fish?" Brow wrinkling, it was obvious that Paul was perplexed.

"Sure, you know, fool, idiot...don't they use that expression down South where you come from?"

"Oh, yah, we just didn't at our house," mumbled Paul, making the 'yeah' sound like it had two a's the way he did when he was speaking 'deep southern' rather than 'light southern' his ordinarily melodious speech pattern.

"Anyhow, I lasted two deliveries and it took me hours. I probably averaged all of fifty cents an hour. Lyle ended up telling me that the older kids used to dump most of the papers but I was too ethical for that. Dumb me."

"Poor, poor exploited child," Paul murmured, pressing his face to her soft, unruly hair, "but be honest. Did you fall on your cute little ass making the deliveries?" His tone was serious but she could feel him shaking with silent laughter.

"I resent that," Pat retorted with feigned outrage, jerking her head up so her hair flew wildly. "I can handle snow and ice perfectly well. You're the one who knocked me over, you big lummox."

"And you looked so cute—an absolute baby doll. All that lovely wavy hair and those big brown eyes. I just knew I was going to have to take you home as a souvenir." He surveyed her affectionately, reaching up to stroke the unmanageable curls. He had learned to love her more than he would have ever thought possible.

"Really?" she smiled shyly, relishing every compliment he was willing to bestow, as she snuggled in his embrace.

"Sure, especially after I saw that lovely smile, those lovely teeth, each a perfect pearl."

"You're so poetic but I wasn't smiling. I was gritting my teeth in agony and trying to keep from writhing in pain."

"I like it when you writhe, squirm and quiver. Your quivering is nice, outstanding in fact. Want to quiver some now?" Paul suggested quietly, emphasizing his point by softly breathing into her ear.

"Now?" she shivered slightly. "Aren't we supposed to be rushing out to the beach and posing for travel pictures?"

"I've already got those."

"Those ratty old things in your study!"

"Hey, don't knock those. Besides, you're too red to be on the beach now." He pressed a finger firmly against her shoulder, surveying with concern the white pressure point against her overly rosy skin. "Why the hell didn't you let me put sunscreen on you yesterday?"

"How else would people know I'd been in the tropics?"

"I thought people from Minnesota were supposed to be smart... at least the ones who managed to escape." This time he burst out laughing and shied away as she reached for a pillow and started hitting him.

"Stop bashing my beloved Land of Ten Thousand Lakes, or I'll show you bashing." By now Pat was straddling him, pounding his head with the pillow and he'd folded his arms over his face to ward her off attack.

"Ouch, ouch, you're mean and dangerous too." He grabbed the pillow from her and pulled her to him.

"Well you should talk, you're red too." She poked his shoulder hard enough to elicit a slight wince and looked into his green eyes which were mere inches away—mesmerizing. Sea green, she thought, and near enough to dive in. Warm sexy sea green like the Caribbean where they had been cavorting the afternoon before.

"Ouch again. Very mean. Besides, I couldn't help myself either. When I was a kid, I used to dream in the winter about escaping to a tropic island. I had a roommate once who owned posters of Jamaica and Barbados that I coveted, pure and simple. Those are the ones I have back at the house and why I still prize them; I had to tutor him in English for a whole term to get them," Paul sighed in remembrance. "And I'd think about how nice it would be to run away and end up living under a palm tree. And have a pretty little island girl," he added, his eyes appearing even greener and more seductive.

"I didn't think it got that cold in Alabama."

"Alabama? Oh, it gets cold there sometimes... they've even have snow sometimes... hyperbole, ok?"

"Besides, I'm not a little island girl."

"You're a girl, you're little, this is an island."

"Pedantic and too logical. Just what I'd expect from a lawyer. Is that how you learned to skate? Ice in Alabama?"

He laughed, "Not much but there are ice rinks."

"Ah. But what, you were in boarding school or something to have a roommate?"

"Oh no, that was Tulane. I was just a young college student, not a mature one like you." To divert her, Pat later realized, Paul started tickling and then suddenly he'd pulled her down on top of him and was nuzzling her. "Nice earlobes, tiny, pretty like you."

"Hmm," she murmured, feeling more little shivers.

"Is that writhing, I detect?" His hands were moving sensually and softly down her back. "Got to be careful of that sunburn. Definitely need to stay inside more today."

"Hmm," she sighed again.

"Bed rest, I think. *Très belle derrière*," he whispered as he cupped his hands around hers. "*Très jolie, ma petite.*"

"New Orleans must have really furthered your education," she said, breathing into his ear.

"Oh yah," he agreed as he shifted her completely onto him. "Oh yah, *très, très jolie. Mon Dieu*, you feel good. *Je t'aime beaucoup...toujours.*"

Pat's eyes were closed and she was breathing deeper, lost now in the sensuous motions as his fingers and tongue teased her. "Don't...," she started to say. His eyes shot open and he looked at her, the expressive green eyes surprised. "...stop, don't stop," she finished breathlessly. He smiled and shut his eyes again, continuing to nuzzle and probe, creating all sorts of tantalizing sensations.

"*Je t'aime aussi*," she whispered, dredging up one of the few French phrases she'd learned.

He laughed at her heavy accent—pure Midwestern—and wondered who had taught her such excruciating French.

Someday he'd have to ask, someday when hopefully they could exchange all their secrets during their pillow talk and maybe he'd teach her the words of love in proper French, the way it should be learned. For now though, he had her slim, firm thighs pressed firmly to him, and was interested only in them.

Pat felt as though a little current were running up and down inside her. She'd never felt so sensitive before, so, so ... she didn't have the words to describe the feeling. And then she didn't worry about words as she began to tremble and Paul was holding her tighter, thrusting further into her.

She had started gasping and he was gasping too, "Good, *c'est bon.*" Then he let out a moan and pulled her down completely on him. "Writhe, you writhe so nicely. Bed rest, definitely lots of bed rest, once, twice, all day," he breathed heavily, clasping her gently.

"You're my doctor," she said, lying across him, utterly exhausted. "Just as long as you make house calls."

"*Toujours,*" he whispered huskily. "For you, always."

It was noon when they finally got out of the room and definitely too hot for the beach. So they had a leisurely lunch served under a palm tree—fulfilling another one of his fantasies, he remarked, although curried goat and mango chutney weren't something Pat ordinarily would have ordered. "Got to be adventurous," Paul admonished, and to her amazement the meal was excellent. After, they arranged to go into Montego where amid the stalls of the straw market, he ended up buying her a huge straw hat covered with flowers. "Now," he said satisfied as he plopped it on her head, "you'll be ok in the sun."

"Ok!" she complained, "I'll never get to see it! This thing is so big I could live in it!"

The vender, a stout ebony-hued woman, overheard and burst into laughter. "Way to go, mon! She is a teeny t'ing."

"But precious." Paul flashed a smile and Pat felt herself turning red. "Besides, you'll be cheaper to take care of that way, and we won't have to worry about a garden either," he teased tapping the brilliantly colored straw flowers with a long, slender finger before cautioning, "From now on, lots of sunscreen too. I intend to administer it myself."

"Certainly, doctor," she grinned flirtatiously. "Do I get to return the favor?"

"Oh, most definitely." He picked up one of her hands. "Ministering hands. Beautiful little hands, velvety, sweet like flower petals, just like the rest of you. Definitely you can do me that favor."

The vendor, who'd been watching, chuckled softly, nodding her head in approval, but neither Pat nor Paul noticed as they walked off, hands still clasped.

That evening they were back to the table under the huge palm, sipping the island's famous rum punch—"One of sour, two of sweet, three of strong and four of weak," according to Marcus, their jovial waiter with the brilliant smile. It took Pat a moment to decode the ingredients as lime juice, fruit syrup, rum and water. Prudently she filed the information away for future use.

It was a rich, seductive night filled with warmth and romance as though ordered especially for the two of them. Nearby were buffet tables heaped with a feast of seafood and barbecued meats, plus masses of the local fruits, practically a tropical sunset in warm variations of yellows, oranges and reds. Tall torches were spouting flames and in the background a reggae band was energetically performing. When it came time for the evening's 'required' limbo, Pat teased and cajoled, "Come on, let's try it."

Shaking his head, Paul stayed in his seat until Pat jumped up, grabbing his hand, pulling. "I dare you."

At last hesitantly, a slight smile on his face, he agreed to try. He actually did fairly well, demonstrating the flexibility of a good athlete, but she was the one who became a finalist and he grouched about her unfair advantage.

"Well what did you expect," she observed cheekily. "You're built like a bean pole," although this wasn't strictly true since Paul had broad shoulders and a strong build. Lanky yes, but with well-muscled arms and legs. It was easy to see why he was a skier and hiker.

"And you're my pocket Venus. Hell, you could practically walk under the damn thing, Miss Five Foot Two, though no Eyes of Blue." With an impish grin, he began to hum his parody of that little ditty.

"Five foot two and proud of it, mister. You're just like those hot shot lawyers that used to argue against Cesar Chavez and his farm workers' union saying the lettuce pickers didn't need higher wages because they were all little Mexicans—you know, closer to the ground so they didn't have to bend as much," Pat countered, deciding she'd never admit she was only five one. A girl had to have some secrets.

Paul burst into laughter. "Jesus, you are an economist to the soul and a damn pinko besides. But then what can I expect from someone who went to Wisconsin."

"Are you referring to my sunburn, sir, or the reputation of my esteemed alma mater?" Pat responded in her haughtiest tone.

"Too much, my little Marxist."

"That was the Madison campus—not mine. They churned out radicals even in the 1900s, until revisionism made most of those people mainstream. I mean look at Dick Cheney, not that he finished their PhD program." Paul's eyebrow shot up and Pat shrugged, not wanting to get into politics and said hurriedly, "Well I had to go to Milwaukee, which offered a master's—the urban campus open to all. Much more egalitarian, you know. We all couldn't attend fancy private schools like you."

Paul politely refrained from mentioning that Pat had attended Minnesota's prestigious Carleton College as an undergraduate. She no doubt would have lectured him on the life of a scholarship student. Instead he pursued their pseudo debate. "Are you going to give me a lecture on the economies of banana production in Jamaica and the evils of former colonies exploited by capitalism?"

"It's more likely to be ganja here that makes the real profits," she said quietly,

"Oops, maybe we should change the subject." His voice lowered, matching hers, another touch of reality intruding into their didactic game. "I don't want one of the local posses after us because you're charting the island's marijuana crops. I'll take on the lettuce pickers any day. Actually, I probably would have liked to have argued for them. We studied a lot of those labor cases in law school."

"Pro bono? Your fancy firm does pro bono?" Pat was curious. Her friends 'in-the-know' had told her that Paul's firm of Beck and Stringfellow was where the big boys went. Highly respected but sometimes political, it was considered to be Washington's top drawer entry into international law. Without even meeting Paul at that point, they had been impressed.

"Some, not much. I guess they did a fair amount when they started but that was with the earlier partners...they're gone now. My dad used to do a lot of pro bono, so did my grandfather."

"I didn't know he was a lawyer too." Pat realized that there was a lot she didn't know about Paul and his background. They'd talked so much but usually about mutual interests and about her life, to be honest, rather than his. He had mentioned his college years a few times but not much else.

"Oh yah, both were lawyers."

"Your dad didn't work with him?"

"No, Grandpa got involved in government work. Dad stayed with the private sector."

"That's why they were in Montgomery, huh?"

"Montgomery...oh, sure, the state capital. Lord, yes," Paul gently drawled, suddenly recapturing the sound of the deep South.

"Is it pretty? Aside from going to Atlanta a couple of times, I've never been South."

"Atlanta doesn't count."

"Scarlett O'Hara wouldn't agree with you," Pat argued.

"She was fiction. Atlanta's just a big city—nice but big despite having quaint street names like Peachtree. I'll show you the real South someday—New Orleans too when all the camellias and gardenias are out and it's more recovered," he added sadly.

"And let me sit under a magnolia tree with a blossom in my hair?" Paul snorted at this remark. "What's so funny?" she responded a bit defiantly.

"Some of those magnolia buds are as big as your cute, little ol' head, sugar," he replied now with a greatly exaggerated southern accent. Then he added in more normal tones, "Also, unless the lower branches have been trimmed, the trees have leaves right down to the ground. You may be tiny, Pat, but even a little pixie like you..."

"Don't disillusion me," she chided. "And Montgomery? You'll show me where you were a little boy?"

"Sure, some time, but I like islands better, especially since it's winter and cold back there. We'll have to collect islands, darlin'." He leaned over giving her a kiss. It and the rum and the lively, exciting music made her return the kiss, her tongue sliding into his warm, soft mouth. All her thoughts of Alabama were fast dispelled. Now interested in the present only, she drew back looking at him speculatively. His eyes had that sexy, sea green color again and it was apparent that the interest was mutual.

"You look tired," he observed, standing and helping her up. "I'm tired too," he added softly. "Long day, more bed rest needed. Must be the tropical sun, very fatiguing." She nodded her head in agreement and his arm slid around her. "Have to help you back to the room," he murmured. "Wouldn't want you to fall and hurt yourself again."

"Right," she agreed. "You're good at helping."

"But this time I get to come into the room, don't I?"

"Without doubt." Pat leaned against him, acutely aware of the comforting warmth of his body as they slowly walked back to their cabana. Her senses were all alert, feeling his hand sliding up and down her arm, touching his firm physique, smelling the spicy fragrant scent of his aftershave lotion, hearing him softly murmur endearments, and looking at him appreciatively. "Bed rest, good idea," she breathed, although of course it was some time before either of them rested and by then she had added taste to complete the list of sensory perceptions.

Yes, the Jamaican honeymoon had been exactly what a honeymoon was supposed to be. Spending lazy hours on the beach and watching spectacular sunsets with tall cool drinks in hand. Eating all the wonderful fresh tropical fruits for breakfast—sweet golden pineapple, juicy rosy mangos, tart little green bananas and huge slices of bright orange papaya sprinkled with tangy lime juice. In the evening they'd indulge in fresh seafood and sometimes at night they'd sit out on their own little veranda, blissfully alone, and look at the moon and stars shining over the ocean as their hands entwined and they again began their physical explorations. During the day, they'd soak in their private jacuzzi, surrounded by the vibrant tropical scarlet, which she could now identify as bougainvillea, cascading over the patio walls.

Somehow, they did manage a few of the usual tourist things too like climbing Dunn River Falls and rafting down the river, and Paul tried to show her windsailing, which he'd done in Hawaii—site of a future vacation, he promised. But, mostly they spent their time alone at the bungalow getting to know each other, investigating each other's bodies, probing each other's psyche, and being deeply satisfied with their discoveries. Halcyon days.

CHAPTER 5

When they returned from the island, Pat officially moved into Paul's nearly empty town house in Ballston. Although her boxes and furniture had been sent earlier, she had spent the last few days before the marriage with a friend from work, the office administrator. Fortunate enough to sublet her apartment almost immediately and not worry about having to finish her lease, she'd still had several days until the wedding. This interim move had puzzled Paul. "Why don't you come straight home with me?" he'd asked.

"Hmm, ah," Pat prevaricated, before adding embarrassed, "propriety."

"Propriety? We've been sleeping together since New York!"

"It's a girl thing, ok?" she'd responded and he'd nodded his head, amused. But Pat knew if Paul and she had decided to delay the marriage after their affair commenced, she would have kept her own small studio in Rosslyn, retaining some independence until they had made their final pledge.

Once, during graduate school, she had lived for several months with a fellow student—Ronnie, another aspiring economist, but she felt in retrospect that had been a mistake. There were all the drawbacks of doing someone else's laundry and cleaning the bathroom but none of the status of commitment. Never again, she'd fervently vowed once she'd broken up with her lover, and although Pat did have several other sexual experiences during the next few years, she remained true to her concept of independence.

None of these subsequent liaisons lasted for more than a few weeks at most and for the year or so before she met Paul, she had avoided any—especially after the unnerving episode with the man from the subway. Sex was supposed to mean more than just physical gratification. With the changing social scene, Pat remained adamant that she was better off not venturing into short-term relationships or worse, like Betty, one night stands.

So she hedged about the move and Paul had teased, "In that case, I guess we'll just have a large celebration once you do move in and officially announce the union to one and all. Trumpets, ok?"

"Of course," Pat laughed, "and a drum roll too."

"Hmm, that's not a bad idea," he declared to her amazement. "I've never given a party out here and now that I'll have someone to cook and clean, maybe it's time."

This time Pat was the one to 'hmm' and Paul burst out laughing. "Just kidding, Pix, unless you do it with fairy dust. Don't worry. I'll take care of everything. We'll have a large open house for friends when we get back from Jamaica— kind of a combined wedding reception and April Fool's party since you missed having the former by running off with me."

"And I'm the fool?" she asked saucily, batting her eyes provocatively.

"Nope, *au contraire*, Madame, you're making nearly as wise a decision as I. It's merely the weather and date and remember we're off to Minnesota a couple weeks after. Praise the lord, Easter is late this year," he'd keened as he shivered theatrically before grabbing her and giving her a big hug.

"Conceited and a thin blooded southerner besides."

"Sure, I have reason to be conceited. I got you, didn't I? But I resent that remark. I thought I proved myself to be fairly hot blooded." Paul looked so smugly self-pleased that Pat felt like laughing but she wasn't going to give him the satisfaction.

"You're just too full of yourself," she chided though she had an appreciative glimmer in her eye. "And what if March leaves like a lion and we're under feet of snow so no one can get to this fabulous party?"

"It'll never happen," Paul answered with great confidence. "It didn't snow nary a bit when we got married just as I predicted then. Besides, if it did now, you and I would have a private little party until the thaw and I'll demonstrate the rising of my blood temperature again."

This time Pat did burst out laughing and then 'too much' was her reaction again when not only was Paul correct about March leaving like a lamb but she had begun to comprehend his preparations for the proposed open house.

True to his promise, it was immediately apparent that she would have to do none of the work save provide a list of people to invite. "Are these all?" he'd complained scanning the dozen or so names. "Surely you have more friends just from work."

"Well…" Pat wrote another half dozen.

"More," ordered Paul. "Everyone. Just like a real wedding. I'm serious about this. I want to meet them all. So let's just get this over all at once so I can keep you to myself after."

Pat took him at his word, embarrassed at the length of the growing list.

"Better, much better," he finally conceded. "Now just let me have your address book and I'll have my secretary send out the invitations."

"Is that kosher?"

"Hey, she owes me," he smiled. "Not to worry."

So, by the time they'd flown off to Jamaica, he'd had already arranged the details, including hiring a catering service to put on a large spread way beyond her expectation.

For once, not having a lot of furniture in the town house was a definite plus when she finally realized the number attending. Several people from his office, including the senior partner, Wesley Beck himself, showed up but the majority of the guests were her friends and co-workers—Paul seeming to have found even more than she'd put on her list. At one point it looked as though there were a hundred people milling about, if being packed like sardines counted as milling. By and large, it was a happy, boisterous crowd, clearly enjoying the occasion.

One strange occurrence took place when the imperative Mr. Beck approached her, asking, "Why don't you give me a guided tour of your house, my dear?"

"Our house?" Pat was bewildered and afraid she showed it. Why on earth would someone like Wesley Beck be interested in their simple, non-pretentious town house? It was hardly more than a cookie cutter replica of thousands more in the greater D.C. area although the fact it was Paul's and now hers too made it special of course to them. Slowly, she hedged, embarrassed.

"Well, if you'd really like to see it, but there isn't anything unique. We have this combination living/dining room, a small half bath and the kitchen on this floor," she gestured vaguely, feeling like a flight attendant pointing out emergency exits. "Then upstairs we have two bedrooms and baths and a small office. Downstairs, we haven't done anything yet. But the space...it's just roughed in for the laundry, a bath and utility or recreational area if we want. Are you certain you want to see it?"

"Oh, quite. I like to know how my up-and-coming young people live." Beck's small, alert eyes were earnest and he was acting as though each word she uttered was important. Most perplexing.

"Well, sure. In that case, would you just follow me. Up or down first?" Flustered, Pat looked around frantically for Paul but he apparently was in the kitchen and no one else was noting this peculiar episode, all too busy having a good time. Meanwhile she wondered why the man hadn't seen the house when it belonged to the previous owner, who had been Paul's predecessor at the firm. That is if it was Beck's habit to walk through his employees' homes. Or, was it the furniture he was nosy about since obviously theirs was lacking? It had to be a test of some kind.

"Down, I think." And that was what they'd done with Beck spending several minutes silently contemplating the piles of boxes she and Paul had not yet unpacked. Disconcerted, Pat murmured, "We still haven't decided what to do about combining our stuff."

"Time," Beck replied, "it takes time. I assume this is all Paul has too."

Pat stared at him mystified at the odd comment and made an inane remark, "Well he doesn't have any family, you know. I mean he didn't until he married me." In response, his boss made some equally inane reply.

Later she told Paul about the weird request and Beck's interest but he'd just laughed. "Wesley Beck has a reputation of being eccentric and sometimes downright plodding even if he's still considered to be brilliant and pragmatic."

In spite of that one peculiar incident, the occasion had definitely been a success. Paul had also surprised her by having a florist come in to decorate for the party resulting in the main floor being festooned with floral arrangements. There were multi-colored mixtures of carnations and gladioli, and potted tulips, crocuses, dwarf lilies, plus pale yellow jonquils and sunny yellow daffodils—all in radiant bloom.

The overall effect was as if one had walked into a spring garden, which Paul said, with a sly smile, was how these delicate decorations would later serve.

"Can't depend on just your Jamaican straw hat for our future garden, sugar." He leaned over to give her a little kiss. "I couldn't let you wear it today or people might not have seen you." Pat didn't give him the satisfaction of a rejoinder although there was an amused gleam in her eyes belying the mildly indignant scowl on her face.

Through the caterer, Paul had rented folding tables and chairs as well as making sure there was a well-stocked bar. In addition, there were cases of champagne, French no less, and an array of hors d'oeuvres ranging from giant chilled prawns to thinly sliced beef sirloin, a variety of pâtés and platters of sushi, baked brie and ornately carved vegetables surrounded by various dips plus curried patties in remembrance of the Jamaican trip. There'd even been one waiter circulating with a platter of hot, sweet oysters coated in the lightest batter imaginable. "A taste of New Orleans," Paul said, promising again, "we'll go there too."

Trays of elegant pastries—including a tower constructed of tiny cream puffs, colorful jewels of petit fours, and miniature fruit tarts completed the repast. Or so

Pat thought for suddenly, there was a great musical fanfare from the trio Paul had also hired—drum beating and a trumpet even, just as he'd promised. And out came one of the servers with a small three-tiered wedding cake. Pat's mouth dropped open. "You weren't kidding."

"Who, me? Would I lie? I'm a lawyer, remember?"

Pat laughed, looking up with happy trustful eyes, and Paul reached down to pick up an elaborate cake-cutter. It was GG's! The prized object had been used at all the weddings of GG's female descendants, but Pat had never expected to see it here and gasped in surprise. Perhaps her mother had forgiven the court house ceremony; at least she'd been in contact with Paul. Somehow, the little piece of silver made everything official. Next it would be used by one of Pat's nieces, and then…maybe…one day a daughter. With this glad thought, Pat rewarded Paul with an especially radiant smile. Paul grinned back and taking her hand, they cut the cake to great applause

Meanwhile well-attired and efficient waiters were carefully presenting trays of champagne glasses filled to the brim so the guests could toast the happy couple and the equally dapper bartender, also in attendance, continued his cocktail magic for those not into bubbly. Most daintily, Paul placed a small morsel of cake in Pat's mouth and then sealed it with a kiss. After he whispered teasingly, "No garter tossing. Don't want to share the view." Pat let out an abrupt laugh, quickly covering her mouth for fear she'd shower him with crumbs.

As the evening lengthened and the crowd began to ease, the tables were folded or moved to one side so that room was turned into a small dance floor. Soon, those that remained were out dancing and to Pat's surprise, the party seemed to go on for hours. Everyone had had a spectacular time as more than one friend told her later and Betty had practically gushed over the live trio, "The height of chic, Pat. You didn't tell me you were marrying a millionaire!"

Pat had merely shaken her head in polite denial. Still, the unexpected opulence had been a shock and later, when she realized the extent of the lavish production, she asked, "Jesus, Paul. Can we afford this?"

"No problem," he replied with complete indifference. "My treat."

"We were supposed to be doing this together. Almost all of the people who came are ones I know."

"So, now I know them too. Besides, I'm independently wealthy," he jested amicably. "And, once I become a partner in the firm, this is the way we'll always entertain."

"Are you sure?"

"About becoming a partner? Most probably. That was the selling point of joining Beck and Stringfellow. About the other, absolutely. I've been saving myself and my money for you for years," he answered sincerely although she could see the twinkle in his eyes. "You're the fairy princess my mother promised me."

Embarrassed, she snorted, "Sure, especially about saving yourself."

"Hey, a little practice here and there, but only practice."

"Hmm," Pat replied neutrally for neither of them had as yet really discussed former relationships and this didn't seem the appropriate time. Not that she wasn't fairly suspicious of one, remembering the glamorous woman lawyer she'd briefly met at the first formal occasion she'd attended with Paul, and noticeably not a party guest now. This occurred just a week or so before they'd gone to New York. In fact, Pat had sometimes wondered if that meeting had precipitated Paul's invitation mere days later. Yet, in his actions and all the time they'd spent together before and since, he'd never given her any reason to believe she might be a rebound.

Now, as Pat waited and worried about her missing husband, the thought resurfaced. It was one she didn't want to consider even though it might be the explanation. Miranda Nicholson. If Paul didn't return, should she call the woman? God, she'd refrained from calling her own friends or Paul's co-workers. How could she consider contacting that woman—and worse, what if he were there? It wasn't until now that Pat realized that subconsciously she was jealous of what the relationship might have been, or worse, be. How humiliating.

CHAPTER 6

Everything was humiliating and nerve-racking at this point, and Pat couldn't understand why. Everything had gone so smoothly from the very start, even the Easter trip to Minnesota, which took place a few weeks after the open house. Although Paul said nothing, Pat knew he was apprehensive about meeting her parents. And, there was some reason for this concern, particularly in regards to her mother. For all the cordiality after Pat had broken the news, she knew that her mother had been deeply hurt that her daughter—the baby, no less—had decided to get married away from home. Weddings just weren't supposed to be simple courthouse affairs. Worse yet, ones taking place in distant Virginia without the family's having met the groom, even if the cherished cake-knife had been sent to endow the union.

Pat remembered telling her mother that Saint Paul was far off and she'd been on her own for years. As diplomatically as possible, she had reiterated that her current friends were in D.C. and at best, it would just be family attending a ceremony if they came to Minnesota. Why then bother with the additional expense and worry? She promised they would get to meet Paul in the spring—a matter of two months at most—when there'd really be an opportunity to know him, not just attend a formality. This reasoning had really rocked her mother and Pat knew she'd made a tactical error but she wasn't prepared to change her... well, to be honest, Paul's plans.

That pivotal conversation had haunted Pat after. Would her mother forgive her, and by extension, Paul? But, her and Paul's worries were needless. Nora and the rest of the family loved him on sight. About her father, Pat had never been concerned. Donald Strom and his youngest child always seemed to be on the same wave length. And, it soon was apparent that Paul was not just relieved but was actually equally delighted to be welcomed into the large gregarious group. Having numerous relatives, Pat really hadn't considered what life would have been like without them so she was pleasantly surprised by her husband's reaction. Moreover, the all-important maternal stamp of approval was reinforced by her older sister and brother telling her that even though she'd waited so long—as though approaching thirty were the end of the line—she'd come back home with a winner. Well, Pat really had, or so she thought until these strange episodes occurred.

As she and Paul took long walks through her old neighborhood in Saint Paul's time warp Midway district, she could see he was vicariously drinking in her memories as well reconnoitering the area. First the nearby golf course where she'd gone tobogganing and sledding in the winter. This was bordered with Minnesota's famed lilac bushes, which alas were still a month away from having their deep purple blooms, so overpowering in rich fragrance. Something she was sure would rival the Alabama flowers that Paul so often mentioned and something which she knew she had to add to their planned garden.

Then there was the narrow park-like road by the Mississippi River where she'd biked and hiked. And her grammar school where Pat made a production of showing Paul the exact location of the famous winter ice rink, not mentioning that here one shadowy night her eighth-grade classmate Ben had given her a first kiss. Her embarrassed giggle in response had left the two avoiding each other throughout the rest of the year and Pat had guiltily been pleased when the boy moved the following summer and even more so that no one had noticed the happening.

Everything he saw interested Paul and Pat's own private apprehensions about the visit fast disappeared. These qualms, in fact, she had never mentioned to her new husband. But, basically, she realized it wasn't just her mother's reaction she'd feared. She had also been afraid that her parent's modest 1920s bungalow and its shabby old furnishings might not live up to Paul's expectations. During the months she and Paul had known each other, it had become evident to her that he had come from a well-to-do southern family.

That worry was soon dispelled. In fact, charmingly so when Pat discovered yet another unexpected interest of her likeable spouse and one that immediately endeared him to her father. Paul was apparently an incipient carpenter and to Don Strom, who viewed tools as much a pleasurable pastime as part of his profession, this meant immediate rapport. It also gave Pat a clue as to what would soon become her and Paul's future hobby. Both men bemoaned the fact that the old time hardware store was being replaced by places like the one her father managed.

"I know it's heresy," Don laughed, "but I'd give anything to have a little shop where we could sell one screw instead of a package and had the kinds of open bins they used to."

"Me too," agreed Paul enthusiastically. "I remember my dad taking me to a place like that in Alabama—old pine board floor, pot-bellied stove for winter, and stuff that looked like it had been used in the Civil War."

"Probably had," chuckled Don. "There was one like that near my home in Lester Prairie when I was a kid. Even here in the Twin Cities, our store was something like that when I first went to work. I doubt there're too many of those places left. Damn shame too."

Pat could well recall when her father's store was bought out by a large chain and turned into the modern, impersonal mart. No, never completely impersonal—not as long as Don Strom was in charge. She also knew her father had been thankful he'd been able to keep his position. Yet in spite of that fact, she was well aware how much he missed the somewhat dusty and dingy old building where a customer could still purchase nails by the pound or even borrow a tool for one-time use rather than have to buy it. Operating that way may not have been good economics, but she personally agreed with her father, remembering the days when good will was what had brought the customers back as much as the products.

"There're still some places like that in Europe," remarked Paul. "I remember when I went down to Athens once. There was a whole street that had such little shops. Same thing in Asia."

"That I'd like to see."

"You'll just have to come with Pat and me sometime," Paul answered casually, but with obvious sincerity. Pat was sure her father probably never would, but the simple remark endeared Paul to her father instantly. She therefore wasn't a bit surprised that the Saturday before Easter, instead of helping her and her mother dye eggs, her husband was up early and off to Don's store with him. The men she most loved had now established a bond—both real tool time guys. And, later after the return to D.C., many of the incoming e-mails from her father were tips to Paul about new items being carried by his chain. Ronnie never would have gotten these, that she was sure.

It was also soon obvious that Paul genuinely enjoyed every minute of the visit and especially the part of being with a real family. When on Easter Sunday itself they drove to her paternal grandparents' home just outside the tiny hamlet of Lester Prairie, some fifty or so miles from the Twin Cities, he was overwhelmed—in fact actually flabbergasted. The look on Paul's face, when they got out of Don's car and he realized how any people were present, was priceless. Almost in awe, he queried, "You did say just family, didn't you?"

"Sure, besides us guys, those are the aunts, uncles and cousins."

"Good lord, Pat, are you related to the whole state?"

"How can you say something like that! Probably only half," she giggled. She hadn't told him on purpose, not wanting to overwhelm him, and was now sure he could understand why she'd immediately concurred with him on their quasi elopement. The logistics for a wedding in her family were daunting unless of course one didn't mind hurting some distant relative's feelings. Or close for that matter since 'immediate' to the Linds and Stroms still meant practically a cast of thousands!

"Well I'll certainly remember not to get in an argument with you! You'd have a whole army backing you," Paul quipped once the shock had somewhat dissipated.

"I should hope so," she said, giving him a kiss.

Her brother Lyle, who'd come to greet them, turned to his pre-pubescent daughter, Sally, and murmured theatrically, "Newlyweds are shameless so remember that, and I won't have to stick you in a nunnery when you grow up."

"Oh Daddy, really," groaned Pat's niece, mortified as only adolescents can be by their parents, and everyone broke into laughter. But soon the girl had run off to join the annual Easter egg hunt. This was followed by appropriate 'egg games' as the Strom clan called these traditional exercises and had even Paul readily participating, somewhat to Pat's surprise since she remembered his reticence trying the limbo. Laughing in delight as though he'd never been to a family gathering, he was soon egg rolling and egg tossing and carrying eggs on spoons. This without the slightest embarrassment since it was soon apparent that among the Strom clan, not only the children but all the adults took part.

By the time the family lined up for their habitual Easter dinner, Paul was dumbfounded, particularly at the abundance of food. "How the hell did you stay so tiny?" he asked as he watched Pat carefully select and then precariously pile an enormous stack of edibles onto her plate.

"You think that's a lot!" interjected Lyle, a towering Viking giant standing next to them. "You should see what she eats at Christmas. Joan and I always wanted to weigh her after dinner to see if she'd doubled her size like one of the nestlings that devour twice their weight."

"And Mother never let you," replied Pat smugly with a self-satisfied smirk. Then refusing to spar further with her brother, she explained, "It's only Easter and Thanksgiving out here at the Gramps. Wait until you see what they do for Turkey Day." With that, she added some chunky chicken salad permeated with celery and water chestnuts to the generous slices of honey-baked ham, three kinds of pickles including her grandmother's prize olive oil ones, various cheeses, hot rolls, spiced apples, olives, radish 'flowers', three-bean salad, sour cream and cheddar-stuffed potatoes, honey, and homemade jams. "Can't take too much," she said demurely but with a wicked gleam in her eyes and a haughty nod at Lyle, who merely laughed. "Have to leave some room for the desserts."

"Desserts? You're jesting of course," commented Paul who now appeared to be truly shocked.

"Nope, coconut cake, banana cream pie, hot date torte with whipped cream, rhubarb parfait...do you want me to go on?"

"My lord," Paul uttered in hushed reverence, "they must have been cooking for weeks."

"Months," mumbled Lyle, who had already bitten into a radish from his plate, which more than rivaled his baby sister's as a towering mound of provisions.

"Sure, didn't your grandparents do things like this?" asked Pat.

"Not on this scale although Grandma made the best pecan pie, bar none, and ambrosia too: coconut, oranges, bananas, nuts, cherries, pineapple and a dash of bourbon for the big people though I usually sneaked some of theirs too." Paul's face lit up in memory. "Yah, she had her holiday specials. Her toasted pecans in hot salted butter, I could have gobbled them for hours and those creamy pralines! My, my, they were downright delectable plus the chocolate rum balls and whiskey cake."

"Hmm...sounds good to me. Were you ever sober?" asked Pat innocently and Lyle snorted before drifting off to find his wife.

"Bad, Pat," Paul chided but he was looking around the varied group, ranging from small toddlers to Pat's grandparents, now well into their eighties. "I had no idea anyone could have this much family. How do you keep all their names straight?"

"Simple. If they're older, I just say 'aunt' or 'uncle' and

if they're my age or younger, I call them 'cousin'. That takes care of even the shirt-tail relatives as Joan would say."

"Very clever. You should go into the diplomatic service."

"Well, it works. Next time we come out, you try it too and later they'll wonder which branch of the family you belong to."

He laughed. "I will and I'll like that."

"What?"

"Coming out here again. Belonging. Your Twin Cities are nice and so is your family. No wonder you are."

Pat grinned, delighted by his remark. "You are too. I guess I'll have to see Alabama to find out why."

"Sure thing..." he drawled, his heavy duty-version, but made no mention of when such a visit would happen.

But at least in Minnesota, everyone, it seemed, liked Paul. For that matter, back in D.C., it appeared much the same. Not only Betty who always had that predatory eye for an attractive male, but also the rest of Pat's friends, her co-workers, and his co-workers were pleased to be in his company. Since their wedding, invitations had become *de rigueur*, as Paul would put it, making Pat a bit cynical about the social value of a pair versus a single female. Was it like poker, where an extra matching card won the hand? It was only Paul's long hours or the fact that they still wanted to spend time alone that kept them now from practically a nightly outing. So much so that as it was, Pat of late had been ready to beg fatigue, if nothing else, and Paul had cajoled her, saying age did that to one, not that he was particularly a party boy himself.

Well, Pat was fatigued right now—no, stressed—and she very much doubted that Paul was out partying unless as half a pair. So, what the hell was happening, she wondered as her reveries ceased. For a moment, she sat in discouraged silence and then suddenly she started thinking about what had transpired this weekend and she felt very lonely and afraid. Had she rushed into everything too fast?

Paul had been, if she were to be honest, the dominant

partner when it had come to the speed of their sexual relationship. Starting out so hesitantly and then taking over once he had decided it was time for them to become intimate, even brushing aside her more cautionary objections about waiting to marry. But then, what about the actual marriage? Did Paul really dominate there? They'd moved into his house but he was the one to already own one whereas she was just a renter. In addition, it was convenient to work for them both and more than large enough for a couple. Certainly there was no reason to seek or want another house at this point. So it wasn't really a question of his making that decision as to where or how they would live.

What about decisions about work? As of yet, there were none. He had his profession, she hers. He said if he had any offers out of the area, they would examine them jointly and she really hadn't considered anything else, content with what she did and where she was. But other questions? Children, well, that subject obviously hadn't been discussed in depth so there was no pressure from him to have them or by contrast, none to avoid them. If she were to be totally honest, Paul had never actually said he wanted any—a fact that now disturbed her greatly. After all, weren't children the final bond in a relationship?

What was now making her so apprehensive about everything besides the startling event that had taken place? As if that wasn't enough! From her blue collar but still solidly middle class background, Paul was obviously a real catch. Attractive, charming, well educated, intelligent, and a successful professional on the rise. He was just what her parents would have picked for her in days of old.

Momentarily her always active imagination allowed her to envision the serious betrothal negotiations that would have taken place centuries before. Another Walter Mitty escape, which she herself often undertook in times of stress. Perhaps she would be in Mediaeval Venice, which had always seemed particularly romantic. Her father, no doubt goateed and garbed in tights, talking to Paul's similarly outfitted father. The mothers probably fretting over their delicate handiwork in their respective homes—nope, mansions or palaces—palazzos—at least. If one is going to be imaginative, one might as well go all the way, which had led to her ongoing argument with Lyle as a child, he always being ready to mock her daydreams. She seeing herself being rowed in grandeur down the Grand Canal whereas Lyle would torment her by saying they'd be chained to the oars and then laughing when she said the Venetians didn't use chains, that that was for galleys during Roman times, as if she'd really known. Ultimately she'd stopped telling her brother her fantasies. Well Lyle wasn't here and Paul was the subject of her current fabrication just as he had been during the months before they wed when the prospect of actual marriage seemed to far exceed her romantic dreams.

So for a little while, she escaped into her safe imagination. There she knew Paul and she would be totally oblivious of the weighty discussions between their families, who would have known all of the significant details about him. Yes, those all important details—their lack now a bane. With luck, she might even have seen him before the wedding although carefully chaperoned since naturally they would have been hot-blooded teenagers and it would have been inappropriate, if not downright dangerous, to be alone. After all, look what happened to Romeo and Juliet, even if that was fiction. But hell, in this more modern age, an older Paul and she still were hot blooded and maybe there still was some danger.

That reality jerked her back to the present, which was just as well. Her family probably wouldn't have been able to come up with sufficient dowry and her father would have hated tights, much less a beard. Just like Lyle's cold realism to intrude again. But, Pat mused, she never would have known then if she'd lost Paul or would she? He had become so important to her so fast that she wondered if perhaps she had always known he was out there somewhere and they both had been waiting for their encounter even though it had taken years longer than those Middle Age adolescents would have had to wait, not that the odds of longevity were too great back then. Whatever, it was much, much better to be in her own time and society and wooed and judged for herself with hopefully the expected life span of the twenty-first century.

Compared to Paul's family now that she herself was being realistic again, her own background was obviously a step further down on the scale of the American dream. Don, her father, successfully managed his small hardware store but that was as far as he was going to go in the competitive business world. As the youngest in his large family, there'd been no money for college or particular guidance from his parents, who had not had the benefit of higher education. Also, he had married so young. Basically, he was just a sweet, complacent man, lacking the ambition that his son, Lyle, and even Pat herself demonstrated.

No, that wasn't entirely true, thought Pat. Success per se just wasn't that important to her father. As long as he knew he could adequately support his family, he was satisfied. Work was meant to be undertaken competently. An honest day's labor given, but it never dominating his total existence; and clearly, he could also never understand the sixty-hour weeks Lyle put in or the sometimes longer time Paul, and occasionally she, devoted to their professions. Moreover, in some ways, Don was a dreamer like Pat, which probably was why they were so close. But most important, Don appeared to be satisfied with the life he had. If nothing else, Pat knew her father was a contented man.

Nora, her mother, coming from Mary Patton Lind's more determined background, had thought about teaching but she was just out of high school when she married Don. Then Pat's big sister Joan arrived within a year, curtailing forever that vocational aspiration, more than a slight disappointment to the Linds although they otherwise found young Donald Strom most suitable. Both Pat's parents espoused the concept of the mother at home even if it meant less material acquisitions. Yet, by contrast, there was always someone there to go to parent-teacher meetings, to serve as a den mother or Brownie leader, to bake cookies for class parties, and to live up to all the other Brady Bunch ideals. Moreover, in her family's case, the scenario had worked in reality. Don and Nora Strom had a happy home and Pat knew how lucky she had been and still was in that respect. Later when Pat the baby had finished grammar school, her mother began clerking part time in a drugstore to contribute to college funds. A career woman she had never been, nor the teacher outside of what she had imparted to her own brood; but like her husband, she was satisfied.

Still, Pat's parents were not without ambition for their children—possibly because each understood, at least subconsciously, what they might have lost through their early marriage. Joan received a teacher's certificate and did teach before Pat's two nieces arrived; now that the younger girl was approaching her teens, she planned to work again. Lyle had turned out to be a computer whiz and as a result was making big money and had married his Summit Avenue princess from that fashionable St. Paul neighborhood. Pat herself had been dubbed the family intellectual with scholarships to the very selective Carleton College and then a graduate fellowship to the University of Wisconsin in Milwaukee. This in turn led to a fast-track internship at the Department of Agriculture and her decent, reliable government job where, in tribute to Mr. Cruz, her favorite government teacher, she sincerely worked to make a difference.

No, Paul was just the sort of young man that her parents would have chosen for her. The fact that he wasn't a good Lutheran, shades of Garrison Keillor, Minnesota's and Public Broadcasting's homespun answer to Will Rogers, or that he came from the South, were to be overlooked in this more liberal time. He was probably even a Democrat! Not that there hadn't been some of those in the extended family tribe, even if they did seem slightly suspect to Grandpa Strom, who by far was the latest chief conservative in a long line of staunch Republicans. These dated back to territorial days. This link was initially established by one of the Stroms joining Minnesota's famous first volunteers in the Civil War, proudly marching off to fight the Northern cause when the new state offered the first troops to the besieged union. And, sadly, to fall at Gettysburg where these same troops had served with special gallantry, a fact Pat emphasized to Paul whose ancestors of course had been on the opposite side. But that was just history. More important was the fact that Paul was just the man Pat had always wanted and still did, regardless of what was happening.

Yes, just whom she wanted and with that thought, Pat decided she'd played Walter Mitty long enough. Picking up the phone, she dialed Paul's direct line at work, wondering if perhaps some case was bothering him and he'd gone to bury himself in work—maybe even collapsing late at night on one of the office's handsome burnished top-grain leather sofas, which put their own little living room futon to shame. But, in spite of a dozen rings, there was no answer, not even a pick-up of his voice mail, which had been a recent addition to the conservative firm. Then she called the main number, receiving only the recorded message detailing office hours and emergency numbers if needed. Exasperated, she hung up and stared at the phone, her lips pursed and her fingers drumming nervously. It was Sunday morning and Paul had now been gone for twenty-four hours. Wasn't that the magic number of hours when one could call the police or the hospitals? Still, what could she say? Her husband had walked out of the house of his own free will after all.

Maybe it was time to contact one of his co-workers or even Mr. Beck himself. No, she couldn't do that. Paul and she had never had a fight, but somehow she knew he would be furious if she were to try and track him down by calling any of his professional constituents. Although an engaging individual in public, he really was a private person. It didn't matter that at home he usually projected lively, good humor and was a terrific tease. Instinctively she knew that if nothing else, her congenial Paul would never want others to know what was happening now. Not that she did herself.

And suddenly, she realized, she didn't know anything substantial about him personally other than what he'd told her. Be analytic about this, Pat thought, trying to keep from panicking at that scary observation. Review what she did know.

First, she knew where he worked. That was definite. She'd called him there. That after all was how they'd initiated contact after the Pennsylvania meeting, for God sake. She'd visited his office. She'd met people from the firm. They'd even attended a party or two when they began dating where she noticed that more than one of the female staff members was eying her speculatively as if questioning what hidden attributes she must have had to snag one of the firm's newest and most eligible bachelors. She had also gone with him to a business dinner and subsequently been invited to accompany him to more parties given by his colleagues, who seemed to enjoy his company since Paul was becoming known for his keen wit. So, without doubt, he did work for Beck and Stringfellow and apparently was considered to be an up and coming member of the firm. Hell, Wesley Beck himself had said so, what further proof was needed!

Second, Paul was a graduate of Tulane with a law degree from the renowned Stanford Law School. That had to have been substantiated. Surely the law firm wouldn't have hired him if they hadn't checked his references so that was true as well. Besides, she'd seen alumni appeals in the mail and his diplomas on the office wall at Beck and Stringfellow. And he'd sometimes said he should have stayed at Tulane because of their stress on European law but three more years of muggy New Orleans had seemed too much. Instead, he'd gone west, 'to see a bit of the country,' but where scholastically the big emphasis internationally was the Pacific Rim. Although Stanford had a cooperative program with Johns Hopkins and sent people to the latter's Bologna Center to address the European issues, he'd quipped he really wanted to be a surfer. When told by Pat not to be a smartass, he'd looked convincingly hurt, except for a sight gleam in his eye, and asked, "What's wrong with surfing?"

"Nothing. I just don't think you'd look that great in a sarong."

At this, his expressive face looked truly wounded. "Next you'll tell me I can't wax the surfboard in the living room."

"Oh, Paul, you can plant a coconut tree there if you want."

"Really?"

"Really, so why did you go west, young man?"

"I hadn't considered Europe at that point. Besides, I didn't realize how difficult it would be to learn Japanese or Chinese compared to good, old reliable French."

Right, the French. Paul had won a prize for an essay in French at Tulane, the Bouvier Prize or something, so obviously he'd retained a love of the language. Then, as it turned out, he had gotten his European experience after all. He'd served in the Air Force—a lieutenant attached to the Judge Advocate General. First he was stationed in Germany and then in Hawaii, where windsailing not surfing turned out to be the sport of the hour.

His discharge papers were supposedly in a file in their joint study although Pat hadn't ever gone through them. Maybe she should, she speculated. Maybe she should look at all his meticulously ordered files in the small steel cabinet upstairs. Maybe she should see who this strange Paul W. Martin, her husband, was. She wasn't the real Mitty of the family. *The Secret Life of Walter Mitty* or Pat Strom's own seemed to have nothing on Paul's and she, for one, no longer was pleased about her own version of Thurber's *My World and Welcome to It.*

Hell, for that matter, she still didn't know what the W signified. Paul had told her it was nothing. "It's just a letter, darlin', a middle initial so I won't have to be called NMI for having none." At other times he'd rattled off a list of W names, whimsical like Wigglesworth or tongue twisting like Wszolek and then laughed, "Hey, it's too embarrassing," adding dramatically, "Tell you what, when we celebrate our Golden, I promise I'll tell you as an anniversary present. Besides, I need some mystery," he told her, "and W stands for wonderful."

"Ridiculous, Paul. If the initial were R, I'd know you were really Rumpelstiltskin."

"Too tall," he'd countered.

That she didn't pursue further. After all, the evil little gnome had wanted the queen's first born, something she'd gladly give Paul, but for which he'd never asked. So instead she said, "W, I know for a fact, stands for weird. So there!" And he'd continued to tease her until soon she'd forgotten since what did the letter W really matter?

Well, now it appeared it did and he was and there were too many things that hadn't been said or asked.

Despondently, Pat went to their little study. It was neat, just as Paul was, and she looked at his desk and the small file cabinet next to it. It wouldn't be the first time she'd glanced in. More than once, he'd asked her to pull out some needed information for him when he was working late, the occupational hazard for young lawyers. In it were bills, receipts, check stubs, tax information, the book for the mortgage payments, plus files carefully labeled 'insurance' and, yes, the one on 'military service.'

Her own papers were stacked in a cardboard box next to the desk. Once they started filing taxes together, she'd planned to integrate them into his system but since they hadn't married until after the first of the year and wouldn't face joint returns until the following spring that was something she had been putting off. Per usual. Knowing her, that probably would be next March or worse yet, mid-April like about the fourteenth. Something that had nearly happened this year although she hadn't told Paul. Pat smiled half-heartedly in recognition of her weakness. But not Paul—no, he'd have those returns ready weeks in advance. It was odd; she didn't procrastinate at work or in keeping house, but with onerous tasks like personal taxes, she did or worse yet, avoided them completely, depending on what was happening. Deep down, she knew that she preferred to subscribe to the school of thought that if one waited long enough, the problem would go away. That or she could hide in a fantasy.

Should she look at his things without asking she wondered or remain a Mitty? Be an ostrich with its head buried in the sand although she knew that was a fallacy. The big birds were merely listening for sounds much as Indian trackers purportedly did when scouting in the far west. Still, was she again avoiding an onerous task? One far worse than waiting to prepare her taxes late the night of April 15?

She could have examined Paul's records at any time, Pat realized. There was no lock on the sturdy little cabinet and he had never said anything to her about respecting his privacy when it came to whatever might be within the house. They each had their own checking accounts and credit cards so she had had no reason to see his. Then somehow, once married, the bills just started dividing naturally. He'd taken care of the house expenses and she assumed responsibility for the groceries while each was accountable for personal purchases and individual cars although there was a definite contrast between her trusty old but unassuming two-door Saturn and his sporty little Miata convertible. That he had informed her represented part of the bonus he had been paid when he joined the law firm.

"Nice bonus," she'd commented wryly. "Uncle Sam was never that generous to me. Are you sure you have enough room for those long legs?"

"What, jealous?" he mocked good-naturedly. "Hey, there's plenty of room for my legs. Besides, your car isn't all that roomy and it's noisy too even if it is dependable. Also, Uncle doesn't expect you to put in extra-long hours gratis," he retorted referring to the time-honored but true lament of legal associates nationwide.

"Uncle doesn't pay me as well either and I have lots of room for my legs."

"Well there's room for your pretty, little legs in my car too but you made your case."

She did though understand that long hours, including ones during the weekends, were part of the legal game. Some of Paul's peers regularly clocked eighty or more hours a week and wondering once, she had asked why he got off with a relatively lesser amount plus time for the honeymoon and the extended Easter weekend.

"My languages," he'd said simply, referring to his apparent fluency, not only in French, but German as well, plus a smattering of Italian which he belittled as menu level. Still it sounded fairly proficient to Pat when they were dining out or the time they attended *Tosca* and he didn't once glance at the libretto.

So although it was obvious to her that Paul's financial resources far exceeded her own, somehow the question of who was the major breadwinner had never come up. Yet she did realize he was in affect her main support. When Pat finally mentioned something to him, he told her he earned over twice the salary, which she was sure was true, so she might as well put as much money as she could into her government retirement funds and pay off old school loans. Those, he said, worried him for years until at last he became a high-priced lawyer out to exploit the masses.

In response, she'd chortled merrily. "Just what I always thought."

"Sure, it's a required class: *Screw the Masses 101*. Then we have *Medical Malpractice Suits 201* and *How to Sue Everyone and Anyone 301*." Snickering, he proceeded to construct a whole curriculum of classes for the successful but unethical lawyer ending up with the advanced required seminars of *Self Plea Bargaining, Bribing Judges,* and *Successful Jail Breaking as Needed*." When Pat finally stopped laughing and accused him of reading too much John Grisham or David Baldacci, he told her he saw himself more as Scott Turow even if he had failed drama, which was the reason he didn't handle trials.

"What, you're a bad actor?" she quipped before mumbling something about maybe they weren't talking law and since he was a poet, they should be considering Lord Byron.

At that point, Paul answered with a leer, "I don't limp but I could be persuaded to discuss my other Byronesque qualities later."

"Maybe," she hedged, but she was grinning.

"Right, but hey, you should save the rest of your money. One day we might want a bigger house." She'd nodded in agreement although at this point their—actually his—Ballston town house seemed more than adequate.

Maybe, if they did decide to start a family, that would change, Pat had thought, but for some strange reason she still hadn't mentioned this possible aspect of their relationship. In all the speed with which they had rushed to marry, the question had never adequately been discussed. In fact, it hadn't been discussed at all and Pat had intuited that there was some reluctance on Paul's part when she'd almost made the Rumpelstiltskin quip. Yes, be honest, she herself knew that someday she wanted a child or maybe two and that she always had.

Paul certainly had enjoyed her three nieces during the Twin Cities visit and seemed to like children in general. Still, even then he had said nothing about their having any of their own and she comprehended now that she had never asked when or if they would have children. Since she'd turned thirty at the beginning of the summer, she realized she was thinking more about this, but they'd been married such a short time, she really hadn't wanted to push the issue yet. That obviously was something else that had to be addressed, particularly as her biological clock ticked on.

Did love make someone stupid, Pat wondered? What else hadn't she asked or found out before she married? Had she been so desperate to get a husband that she hadn't cared? Ridiculous, she loved Paul, plain and simple, or she never would have become his wife. She just hadn't wanted to intrude in his private place, believing that slowly he would reveal his secrets. So aside from his work and her so favorable impressions formed over their months together, she knew nothing about her husband. What a fool she was.

Placing her hand on the file cabinet, Pat stood silently, deciding whether to open it and see what it contained. No, she thought, not yet. It wasn't procrastination this time, she assured herself; it was a matter of respecting that privacy. When he came home, she'd ask him. She'd ask him everything this time. Then she reflected dismally, what if he didn't come home? The thought was sobering but then so was the whole situation. Pat started gnawing at an uneven finger nail, cognizant that this was a nervous habit to which she hadn't succumbed for years. Not since graduate school actually when she had been mortified to realize she was doing it during her orals. God, she had to get a grip on herself.

All Sunday morning, she tried to keep herself busy but it seemed as if she couldn't complete the simplest task. She'd brought a report home from work but after five minutes of staring at the seemingly endless pages and obviously comprehending nothing, she stuffed it back into the briefcase. Instead she found herself fidgeting, anxious to get to the real subject dominating her attention: Paul.

Then she thought about calling her mother. Hell, the call she should make was to the police! It was definitely more than twenty-four hours now, but somehow, she couldn't bring herself to take that step. Her mother, though, that was different. That call was something Pat made almost weekly and it was expected; but what would she say if there were inquiries about Paul and what they were doing? Such questions of course were a certainty.

Pat decided to take the easy way out and send an e-mail to the whole family, knowing by now her parents would probably be off to church. Using the excuse that unexpectedly she and Paul were going to be out the rest of the day as well as the next few nights, she promised that she'd call later in the week.

Lyle had finally talked his parents into joining the information highway and had presented them with a user-friendly, shiny Apple the previous Christmas as well as signing them up with internet service. Mostly her mother seemed to enjoy routing and rerouting the net's endless humor and chain letters, but her father had become a surfer par excellence and was rapidly learning one new program after another. Pat now thought she knew where Lyle's creative programming talent and her own flare for numbers had originated. Lyle had even been approached by the highly respected Boston firm of SofTek but preferred to remain a Minnesota boy. Such a shame her dad hadn't had the money or direction to attend college, Pat thought, not that Don Strom ever seemed unhappy with what life had brought. So, as she hastily keyed in her terse and overly cheery but casually pseudo message, she thought, God, I'm even lying to my parents now, but she knew she'd break down if she spoke to either.

Actually and fortunately, she and Paul had had no plans for the weekend other than starting on their latest furniture project so she wouldn't have to make false excuses to any of their friends. She, in particular, had looked forward to their lazing around the house. Maybe a few quick errands Saturday morning while Paul busied himself with the wingbacks but a quiet evening at home that night and a romantic dinner and all the good things to follow. Candle light and wine; she'd had the whole thing planned, even buying some veal for her prize scaloppini, which Paul so enjoyed and she knew would earn with his day's efforts. They'd both been so busy the last few weeks and he had been working long hours on a European project that some time alone had seemed very desirable.

Well, she was alone all right but where the hell was he? If it weren't work, was there another woman? That vision of the glamorous brunette lawyer passed before her eyes again, which she was sure were slowly turning from brown to green and a dark, acid green at that, not Paul's rich color. Or worse yet, a man? Paul had been so slow starting their sexual relationship initially that even that thought had entered her mind after the first few weeks of dating him. Then once he did begin making amorous overtures, she'd had no doubts that women were the sex of choice as far as he was concerned.

Well that was a strange observation to suddenly reconsider, that her husband might be a closet homosexual or bi. No, definitely not. In spite of the bizarre encounter yesterday and the other two months before, what after all could have been more heterosexual than the way he'd treated her? Crude perhaps but definitely macho all the way. But, the possibility of another woman? They'd only been married for seven months! There had never been any indication that there was anyone else when she met him except for the sultry, arrogant brunette, whom he'd never mentioned after the one encounter. But then her husband never dwelled on previous evolvements—another absence of information on his past. No true confessions for Paul.

The couple of times he'd had to go out of town since they'd wed, he'd begged her to go with him and the one time she'd had a business trip, he'd flown down to Atlanta for the weekend to join her and, he'd said, prove to her that Peachtree was not the old South. When she'd asked if she should take an extra day or two leave so they could drive over to Montgomery, he'd replied that he only had the weekend free. To properly visit the Cradle of the Confederacy, Heart of Dixie, Cow Town of the South, and a whole string of other titles he drawled out, more time was needed. Odd, she hadn't thought about that excuse to avoid Alabama. And no, she really didn't think it was another woman unless he'd been the best actor in the world throughout their brief marriage.

So, if it wasn't sex and it wasn't work, then what? Family, he had none. She kept returning to that fact but what if he was lying to her? Was he the son of some Ku Klux Klan Grand Wizard or did he have an earlier wife and six children secreted in the Confederacy's Cradle? After all, there was a rumor about hot blood boiling early down South, Pat thought facetiously. Still was there some reason equally devastating why he couldn't or wouldn't take her to Alabama? He didn't even keep photos around! A sole exception was a small simply-framed snapshot on the desk that he'd told her was his parents. He must have been around two or three when it was taken for he was sitting on his mother's knee.

Paul looked so delighted in the picture—a pretty, healthy-looking little boy secure with his family. They were in a garden somewhere and his mother was laughing. She was a beautiful blonde woman, probably in her mid-twenties. The image of his father was less clear. He was kneeling next to them, an arm protectively encircling his wife and child, but his face was turned slightly so that his features were partially obscured. Still the familiar pronounced nose was apparent. From what Pat could see of his father, Paul obviously favored the man in more than facial features for his parent was also dark and lean and tall. All three had looked so happy in the little photo—one of those precious moments captured for the future.

"My mom died a couple of years later," Paul told her, his countenance long and sad and his voice bleak. Pat had felt she wanted to cry as she listened to him, grasping the obvious trauma of his loss. "There're other pictures, including some of my grandparents and school days down in the basement in a footlocker. I guess someday I'm going to have to finish unpacking…I guess I've just been putting that off," he added softly, inferring of course that it was too painful.

Since Pat didn't surround herself with photos, she hadn't thought much about their lack or the absence of other mementos. Her own exception was a small framed collage hung in their bedroom with snapshots of all her family, which had been given her by her sister the year she'd moved to D.C. Paul had had no one to prepare anything similar after his painful adolescence. Yet when it came to other keepsakes, Pat certainly had a wide array. Where were Paul's? Surely they couldn't all be in that single footlocker and the two or three taped cartons.

Of course there was a logical explanation for the lack just like his departure from Alabama for college and the military. How much physical baggage did a young man—boy actually—alone in the world, carry? There had to have been plenty of the emotional variety, Pat speculated, but Paul didn't speak much of his family afterward other than saying how much he'd missed them. That she sure was a genuine sentiment.

She herself had some yearbooks and photo albums from earlier times stuffed into one of the boxes she'd brought from her studio apartment but she wasn't overly materialistic or sentimental when it came to packing around souvenirs of her past. If someone were to wonder who she was, what would they find in this little town house?

There were her few possessions: CDs and an inexpensive player which she'd been meaning to donate to the Salvation Army since Paul had the latest updated version; a laptop computer on long-term loan from work; the small TV they now kept on a kitchen counter; books; a few collector movie posters in K-Mart frames dating to the '30s and '40s—usually selected because she'd watched the films with GG during their late night TV marathons; and her sparse selection of furniture. This consisted of the futon sofa in the living room; a pair of bookcases; a small oriental rug— a Turkestan, her one great extravagance; and a desk, table and chairs from Ikea. Only the matching pair of Italian smoked-glass lamps and the comfortable old easy chair in the study, which she'd brought back from her dead grandmother's house, had any family connection. These items had helped fill out Paul's practically empty town house and to her knowledge, everything he owned was there.

When they first met, he explained, "This place was a real bargain, which is why I jumped right in. One of the single guys at work was leaving and apparently needed money fast—some family problem out west, I think. Rather than the uncertainty of having a realtor and an undetermined period of waiting time, he was willing to sell at his bottom price as is minus what would have been the realtor's fee so actually he got about he would have without the hassle of waiting a few months and more expenditures during that time. For me it's a sound investment since I was entering a new tax bracket and could use the mortgage write-off. Besides, I needed somewhere to live and it's convenient to the metro so I don't have to drive to work. Even if I do love the Miata, as you accuse, there's no way I'm stupid enough to want to face work-day traffic. Besides, I can't even get on

Route 66 during the restricted HOV peak hours, even though we're only a few blocks from the exit. Now weekends, that's a different matter. Especially if I have to zip down to Rosslyn to see someone special." Pat had blushed.

But, during her first visit, she was shocked to discover that Paul had acquired only a king sized bed, TV and some other electronic gadgets, plus a few other pieces of furniture like his card table and office items since as of then he spent most of his time out of the house. "What else does a bachelor need," he'd quipped so cheerfully that she wasn't sure if he knew exactly what he was saying, especially since they had not as yet progressed beyond the platonic stage. Worse, she was beginning to wonder at that point if they would. She found him so damn attractive, but she had too much self-pride to make the first overture. In some ways, she remained an old fashioned girl. Later after their New York sojourn, she'd of course agreed with Paul's assessment of what the townhouse needed. By then she was also sure he'd known exactly what he'd been saying earlier.

"Sex fiend," she often accused thereafter, while cavorting in the commodious bed, since being old fashioned only went so far. And subsequently been delighted too, when he'd acted like one. For that matter, so had she, shades of Cleopatra, Madame du Barry, Catherine the Great and other famous women of the past known for their amorous adventures. After all there was old fashioned and there was old fashioned!

In addition Paul also had a few hangings including some batik fabrics from his tour in Hawaii, and the tattered but prized Caribbean posters. There was also an extraordinarily beautiful mountain scene from Switzerland with tiny figures on skis racing down its slopes. Made from an actual photograph, this had been expensively mounted and framed with stainless steel, completing his decor. "You skied there?" Pat had asked, impressed by the stark and majestic scene. Obviously her spouse was a much more proficient athlete than she had realized.

"I went over from Germany."

"It's an old poster too, isn't it?"

"Not that old. I found it in a little shop and liked it."

Still it was evident to Pat that a bed, her few pieces of furniture, and Paul's posters, no matter how loved, did not constitute a furnished home and that accomplishing that objective would become a priority. Pat had discovered a bit to her consternation that once married, her mother's nesting genes were emerging. Paul, by contrast was more hesitant so they compromised. Slowly, on weekends, they began to acquire other items here or there to turn the place from a convenient but impersonal residence to a home.

Their hobby started when the two would stroll through Georgetown or some of the other places Paul liked to walk, stopping to peer into shop windows. As the weather improved, they began instead to go for rides out into the countryside. Then between sightseeing in the region's small towns and sampling local cuisine, they'd also wander the streets, turning into little antique or second-hand shops. Here they'd pick up something if it appealed to them. There seemed to be no hurry to furnish the house just for the sake of filling it up and as of yet, the rooms were still fairly empty.

"We have all the time in the world," Paul convinced her. "Let's pick the good stuff when we see it or buy something that we think is fun." And keeping that in mind, they purchased wild and wonderful decorative items like a hand-carved wooden screen from India with marvelous swirled leaves and flowers, as well as an intricately tooled brass table from the Middle East. They even found a pair of lead lamps studded with huge chunks of colored glass, which a Moslem friend told them were Ramadan lamps.

"Rather like Christmas lights all year, Pat," Ali explained.

"That's good," Paul replied. "I met her surrounded by Christmas lights and she looked like a little doll so I decided I'd ask Santa for her."

"So that's how it happened," remarked Pat slyly with a saucy toss of her curly hair. "I thought boys didn't play with dolls."

"Only little boys; big ones know better," smirked Paul, reaching over to tug gently at one of the provocative ringlets. All three broke into laughter and that night after their friend left, Paul smugly confided that the best part of playing with dolls was taking their clothes off. Then he proceeded to do just that slowly in a most tantalizing and satisfying manner as far as Pat was concerned. In any case, the continuing quest for furniture per se remained a gradual process and usually a small private adventure besides. Like the damn wingback chairs were supposed to have been, she now thought in exasperation.

In addition, augmenting their possessions were all the gifts received after their marriage. This wedding largesse from her friends and family actually had surprised him. "I thought you got things when you had a real wedding."

"We did have a real wedding, just not a formal one. This way if people give us gifts, it's because they really want to," Pat explained.

"I like that," Paul said smiling, but he'd still been astounded by the number of items that slowly filtered in. He hadn't wanted announcements, asking, "To whom would I send them?"

That had upset Pat's mother, who had been brought up on Emily Post. As a result most of the gifts of course were from her family, the large and extended one that had so surprised Paul during the Minnesota visit. The Stroms, Linds and Mary Patton had arrived in the fruitful Minnesota farmlands throughout the nineteenth century and stayed to be fruitful themselves. Indeed, Nora was one of five children while Don had seven brothers and sisters. Pat couldn't count all her first cousins much less those more distantly related and in actuality, had been thankful that she didn't have to go through the kind of wedding her older sister had had.

This of course was another reason that Pat had been inclined to agree to Paul's wedding plans. And regarding the gifts, she pointed out, "Also, we probably won't end up with three fondue pots like Joan or the six carving sets my sister-in-law received." Pat had been only fourteen when Joan married into another large family after finishing university, but she well remembered the months of planning and had sometimes thought her sister and mother were going to have nervous breakdowns. Probably her father too, when the bills were taken into consideration.

Her brother Lyle then married an only child and if anything that was even worse. Elise, his bride, was from such a prominent Saint Paul family that money was no object, leading to prenuptial social activities ad nauseam. It was a good thing that her sister-in-law had been worth the effort, Pat always thought. No, marrying at the courthouse had a lot to be said for it. Never, at her age, would she have considered going through all that hassle even if it had resulted in disappointment to her mother. Wryly, by contrast, she realized her father was no doubt delighted that she'd taken the easier course and not just because of the cost of the wedding.

Another reason her mother had been upset Pat knew was because the marriage wasn't performed in a church. Well, Pat thought, aside from times at home, she herself wasn't much of a churchgoer and Paul had said nothing about his religious preferences. His mother had been Catholic and his father Protestant but apparently there had not been any great religious influences in his life although occasionally he'd come out with some revivalist rhetoric and had an amazing repertoire of old spirituals.

These she gathered he'd learned from a family retainer and visits to her A.M.E. church as a small boy. Pat hadn't been clear at first on this, but Paul had explained that even in religion, the blacks and whites of the south remained separated and that the African Methodist Episcopal Church was one example, evolving of late into a neo-Pentecostal denomination with mostly middle-class parishioners. "But always highly spirited," he'd added with a fond grin. "Certainly beat my grandparents' relatively staid Episcopalianism and a lot more fun as far as I was concerned." Pat refrained from adding that too often such separation happened in the north too and not just in worship.

In her own case, it was probably when she went off to college that she had drifted away from regular church attendance. After she started living with Ronnie, she ceased the pretense. It wasn't that she didn't believe; it was just that organized religion didn't seem the answer for her. Perhaps if there were children, she'd reconsider. Again though, religion was something she and Paul no doubt should have discussed before they committed. Where had she been mentally once she became involved with him? So emotionally smitten that she didn't consider any basic questions? It was beginning to appear so and she was getting more disturbed.

As if to prove the point, Pat looked down at the ragged nails on her small, well-formed hands. She had been biting again. She knew she was overly vain of those hands and nails, although Paul too had often remarked upon them. For that matter, he'd often remarked about most of her anatomy, seeming to be pleased by what she had to offer. This was one of the more satisfactory aspects of their relationship for deep down, Pat had often envied her sister's blonde beauty and height—a full six inches taller. Yet at the same time, she'd been also pleased that she favored GG, her family heroine. Still...she couldn't help but wonder at times what it would be like to resemble tall and willowy Joan. Until now, Paul's noticeable attention had dispelled that slight feeling of inadequacy although the annoying brunette lawyer was showroom tall. The woman easily could have been a model.

The thought then went through Pat's mind that she also had appreciation of her partner's physical attributes. Maybe too much so if it meant she'd ignored valid considerations when she jumped into their marriage. Right, a real mutual admiration society they were or had been. Damn, she'd nibbled off all the nails on one hand. Clearly she wasn't paying much attention mentally now either.

And the matter of the former relationships, another big question now looming in her mind? It had been evident to both that there had been others in their previous lives. Heavens, they were as late into their twenties as one could be. But, the issue of identifying these unknown individuals had been avoided not that she wouldn't have told Paul if he'd asked. He just hadn't and she somehow had been reticent to quiz him.

Certainly when they met, it was apparent that there was no one special for either. Within a week or two, they were spending all their free time together and talking long periods by phone on days they didn't meet. If Paul's work hadn't demanded so many hours, she was sure they would have seen each other daily even then. That again was another reason why she'd been puzzled that the sexual relationship had progressed so gradually.

Later she'd decided it was a matter of respect. In any case, by the time he did ask her to come to New York with him for that first weekend, she was more than ready. Just because she didn't believe in sex for sex's sake alone didn't mean she was immune to its attractions. It had been a long time to be celibate as far as she was concerned and Paul definitely was the man she wanted.

That weekend had been like something out of a film— definitely the most romantic thing that had ever happened to her. Well maybe it all was out of a film, come to think of it. For instance, how did he afford an excursion like that? Even if he was taking down more than twice her salary. And the weekend itself. Her diamond ring, which was well over a carat and clearly an exceptional gem, as the jeweler had assured her. She'd read some place that even a one-carat diamond, if it were of the finest grade, could run over $10,000. Certainly Betty's eyes had practically jumped out of their sockets when she saw it and though Betty may have been flashy when it came to costume jewelry, she had a solid appreciation of diamonds as a girl's best friend. Why had Pat never thought of that! And the extravagant honeymoon at the luxury resort—another romantic dream fulfilled. The open house. Their numerous outings. All of those things had to mount up.

Pat of course had paid for a few of their early outings to a concert or a performance at Arena Stage by merely presenting tickets, but Paul seemed definitely embarrassed when she did so. Nor was he comfortable going dutch as she'd done with most of her previous escorts. Consequently, he gradually assumed the role of the perpetual host although she had cooked several dinners for him, proud to demonstrate her strong culinary skills and which he clearly appreciated as shown by his enthusiastic and robust appetite. There were never leftovers those times when she fed him! But the most that he had then accepted from her, other than food and sex, and that clearly mutually desired and given, was the plain broad gold band she ultimately placed on his finger at the courthouse.

Paul never seemed at a loss for money and she hadn't noticed dunning phone calls or creditors beating at the door but what the hell did his credit card look like? Pat just hadn't stopped to consider all the expenses they'd incurred and here she was the government economist. Jesus, maybe it was true. You get used to spending the taxpayers' money and after a while, you lose sight of real life!

Yes, the New York weekend, the trip to Jamaica, the extravagant house warming, the purchases they did make—not all cute and fun but some actually fairly pricey like the occasional antique that struck their eye. How was he paying for all that? Was he in debt and that was what was making him act so strange? It was time to look into that filing cabinet. No procrastination now, no attempt at denial, it was show time. God, what if they were about to be evicted? She hadn't signed anything pertaining to Paul except the marriage papers at the court house so she figured her own credit was good and she had been saving money particularly since the marriage. Plus there were all those government bonds she'd had automatically taken out of her pay at work; small, sure, but twenty-six a year and she had been working almost six years now. They should amount to something! Maybe they could consolidate his debts and find some way to straighten out the mess. Poor Paul, dumb her. How could she have been so stupid not to realize they were living way beyond their means and why hadn't he told her?

CHAPTER 7

Pat ran back up the stairs, leaping two at a time. The only manipulation she'd been undergoing was within herself. She had allowed her mind to play tricks because she still couldn't accept what was happening. This had to cease now!

With that thought, panting she dragged the desk chair up to the file cabinet, parked herself down, and pulled open the top drawer. Yes, there neatly labeled were folders for Paul's checking account and credit card (personal), so apparently he had a work one too. Next came insurance, medical information, etc.

She opened the credit card folder with trepidation, but the last statement was perfectly straight forward: filling station gas; a repair bill on the beloved Miata; a stop at the state-run ABC store to replenish their small bar although he got their wines mostly from a specialty shop on Wisconsin Avenue—the European connection apparently dominating his taste and rather expensively so she noted; and finally some restaurant charges—these for places he'd taken her. But, more important, no previous charges nor accrued interest penalties.

Next she looked at earlier statements, which were much the same although there were odd items like the pharmacy bill for the antibiotics he'd needed when he'd had accidentally slashed his finger this past July just before the first episode. Could that have been caused by a reaction to the medicine, she suddenly speculated? But then what about the last incident? Paul had no reason to be taking any prescription drugs now.

There was also a fairly hefty tab from one of the men's clothing stores he liked. "Got to keep up the corporate image," he'd said with elaborate casualness while modeling a light-grey three piece wool suit by Brooks Brothers. She'd whistled at the thousand dollars plus price tag but knew in the league he was playing, clothes did help make the man. "Also, keeps the ladies looking," Paul had leaned over and whispered to her with a cocky grin, reinforced then by his hammy, theatrical leer. Who said he'd failed drama—so much he did was melodramatic—a real thespian and she hadn't caught on.

"You're so vain," she'd hummed back but she'd given him an appreciative wink indicating that she, for one, was definitely looking and was rewarded in turn by one of those sensuous looks from his ever-changing rich green eyes.

"Hmm," he answered suddenly serious, "maybe you can unwrap and examine the merchandise when we get home."

"That sounds good," she agreed.

He bent further to kiss her lightly. "Can I do unwrapping too?"

"Without question."

"Good, that's a date then." The cocky smile had turned to a sweet, tender look.

Yet nothing, not even the bill for the antique mirror she'd admired and he had then immediately purchased during their outing to Leesburg, was unpaid. This lovely example of early George III giltwood, resplendent with its elaborate scrolling of birds and intertwined foliage, alone had run close to four thousand dollars. "My first car, and that was a piece of junk Lyle found for me when I went off to Wisconsin, didn't cost half that much!" Pat exclaimed. Then open-mouthed, she'd watched while Paul casually presented his credit card to the dealer after seeing how much she esteemed the ornate object.

"I bet it did by the time you got to Milwaukee," he observed wryly. She'd snickered and had to nod her head in agreement, remembering the long litany of assorted ills for the wreck from hell. If for nothing else, Ronnie had been talented when it came to cars and that in part was how they'd met. His excuse to make a move on the little girl from Saint Paul, he'd told her later. Ah yes, Ronnie who'd heard her moaning over the drawbacks of auto mechanics to another girl in their class and who'd come on like Click and Clack from Public Radio and by term's end was sharing an apartment with her.

Not used to impulse shopping, at least on that scale, Pat was still nonplused by the mirror's price tag. "My grandmother had one," Paul said as if that closed the subject and he, after all, had been the one to sign the credit slip. In any case, its charge too had been immediately paid. Certainly, the fancy framed oval glass made an impressive statement in the small foyer leading into their town house and Pat instinctively glanced in it each morning as she left. Paul wasn't the only one who was vain, she acknowledged. Moreover, it had caused one of their first disagreements and she, smugly, had prevailed.

"Higher, it's got to be hung higher. Eye sight," Paul had insisted as he brandished a hammer and nail. "Paintings and mirrors must be placed at eye sight."

"All very well for people whose heads are in the clouds. What about ordinary people like me!"

"Ones who live under ivy leaves?" he snorted, but then patting her affectionately on the head, he moved the nail down several inches. "Ok, Pix, you win."

Yes, she had, but as she continued her search further back, she let out a whistle when she noted the final cost of the catering firm, musicians and florist. She'd had no idea how much their party ultimately ran and obviously had way underestimated its extravagance. By the time she got to the bill for their Caribbean holiday, she was truly astounded. Paul hadn't let her know the cost of that either. She'd realized the resort was pricey, but not one in the five star range. He'd obviously spent more in the few months they had been married just on credit card purchases than she had grossed in over a year! What about the town house mortgage, utilities, insurances and taxes for goodness sake?

One item though was missing from the statements. This was the price of her ring although she clearly recalled his paying for that with a credit card. Even though there had been no price tags shown her when they were making the selection, she knew the brilliant little gem, now twinkling on her finger, cost a small fortune and that Paul had been taken aside to discuss possible insurance. She had tried to opt for a less luxuriant item but been overruled from the start by the initial selections he insisted be shown her. In fact, he seemed almost disappointed that she'd chosen one of the smaller stones in a simple gold setting even though it was a truly brilliant solitaire. Nor had she wanted an accompanying diamond-studded wedding band, deciding on plain gold to match the one they had selected for him, her purchase. The other rings she'd pointed out were big and flashy and she was neither.

"Hmm...I think you've got flash and you seem just the perfect size to me," he told her, appraising her lissome gamine figure, "but I guess you're right. Wouldn't want you to build up too many muscles on that left side from its weight. An unbalanced pixie would look mighty strange."

"Idiot," she laughed, poking him in the ribs while Paul grabbed the potentially threatening hand.

"Hey, careful there. You'll hurt my feelings. But you're correct. The stone should match your pretty little hand, when it isn't being used as a weapon," and he held it to his lips, placing a gentle kiss. "I love you, Pixie Pat," he whispered. Her answer had been in her expressive face, which shown radiant and happy.

Blinking away a tear at the memory, Pat continued her search. Painstakingly, she perused his banking statements, which revealed a healthy balance more than adequate for their life style. God, maybe Paul hadn't been kidding when he said he was rich although she couldn't find any savings accounts or stock information. No, he'd said there was some sort of investment plan at work and that he took full advantage of it. Certainly he had also shown great interest in the options she had through the Department for that was when he'd urged her to invest everything she could. The more she could sock away, he'd advised, the smarter she was. Sometimes she'd wondered which of them was truly the economist.

Jesus, was it taxes then? Pat looked for that file, and yet there again, it seemed that as far as Uncle Sam, the Commonwealth of Virginia, and Arlington County were concerned, her spouse was in fine shape although the file only contained current information. What tax data was here had not been completely clear although it did show he was taking zero deductions unlike her and that he had no problems with the authority figures. Most of the earlier data, including tax forms submitted in prior years, must be at his office at work or in one of the unpacked boxes in the basement. More probably, he kept all that information on the computer for future reference and was only retaining the previous forms somewhere in case, God forbid, he was ever audited by IRS or some nasty virus knocked out his hard drive. Another menace of the modern world but both she and Paul agreed it was always wise to take precautions in an increasingly electronic world and were constantly updating their virus checks. No such worries when one lived in a cave, Pat reflected—no bills either. Hunt and gather and that was that!

It also appeared that Paul was earning about what she thought as far as salary and benefits. Still, even though this was a healthy income, six grandly imposing figures to her eyes, it didn't explain how he could afford all the extra expenses since they'd married.

If not another woman, nor money, what then? Was Paul in some sort of legal predicament? Worse yet, was he making his money illegally? The thought of drugs flashed through her mind. Was he a Mafia scion, Paul Martini not Martin? Or maybe the dark good looks were narco-Columbian not Cajun? Paul had certainly been in another reality from hers those two times they'd had the bizarre sexual encounters—not just some innocuous fantasy world like her daydreaming. But, there'd been no indication otherwise of erratic behavior. Pat was sure she would have had some clue if Paul used drugs. She did, after all, have some experience, she thought wryly.

Ronnie, her former lover, had begun experimenting

with various substances after she moved in with him. Shit, he'd probably been doing it all along but she'd been too stupid to realize. When it came to men and their secrets, Pat ruefully surmised, she apparently was the last to know.

Although she herself had sampled some uppers once when stressed by graduate school, drugs had never appealed to her. And, being the only person in the world who couldn't seem to inhale a cigarette, for which she was now thankful, Pat was also probably the one person who believed a former president hadn't tried marijuana even if he had plenty of other vices. Second-hand exposure from Ronnie had become another problem and not just the marijuana smoke. In fact, his continued usage was only one of several reasons she and Ronnie became estranged.

Yet frankly, Pat was afraid of drugs, TV hype or not. She had watched a close friend of hers at Carleton gradually become an addict. The girl dropped out of college by senior year and ultimately ended up on the streets in the East Lake Street red light district of Minneapolis when her family gave up on her. It had been a sobering experience for Pat to see the disintegration of her bright, beautiful friend. Worse was knowing that prostitution and all its inherent dangers were Brenda's fate instead of the brilliant political career all the class envisioned when they met this dynamic girl from Duluth their freshman year. For years, Pat expected to hear from one of her classmates that Brenda had over-dosed or, worse, been murdered by her pimp or a customer. No, Pat was sure she would have detected Paul's usage.

So, discounting the drug theory, she concentrated on possible problems at work. But hell, this was a reputable firm Paul had joined and it was apparent that he was well liked even if he had developed no close friendships among his peers. Not only had the senior partner come to their open house but he and Paul's co-workers had given them a sterling silver coffee and tea set, grandly presented and greatly admired at the party. It was by far the most extravagant item they possessed, worth thousands no doubt. Then only a few weeks ago, the main man—strange Mr.

Beck, himself, had taken her aside at a dinner party and told her how pleased he was with her husband's work. When she'd reported that conversation to Paul later, he'd smiled slightly and said, "He's just sounding you out to see if someone's headhunting."

"What? You're thinking of another job?" Pat was visibly jolted by the unexpected prospect.

"No, not really. A couple of other places have spoken to me since I came on board. I do interact with lots of different firms and businesses in my position, but I like where I am. I like D.C. I always wanted to come here. I told you I'd let you know if there were ever another job that interested me. Why? Would you like to go somewhere else?"

Pat thought seriously for a moment. When she'd first come here as a junior economist with the Department of Agriculture, she really hadn't considered whether she'd planned to make the government her lifelong career. It had been a good job offer right out of grad school and after breaking up with Ronnie, the change of location had been more than appealing. For one thing, there was a chance for fairly rapid advancement through the special professional intern program, help with her school loans, the very good prospect that the work would be interesting, and most important a break with the Midwest. The last was especially appealing since Ronnie obviously intended to stay there, at least until he finished his doctorate. Her lover may have been stupid about drugs, like too many of their peers, but at academics he was a whiz.

That was another philosophic difference between her and Ronnie. She might have her own little reveries, but of the two, Pat knew she was the one with common sense and the ability to function in the real world. Another lesson from GG was that common sense wasn't common and it annoyed her that Ronnie felt so superior about his academic achievements and often viewed himself as far better than the masses. Masses perhaps like her parents, who lacked formal education and material wealth. Regardless of her later apprehensions, it hadn't been Paul, in spite of his apparently moneyed background, who was class conscious. No, the one time Ronnie visited her home was the first time that Pat was made aware how humble her background was. Even Elise, who came from real money and sported an Ivy League degree, never indicated that there might be any lesser social status with her new in-laws; nor for that matter did Elise's well-known family, who often included the Stroms in their own activities. Don and Elise's father, in fact, had taken several fishing trips up to Mille Lac, where the latter owned a spectacular lakeside lodge adjacent to the Indian reservation. Pat was hoping that perhaps Paul might be invited one day since he'd mentioned fishing excursions with his father. Going for a Northern Pike she was sure would far surpass the tiny bluegills or even healthy-sized catfish of the Alabama ponds, which he'd caught with pride as a small boy.

No, if anyone belonged in an ivory tower, it was Ronnie and he'd well learned the game to advance in the too often insular world of academics. Perhaps in an earlier age he would have thrived at some place like Berkeley, than noted for its added political agenda, not that getting ahead in any university wasn't politics itself. As it was, thought Pat bluntly, Ronnie would ass kiss, be pretentious, and snow his undergraduate students and even some of his peers with hypothetical rhetoric. Moreover, provided he found someone as besotted as she'd initially been who was willing to help him, he'd even turn out some well-written theses that probably would be published. Not works of actual practical value of course, but still something to further his career.

Yes, she had decided, further academics were not for her even though her written efforts seemed to have helped Ronnie. Economics she believed was a tool to be used in the real world, possibly making a small difference the way Mr. Cruz taught. It was therefore a propitious time to see more of the world regardless of how much she had loved her area of the country. After all, her whole life until then had been in the Midwest and close to her family.

Starting as an undergraduate at small, homey Carleton had been a wonderful experience; but, Northfield still had been only an hour's commute from her parents. At times then she had even considered being a day student, using the room and board fees to purchase a decent car. Oddly, or so it had seemed at first, it was her father who convinced her that the experience of life on campus was more valuable in spite of the additional cost although this was not the argument he'd given Nora Strom. Instead Don pointed out the dangers of driving in Minnesota winters and the fact that valuable study time would be lost in the commute. As if to prove his point, there had been an especially severe winter Pat's first year and Nora never again questioned the decision of her daughter's living on campus.

Attending Wisconsin after had really been Pat's first chance to strike out on her own, but even then she'd picked a neighboring state rather than further away Michigan, not that the more generous fellowship hadn't helped determine her decision. The big city atmosphere of the university in Milwaukee combined with its lakeside location and verdant landscaping seemed the ideal marriage of cement and soil, something the Twin Cities with all its parks and lakes also so fortunately achieved. Yet once Pat successfully obtained her degree, she had no actual regrets about terminating her scholastics; she had better than the required 3.3 and could have continued for the PhD but although stats were a snap, she really didn't enjoy the theoretical aspects.

Also, leaving academia meant leaving Ronnie. They'd had some good times, mostly at the beginning; but within weeks of moving in together, it was apparent to them both that there never would be a good basis for a permanent relationship. And as far as she knew, to date Ronnie still hadn't found one with any of her successors—all of whom seemed to have caught on as fast as Pat did that sometimes some people are too good to be true—a pithy little thought that now was coming to haunt her in regards to Paul.

Ronnie's continued although sporadic usage of drugs, including some chemical and hallucinatory, had ended their relationship as much as his self-serving scholastic attitude. Although Pat had no vindictive feelings toward him, the fact she would have less chance of bumping into her ex-lover by going east had its appeal. In their specialty, there would have been too many opportunities to meet if she had remained in the Midwest and that she didn't want. A break should be just that. So, if she were truly to evaluate their relationship, she would have said it was disappointing and that she'd been a bad judge of character. The unsettling thought was now occurring to her with some regularity that maybe she had been again.

Still, Ronnie had been her first lover and she'd been somewhat sad that things had to end that way. He, though, seemed no more devastated than she, in fact, perhaps less so, which didn't help her ego. Later, when she learned from friends that within a month of her departure he had moved in with another classmate who had also decided to continue working for her PhD, Pat knew why he'd been so accepting. Worse yet, she realized that the girl was even a better writer than she, showing once again Ronnie had been selective in his choice. Aside from Pat's slightly bruised self-esteem, all guilt and regret on her part over the breakup disappeared. At least they'd parted on as cordial terms as one could under the circumstances. And, upon learning of her successor, she made no effort to keep contact. In retrospect, she summed it up as one of life's lessons learned but it was better to have that realization before marrying or worse yet, having children like some of her friends in similar situations.

Her mother, Pat knew, in particular had been upset first about her and Ronnie living together and then almost perversely by the subsequent breakup. Nora Strom knew nothing about Ronnie's weakness with drugs and fortunately never perceived his well-disguised sense of social superiority. In public Ronnie was extremely polite, which also would contribute to his rise. Mr. Congeniality himself, another trait that Pat was distressed to realize also applied to Paul. But Paul had always been so sincere, so honest...Pat gulped at that consideration, that she might have been sucked into a totally fraudulent relationship. And worse, that for some unknown purpose, Paul had never loved her, which was even more hurtful.

Pat's father again had been more realistic about Ronnie and maybe that was a good sign, since he truly liked Paul, which was comforting. With Ronnie though, Pat was sure Don Strom had suspected one or the other of Ronnie's faults but would never have ventured a comment unless asked. Although Don hadn't said much to Pat, it was obvious he recognized the fact that his daughter was a grown-up and respected her decisions. As far as he was concerned, once she left Carleton and assumed all her own fiscal responsibilities, she should be accorded the respect of being a mature woman. "Mothers," he'd said to her, "always have to be mothers. Even when you turn fifty, sweetie, you'll still be the family baby in Mom's eyes." Then he chuckled, "Mine too."

Yet both knew Don would give advice only when asked and never be out of sorts if it were disregarded. By contrast, one could feel Nora's hurt in similar situations. But oddly, once Pat married Paul, she felt there was a slight change in her mother's attitude. Being a married woman apparently counted to Nora as a recognized step towards that elusive adulthood.

So, going to the East Coast was a welcomed challenge in more ways than one. Pat's work fortunately did prove interesting, especially compared to her previous jobs. Those had been mostly temporary and suited only to helping with the expenses of a full-time student. None had truly related to her chosen profession. And, to be honest, Pat enjoyed D.C. far more than she expected. She worked by and large with congenial people, who overall were bright and stimulating. The city was beautiful with countless things to do. Many in fact were free, which was perfect for someone starting out on a very limited budget. Pat also felt she was doing something beneficial, in spite of all the government bashing.

And, most important, she made some affable friends and acquaintances even if of late she seemed to have been drawing away from them, no doubt because Paul had become the very core of her existence. He was the best friend she'd always wanted and she his, or so she'd thought. Life had been relatively easy until their meeting although she'd sometimes wondered if she were being passed by in the marriage mart. Certainly she had encountered a few interesting men but none interesting enough until she had literally crashed into him.

"No," she'd replied honestly in answer to his question about relocating if he were offered another position. "I like D.C., my job. I'm doing ok." Actually, she was doing more than ok, she figured. She'd never rival Paul's salary but she'd managed to progress several grades in her six years at the Department. Further, being a well-educated woman and personable to boot, she believed she even had a shot at becoming a senior exec or at least top mid-management if she were to devote the rest of her career years to federal service. "You'll let me know if you do want to leave, won't you?" She could get a decent job elsewhere, perhaps even with the field offices of the numerous Ag agencies, which were scattered across the country. But over all, she wanted to stay where she was and in federal service, trying to live up to Mr. Cruz and making a difference. Perhaps eventually she might change her mind, but not now.

"I assure you, you'll be the first to know and we'd discuss it before I'd ever make a decision. I let you know everything," Paul had said with what had seemed complete sincerity.

Well she'd believed her 'best friend' had let her know everything which just went to show what a fool she was. All the more reason to see if she could discover his secrets. In for a penny, in for a pound, Pat decided pragmatically, and she began to hunt through the rest of his files, seeking some clue as to what was happening. Finally after an hour of her exhaustive search, she stopped, putting everything neatly back in place. There'd been a wealth of information there about the mortgage. Even the fact that Paul was not only making regular payments, but in actuality slightly accelerated ones for a faster payoff. Moreover this was for a fifteen-year loan rather than the more conventional thirty-year one. The record of his purchases revealed no unexpected items either. There was nothing else truly personal save for the military records which did indeed show his JAG service and postings. Then she looked at his desk again, at the small framed picture of the little family of three, and lastly around the rest of the room for more clues from his other possessions.

The shelved books were no great indication. His law books he kept at work. Most of what was here were university textbooks and recent acquisitions—biographies, light fiction and some volumes of poetry. Oddly enough, there were also several old children's books, a well-worn *Tintin* and some *Babars*, all in French, which she wondered if he'd used when he was learning the language. She knew she'd perused a comic book or two in Spanish like *Fantom* or *Miky Raton* as a student for just that purpose, and especially enjoyed the Spanish versions of Richard Scarry's books although she never wanted to admit what a thrill it had been when she'd first translated his charming little stories on the alley cat like *Ali-Gato El Gran Pintor* or *Viva la Música*. No, it was much better to mention casually how much she'd liked reading Garcia Lorca's plays in the original or *Don Quixote*, even though she had practically worn out her sturdy Cuyas dictionary, now bandaged with the world's strongest tape as a victim of her efforts. Yet, by contrast, there were no French text books or even a French/English dictionary, tattered or not.

What she did see were several French novels including André Gide's *La Symphonie Pastorale*, which ironically Ronnie believed was one of the greatest examples of literature and had as a result frequently equated everything to Beethoven's *Symphony No. 6*, through which the book's protagonist explained colors to a blind girl. The climax being the girl's recovery of sight and subsequent disillusionment to discover that her imagined world was more beautiful than reality. At times, Pat cynically thought it was probably the only foreign fiction Ronnie had ever read. Worse yet, that maybe it was the only fiction, much less that the *Sixth* was the one classical composition he could identify. Ronnie had no great interest in the arts, which hadn't helped their relationship. Be honest, Pat thought to herself, aside from cramming for econ exams together and editing his papers, said relationship was based on sex—hot, carnal and basic.

I'll have to ask Paul if the Gide is really that good, she mused. Or the Beethoven—actually any Beethoven, but of that she had no doubt. Shit, Pat then wondered, was she like Gide's blind heroine? Had she seen everything through some wonderful dream or majestic music and now that she had sight, Paul wasn't as perfect as she thought? One changes in marriage but like this? Did everyone awaken some morning to a stranger? Certainly not her parents nor Lyle and Elise and never Joan and her Tom. Definitely not staid, dependable Tom, the insurance agent who was as much a piece of the rock as the company he represented. Were there clues she should have seen all along to prepare herself? Was she a Mitty here too in believing Paul was a normal, wonderful man with whom she could build a happy life? With Ronnie, she finally realized she had allowed herself to be manipulated and probably that was why she never moved in with anyone else. But, Paul, she married him! Was that just being weak and manipulated again?

Pat eyes squinted as she looked back at the books, trying to find some clue. There was also a dictionary in French only and corresponding, one in German. There was even a French/German one. But, again, there were no text books for that language either although she did see an Italian grammar—to help with those menus no doubt. Odd, she'd kept all her Spanish grammars and the poor, battered and wounded dictionary was still that ever dependable classic Cuyas' Spanish/English, but she knew Paul used the languages regularly. So undoubtedly, he was beyond needing the aids or those aids were all at his office. She'd never noticed when visiting him. So much unnoticed, not considered, unknown.

Then she mentally appraised his other possessions and again conceded that aside from the few antiques they'd been purchasing and what she'd brought with her, almost everything in the house was new or a product of their restoration projects. She smiled sadly as she again remembered his original comment about the lack of furniture, "Besides, I told you all we really need is the bed," this repeated in a soft whisper one of the first nights she spent there after they had returned engaged from New York and were mere days away from being married. Surely it couldn't have just been sex that brought or kept them together—a new and improved version of her relationship with Ronnie, so to speak. Love having been added to the carnal.

Still, Pat couldn't discount the counter argument that Paul had been a student and a military officer and above all a bachelor so there really was no reason for much accumulation. But, it did seem strange now—hell, downright obvious—that for an only child, he had no conspicuous family mementos displayed save the little picture. It was almost as if he'd been an institutionalized orphan or relegated to some sterile boarding school or even, horrors, some juvenile detention center, forgotten by one and all. No, not the reform school. Lawyers were officers of the court or something like that; surely Paul would never been admitted to the bar if he'd had a criminal record, adolescent or not.

Her souvenirs—none criminal although she still didn't eat Heath bars after having been dared to shoplift candy once as a child—were mostly in Minnesota. She hadn't entered the scene of the crime, the small neighborhood drugstore, for weeks thereafter and then only because her mother sent her on an errand. These honest keepsakes remained safely packed in her parents' basement once Joan's and her bedroom was turned into a spare room. This took place after Pat finished college and plainly had no intention of moving back to the Twin Cities. As if to compensate for the loss of her baby, Nora immediately boxed Pat's belongings and then prepared the room for the grandchildren and other visitors. Pat wasn't sure at the time if she or her mother had been more disturbed, but it was

Pat's decision to leave.

Pat had promised her mother she would retrieve these items once she felt really settled. In addition were several pieces of furniture she'd inherited from GG, including an ornate headboard carved by Karl Lind and coveted by both her siblings, The all-important headboard had been her equivalent of a hope chest item and superstitiously, she had denied herself its use until she found the man with whom she wanted to share it. She had assumed that finally, this would be the year to retrieve it and everything else on their proposed drive out for Christmas. Since Paul had only had time for the long Easter weekend, having used his still limited vacation hours for the extra day in New York and their honeymoon, she had also promised her mother they would stay until New Years. Paul had not been overly enthusiastic over the prospect, not that he objected to going to Minnesota again. It was the time of the year and the fact that she planned to drive the Saturn and return with a U-haul.

"Driving in the Midwest in winter! Maybe we should fly and just ship the things," he protested.

"That would cost at least twice as much—maybe even more," Pat argued in turn and slightly disgruntled, he agreed. Well, if his financial records were any indication, she need not have worried about trying to save money although whether in actuality she could ever trust the headboard to some mover, Pat didn't know. Or, for that matter, would she still have someone with whom she wanted to share this cherished item.

Certainly Pat's older siblings had ultimately moved their possessions from the Midway dwelling as soon as married and she well knew that her father had dreamed for years of having some private space of his own in that small, but homey abode. It was after all, only a bungalow—not huge, only three bedrooms, and while Pat was growing up, seemingly bursting with activity and the presence of her siblings who stayed in residence until they too had married. She alone had gone away to school instead of being a commuter to the University of Minnesota campus.

The coveted basement, now housing her possessions, was where the Strom children played at length with Lyle's train, often in the dark save for the small locomotive lights, to make their games more scary. How angry, in fact, the older two were at a younger sister's baby clumsiness; for far too often, Lyle and Joan set up intricate rail systems and built tiny Lego towns only to have Pat stumble into them. Yet down there also, Joan had helped her with a Halloween party during her fourth grade, making costumes of green and orange crepe paper which was one of Pat's first sewing lessons.

And all three children had played marbles on the cellar floor in winter; that was if Pat had any left from the gambling of 'odds and evens', a game she played each spring while walking to school with her friends. Actually highly unsuccessful, she'd ask Santa each year for a new bag although often in pity, Lyle supplemented her dwindling store. It had also been Lyle finally, who had revealed to her the shocking truth that some of the players cheated. He then coached her to watch for those classmates who might hide an extra marble in the pouch of skin between thumb and hand in order to have it ready to add to those in the fist if there were some danger of losing. Lyle might be unmerciful in teasing his baby sister, but others did so at their own risk. Pat smiled at the thought of her sometimes overly protective siblings and wished her big brother could once again somehow magically reveal the truth, shocking or not, about what was happening.

Once Pat's things were out of the bungalow, perhaps her father could have that long desired den. But for now, poor Mother, the family curator and keeper of Pat's childhood treasures, was apparently likely to remain so, at least until this mess with Paul straightened out. And, poor Dad would just have to continue his wait.

In Paul's case, his family was dead and maybe everything had disappeared then. What would a college kid do when his whole family dies? Would she have kept her

Wizard of Oz books and Girl Scout badges if there hadn't been that safe, cozy basement and a doting mother to watch these prized possessions? Yes, Pat decided. She would have, but then she had the option and she also still had the family.

Paul, she thought in mixed anguish and frustration, what's the matter and where are you? Back down the stairs she went, this time slowly as she pondered. There she fiddled away some of the remaining hours of the day trying to read a J.A. Jance mystery she'd missed. It was her first introduction to Joanna Brady, but somehow the lady sheriff wasn't as intriguing as the author's Seattle detective, J.P. Beaumont who had married an attractive and wealthy woman of mystery. Well Pat had apparently wed a mysterious, well-to-do and attractive man. God forbid that she'd gotten involved with a murderer! A mafioso bones maker or whatever the hell crime families called someone who made a hit. Ridiculous, Paul had been a military lawyer and evidently she had watched *The Sopranos* too often.

Next Pat settled down on the futon and spent a few minutes viewing one of the more serious Sunday TV news shows, something she and Paul often did together. But it couldn't hold her attention either. There were still too many unanswered questions and she felt as though her brain was approaching overload. Then she thought of working on the cabled sweater she'd been knitting as a surprise for her husband. Speaking of secrets, but such an understandable one! How often she'd had to shove it under the bed or behind the futon when he'd come home earlier than expected. Rich sea green to match his gorgeous eyes, it was for his upcoming birthday when he'd catch up with her on the BIG-3-0 come the end of November.

"An older woman," he'd baited her when he learned her age.

"Only five months," was her annoyed comeback.

"Hey, just think of all the firsts you had."

"Sure, a tooth, sitting up, solid food."

"Oh I bet there were other things too," he teased. "Girls always mature faster."

"And boys...particularly kids in their twenties who have no respect for their elders."

"Ouch!" he exclaimed, lightly smacking his face and making Pat roll her eyes in mock disgust at his theatrics. "I'll be good, ma'am. I promise. Don't send me to bed without supper."

"I thought you liked to go to bed," she remarked coyly, a sexy little look appearing in her eyes. "Maybe I shouldn't be corrupting younger men."

Paul put his hand to his forehead in a gesture of despair. "I never thought of that. Please corrupt me, Madame. Let me be your boytoy. Maturity becomes you. I shall endeavor to follow your good or bad example, whichever the case may be."

"Fool," she smiled indulgently and then later that night, moving her body against his, she'd whispered seductively "Boytoy," and the term officially entered their own private vocabulary of endearments.

When was that conversation Pat wondered? A week, two weeks before her June birthday when she'd finally revealed that it was thirty not twenty-nine she would be celebrating? Another secret like her height? But her secrets were so innocent...small like her whereas Paul's were like him, large and dark.

Giving up all pretenses of being productive, she wandered into the kitchen and made herself a peanut butter and tomato sandwich and settled down to read the Sunday *Post*. But her appetite was gone and leaving the sandwich half eaten, she gave up on the newspaper as well and climbed back up to the bedroom. A bubble bath, she decided. Cleanliness is next to godliness and where the hell is he? Sinking into the foaming tub, Pat soaked herself, staring blankly at the ceiling until the bubbles were long gone and the water had turned cold and grey, matching her mood. Getting out finally, she made her way into the bedroom, not caring for once that she was dripping on the floor. Throwing herself down on the bed, she lay, again looking up at the ceiling as if she could detect some great secret in the hairline cracks. Perhaps an augury of events to come. Where was GG's second sight when one needed it?

Ceilings I have seen, Pat mused—the tangled tawdry tale of a wretched woeful wife. How many ceilings does a woman see in a lifetime? Particularly a sexually active one, assuming her sex life is dominated by the conventional missionary position? If Paul were here, they probably would be chuckling as they fantasized about what ceilings she'd seen during their short relationship and the secrets learned. He, of course, had had the opportunity to view one or two as well but of course he wasn't here and there was some secret and that was the problem. It was almost 8:00 P.M. now—definitely too early to go to sleep but Pat didn't feel like doing anything else.

Paul, she thought sorrowfully. Where are you? Who are you? To reassure herself, she began to re-itemize what she knew, almost like counting sheep. He was almost thirty—those all important five months younger by which he continued to tease her unmercifully even if he had made an elaborate production when last June 24 had arrived. In honor of the memorable 3-0, he had taken her for an elegant dinner at the Watergate. There he had presented her with a beautifully intricate bracelet, which appeared to be an antique. Tiny diamond chips centered within small matched pieces of polished pink-tinted quartz. Each framed and then linked by fragile twists of white gold. It was obvious this was the work of a real craftsman.

"It belonged to my grandmother," Paul had told her—one of the few tangible mementos of that lovely lady he still possessed. Pat had cried when he put it around her wrist and he'd chided her, "Hey, don't get all sentimental in your old age!" But she could detect a hint of moisture around his own bright eyes as he smiled benignly in response to her reaction.

The story about the bracelet had to be real; surely he couldn't have been acting! But, facts—what facts did she know for certain or what else had he told her? He was from the South, born in Montgomery, and his father was a lawyer who had had a small private practice, which is why he'd wanted to be a lawyer. "It was probably because he always let me play with the magic markers and his flip chart when he took me to work," Paul told her by explanation, a slight smile on his face.

"Sure," Pat agreed. "I bet you still do."

"Oh, most definitely, Madame. I even have a smock at work so I don't get my clothes dirty and they only let me use water-based markers."

"I believe it about the smock," she laughed, teasing him about the extreme care with which he treated his costly wardrobe, not that she wouldn't have done the same. Her $200 suits, usually acquired on sale or from Frugal Fannie's, got plenty of personal attention. "I get to use permanent base and we even have ones that smell like fruit."

He looked at her for a moment. "You're serious, aren't you?"

"Of course, who ever heard of an economist who didn't have cherry red and anise black markers," Pat answered feeling supremely smug and he burst into laughter, shaking his head in mock disapproval.

Paul's mother trained to be a school teacher—science classes in junior high. She probably had magic markers too, Pat reflected rather inconsequentially. But, the woman stopped teaching within a year at Paul's birth. The younger brother, James, was born when Paul was four. There were complications and both mother and infant son died. Then they'd had a housekeeper. Sarah? Wasn't that her name? A nice black woman, old and matronly—almost another grandmother, who'd been there when he came home from school and the one who'd taken him to her church and taught him all those spirituals. And he'd been really close to his father. They'd gone fishing and his dad had taught him to hunt and garden and had helped him with his homework and coached little league although Paul himself preferred soccer.

"Soccer?" Pat queried. "You guys were ahead of us. It's only been the last few years that it's been catching on at home. My nieces play."

"Yah," said Paul dismissively. "The South's gone a bit

beyond hunting with coon dogs or sitting on the back stoop sipping white lightnin' for entertainment. Besides, my dad knew how to play. He learned in England although he started with rugby."

"I didn't know he lived in England."

"He had a Fulbright and did a year at Oxford after college."

"Wow! I'm impressed, truly impressed."

"Yah, he was a fairly impressive guy."

"I'm surprised you didn't follow in his footsteps that way."

"I wanted to be educated in the States," Paul stated curtly. "Besides, who says I was smart enough."

"Paul, Paul, Paul," Pat scolded. "Didn't you tell me you were in the top ten of your class at Stanford and edited the *Law Review* besides?"

"Must have heard me wrong," he muttered, dropping the subject, but of course he had been unless he'd lied and at that point she didn't think so although he'd never shown her copies of the review. No, no lies from what his boss and office peers said. There apparently was even a Phi Beta Kappa key hidden somewhere—an honor she'd just missed, much to her annoyance. Damn English lit and a professor fixated on students writing poetry when she couldn't rhyme worth a damn. It was amazing she still loved the genre. Amazing that she loved a mysterious man who could create it with far more talent than the accursed pretentious prof—another academic variation of Ronnie, she'd later decided.

When Paul's father died in his early teens, he'd gone to live with his grandparents but she couldn't remember if those were his mother's parents or his father's. The fact he stayed in Montgomery probably meant they were his father's. Paul had never really said where his mother originally was from although Pat somehow had assumed New Orleans. Certainly she'd married his father when he started Law School at Tulane. The woman apparently was a couple of years younger. Both his parents were only children, Pat remembered him saying, so there really was no one else besides the grandparents.

That's right. His mother had been sent to a convent school or at least a Catholic boarding school after her own mother died. So maybe she was Cajun, which would help explain Paul's coloring and facility with French. No, that part wasn't right. He looked like his father and his mother was the blonde. The mother seemed the more amorphous of the two, but then hell, Paul was only four when she died. He'd never even mentioned her name, Pat suddenly realized, and then chagrined, she realized she had never even asked. Another mystery name like the irritating W and French no doubt: Adrienne, Blanche, Charlotte?

Paul's freshman year, his grandmother found out she had cancer and the following summer—he'd gone home to work in Montgomery to be with her—she'd died. He'd then asked his grandfather if he should transfer from Tulane to Huntingdon College, which was just walking distance from their house on Thomas Avenue, or maybe to Auburn's Montgomery campus so he could live at home. Thomas Avenue—that was right—the boulevard lined with oleanders, which Paul told her were poisonous—pleasingly attractive but deadly. Pleasing like Paul the consummate flower lover, she reflected, and then stopped short of completing the analogy.

The old man said Paul should stick with his dream, everything would be fine. Well, it hadn't been and his grandfather had died before Christmas his sophomore year—supposedly from a heart attack, but really Paul suspected from a broken heart. Pat suspected Paul's had broken then too.

After that, there wasn't much reason to return to Alabama. Paul devoted himself to his studies in social sciences and languages, capturing that enviable Phi Beta Kappa key and some other prizes. Next he was accepted to top-notch Stanford Law School, financed partially by an Air Force scholarship, which fully paid one year. Pat wondered why he just hadn't taken a loan and avoided the military service.

"I thought about that," he'd answered seriously. "But I wasn't going to be returning to a family law firm and I kind of thought I might like the military—the discipline, the boarding school aspect."

At that comment, Pat had stared at him strangely since none of her peers had considered such a career attractive, save for a few high school acquaintances with no real prospects and one friend who dreamed of being Top Gun; in their cases, the services had made sense. Lyle and Joan had some friends, who had gone to West Point and Annapolis but that was for the academics and prestige since only one stayed on as a career officer. Still hadn't Paul done that too in his own way?

Catching her look, he'd responded, "Hey, camaraderie, all right? Also, there was the prospect of travel and the thought I might want to make it a career. That's probably also why I went for a straight JD although I had considered their Law and Business program."

Consequently, at age twenty-four, Paul joined the Air Force to pay back his stipend and was sent first to Germany and then to Hawaii. "Two choice posts," he'd half bragged, "but I took advantage, learning as much German as I could." No question, Paul obviously had a real flair for languages.

He'd also traveled when he could. That had included the skiing in Switzerland. "Next long holiday," he'd then told Pat, "we're off to Europe or Asia and I'll show you around unless you prefer to stick with the tropical islands, perhaps sampling the Pacific version."

Peculiar again, Pat thought. Paul would take her to the Orient but not to Alabama.

Deciding not to make the military a career, Paul was honorably discharged. "It didn't get to be like JAG on the TV," he'd laughed. "Most of the time I was counseling poor fools who had committed infractions or was chained to my desk vetting contracts. Not overly glamorous work although once I had to review an agreement with a group of native Hawaiians over some prehistoric burial ground. Dealing with them and Indian tribes..."

"Native Americans," Pat chided.

"Depends on the tribe," asserted her spouse. "Buzz words change and you can't lump them together any more than all Africans or all former Soviets, as we and they have been seeing disastrously. Still, it is like dealing with sovereign nations and added more spice than I would have thought artifacts and thousand year-old bones would have engendered. Definitely one of my more exciting projects."

Paul had then traveled for a few months through the Pacific while his applications were being reviewed by various law firms. "Islands, darlin', I told you they fascinate me and who knew when I'd have the time or money again." But there was money, Pat thought. Damn it! That mysterious mother lode that had to be paying for some of their extravagances and would have financed a hiatus through the South Pacific and probably the down payment on the town house, signing bonus be damned.

When Paul returned state side, he'd been interviewed by several prominent firms in Seattle, San Francisco, and D.C., which were apparently the cities that interested him. At last he'd decided to take the offer from Beck and Stringfellow although he'd once implied to her that bonus aside, it wasn't the most lucrative in its starting salary but it was in D.C., his preferred city. Odd about that, even if his paycheck looked plenty good to her. And, obviously, again from what her friends had told her, he had to have been good or he never would have received the very select opportunity. So probably he'd been looking at the long-range prospects, especially since there was so much European business being handled but then why the hell had he picked Stanford for his law degree? Perhaps with the other firms, his work would have been dealing with the Pacific Rim and Orient. Some of his JAG experience as well as the acquired linguistics had to have contributed to the mutual decision between him and his firm for she knew that currently he was involved in legal matters dealing with foreign corporations and wealthy Europeans investing in the United States.

In fact, Mr. Beck had told her at that dinner party how

unusual it was to have an American employee with Paul's strong linguistic capabilities and that in the near future, he probably would be sending her husband on some trips to Germany and France. With the E.U. and a common currency in the Euro, it was even more important for U.S. firms to strengthen their ties with European counterparts so they wouldn't be frozen out of the unifying economy. Also, in a shrinking world, personal ties were intensifying. All of this meant negotiating one's way through a myriad of laws and regulations, domestic and foreign. Wesley Beck clearly saw himself as a visionary and his firm the tool for accomplishing this goal, much less realizing that being a leader also led to further wealth and power. Having staff members that could tackle the issue, especially in more than one language, was the key and a bright young man like Paul fit that profile.

So, linguistic capabilities again—able to mediate in French and German. Pat was still contemplating those foreign dictionaries, the lack of the grammars. Paul was so good he didn't need aids in English? The French from his mother and then Tulane and New Orleans perhaps? And starting German as an undergraduate with the extra time in Germany but would that make someone a linguist? Still, it would have been a second foreign language and that was supposed to be easier to acquire if one had had an early start on another. Pat knew she was fairly proficient in Spanish and in fact had participated in several meetings where the language was used, but this was after four years of high school classes and a minor in college. She'd even taken a couple of follow-up conversation classes at Ag's well-known night school. Yet although she had been an A student and certainly could translate documents with some facility, plus the backup of good old Cuyas, no one would ever call her a linguist. Well, it was a gift and by some means Paul apparently had it. Even his English was so precise with just the slightest touch of a southern drawl. Odd, she'd never thought about that. An Alabama boy who went to Tulane and he didn't have a pronounced drawl except when he was teasing or they were talking about the South? Then subconsciously he turned it on, or was that deliberate?

Also, what was it he had said when they met? She'd been telling him how she was trying to recapture her childhood glory as a skating champ and he'd said something like "Me too. I just thought it would be nice to see if I could still do it." Where would an Alabama boy and someone who'd gone to college in Louisiana and then law school out in California learn to skate? Had there been some period he'd spent in the North or had he learned in Germany? But he wasn't a kid then. He was a young man in his mid-twenties. Maybe she had just misunderstood him although she was sure he'd been referring to childhood. So many questions, she thought, her mind racing, but eventually she did doze off.

CHAPTER 8

When Pat awoke, she heard the sound of water running in the bathroom and Paul whistling. My God, had it all been a dream? No, she was still nude, just as she'd been when she flopped onto the bed although Paul had apparently draped a quilt over her. Her nightgown had fallen to the side of the bed, never picked up, never worn. The still unfinished Jance mystery lay by the bedside, pristine without an additional page turned, and it was now almost 6:30 A.M. The alarm should have been due to ring any moment, except it was turned to the off position. Had she forgotten to set it or had Paul turned it off? She could even smell the aroma of fresh coffee perking down in the kitchen—macadamia no less, her favorite. Up she shot. When the hell had he come home?

Just then the bathroom door opened and he was standing there in his pajama bottoms, a damp towel around his neck and she could smell his spicy aftershave lotion. "Coffee, darling?" he asked, for once completing the word, as he walked through the bedroom towards the upstairs hall.

"Paul," she called and he turned and looked at her, a big smile on his face. "Paul, where were you?" she blurted out.

He glanced at her puzzled. "The bathroom of course." He came back and looked down at her concerned. "What's the matter...bad dream?"

"Paul, where were you yesterday and the day before?"

Now he definitely looked perplexed. "Yesterday? I was here. What do you mean?"

"No, you weren't. You walked out of here bright and early Saturday morning and I haven't seen you for almost forty-eight hours. If you hadn't been here this morning, I'd have been calling the police now."

"What the hell are you talking about?" He sounded angry. "I just got out of bed, for lord's sake. I didn't want to wake you but I have to be at the office early today and I thought I'd get ready first."

Pat reached up towards him, nearly pleading, "Where were you? What's wrong with you?"

Stepping back, he looked at her with shock. "Pat, what's the matter? I don't understand. Is this supposed to be some sort of joke? If it is, I don't think it's very funny. Now cut it out. Do you want coffee or don't you? I've got to get to the office by 8:00 today. If you want to play games, we'll do it this evening, ok?" Then turning, he practically darted out of the room. A few minutes later, he was back with two mugs of steaming coffee, one for him and one for her, but he said nothing, just placing her mug by the side of the bed.

Going over to the bureau, he pulled out clean underwear and she could see from the way he was looking into the mirror that he was watching her. Next he selected a shirt and dark grey suit pants and then he went back into the bathroom to dress—a definite change in their nonchalant habit of dressing and undressing before one another, but something he did when he was that strange, distant man.

Once back in the bedroom, he snatched a tie, solid grey in color. It was not his ordinary deliberate production of selection for she knew he usually chose a light grey with narrow, discrete red stripes to complement this particular attire; nor was he using his customary great care in tying it either. Again she was aware he was surreptitiously surveying her by way of the mirror. She continued to sit where she was, hunched up with the quilt wrapped around her, watching and trying to decide what she should do, besides possibly bursting into tears. She had been nonplused, to say the least, by his reaction and heated denial.

Returning to the closet, he grabbed his suit coat and then walked out the room still avoiding any direct eye contact with her. He was going to the study for his briefcase, she was fairly certain, and a moment later she heard him starting down the stairs. Just before he reached the bottom, she heard him call with cold clarity, "We'll talk this evening."

There'd been no goodbye kiss, no tousling of her hair,

no softly whispered "I love you, Pix," no happy melodious whistle. Not even his corny and usual "In the words of the great Immortal Arnold, 'I'll be back,'" or "*Hasta la vista, Baby*" delivered in an appalling German accent, which for some reason amused him greatly. There wasn't a Schwarzenegger extravaganza he hadn't seen which made quite a contrast to all the foreign arts films he also enjoyed. Christ, while she was Mittying, had he drifted into being Conan the Barbarian during those eerie episodes?

Damn, she thought. This morning's conversation had told her a lot. Dejectedly, Pat got out of bed and slowly, laboriously made her way to the bathroom. She felt like she was a million years old, as though her youth had been stolen—leaving her a female Rip Van Winkle, minus the beard. Not by achieving the mere three decades, but by the last forty-eight hours during which she knew she'd aged immeasurably and lost something she might never recover.

Paul's shaving gear was scattered all over the vanity counter and there was water splashed on it and the floor. The toothpaste tube was missing its cap. That was something Paul never did, always being careful to put things back where they belonged and cleaning up any mess. Further, he had just tossed the towel aside instead of neatly hanging it to dry. Even his pajama bottoms were lying crumpled on the floor instead of being placed into the clothes hamper. Clearly what she had said had disturbed him.

Well it had disturbed her too. Maybe she should just stay home today. Or, better yet, maybe she should get dressed and march down to his office, if that was really where he was going, and demand to talk to him, but she knew she couldn't do that. She'd agonized alone through the weekend because she didn't want to embarrass him. So, maybe... maybe she'd just get ready for her own office where she'd do her best to keep herself occupied and maybe really be able to concentrate on her own work. At least there were no major meetings or reports due today. Then maybe she'd come right home after work and be here when he returned.

That is if he bothered to come. But then he had after all

returned sometime last night and acted perfectly normally this morning until she'd spoken to him. He appeared to be the same Paul he'd been just last Friday night when they'd fallen asleep, comfortably snuggled together. If she hadn't said anything just now, he probably would have been the same Paul he was most mornings even if he was up earlier than normal today. Still, early morning meetings weren't that unusual for him, especially if there was a conference call planned to Europe where it was six hours ahead.

The day dragged. Several people in Pat's section were walking over to L'Enfante Plaza for lunch—a kind of informal gab session that her professional peers did every week or two to catch up on items not brought up at staff meetings. At least that was the theory justifying their little luncheon klatch even if it seemed the actual result was sometimes purely gossip or speculation on office politics as well as chit chat about out-of-office happenings. Usually she joined the group, but today she pled fatigue and said she was behind on a survey she was doing.

One of her smartass cohorts, Todd of course, looked at her laughing and said, "Ah, still the newlywed...so tiring, poor dear. What does Paul look like?"

"Button it up, Todd," she retorted blushing, "or I'll report you for sexual harassment."

"My, my, touchy today," her friend countered, blowing her a kiss and she'd grinned back even if she did feel like shit. In all, it was a long and disheartening work day and once more, she wished she had someone to talk to like the Todd of old, but she knew she couldn't. This was just too personal and she was no longer the Pat of old either, much less God knew who Paul had become.

CHAPTER 9

When Pat arrived home, she changed into casual clothes per usual—another of Mother's rules or actually GG's passed down through three generations and still in force. Then fidgety and anxious, she began her wait. She considered cooking something tasty that Paul liked perhaps as a way to ease into the conversation she knew they must have. But hell, she wasn't hungry. If anything, she felt somewhat nauseated, not surprising with the stress she was feeling. Ease? How could they ease into discussing what had happened? For that matter, she now suspected that she'd never been completely at ease after the first episode even if she'd tried to repress it. As for today, the tension seemed unbearable and she saw she'd succeeded in gnawing off the nails of her other hand. What next, her toes, or fiddling with her hair, or some other nervous habit? What would Mother suggest now? Damn, she truly was losing it.

She should have gone to the health club at work today but then she might have bumped into Betty, who would have wanted to know what was new as if Pat knew herself! Or old or whatever. Still she could jog around the block a few times—something to relieve her stress. But if she did that, she might miss Paul when he arrived. If he did. Instead she found herself pacing back and forth like that pathetic wolf he'd written about in his poem. The town house had been a sanctuary, their den. For a moment, she imagined two great furry mammals curled snugly around each other in that cozy, little den much as she and Paul had snuggled last Friday, a mere three days ago. Maybe she was turning into a poet too. Hell no, what she was doing was acting as though she was the one in a cage or worse yet, back in the apocalyptic cave.

Paul arrived home shortly before 7:30 and at this point, all pretense of Pat's being cool and collected disappeared. He hadn't even put down his briefcase before she blurted out fiercely, "Where were you, Paul?"

"What do you mean?" He looked at her anxiously, his eyes narrowing.

"You haven't been home all weekend. You marched out of here Saturday morning without a word and the next thing I knew you were in the bathroom this morning, acting as though nothing had happened."

"I don't know what you're talking about," he said evasively, and he was no longer looking at her directly. "I think I need a drink. How about you?" He walked past her towards the kitchen.

"It's not the first time, you know," she called, her voice rising as she followed him. Standing nervously behind him, her hands curled unconsciously into tight little fists with the remnants of her nails still sharply digging into her palms. A real effort, that.

Paul turned around from the cabinet where they kept their liquor supply and faced her. "What!" It was obvious from his widened eyes and the sudden loss of color to his face that he was stunned.

"About two months ago. It was the same sort of thing. I woke up, you were looking at me, and then all of a sudden you wanted to have sex..."

"Hell, I almost always want to have sex with you." He poured her a glass of wine, unasked for, and then one for himself. Taking a small sip, he considered her statement. His countenance now moody, he settled into one of the chairs at the small wrought iron kitchen table with the glass top—the ice cream parlor set, supposedly like his grandmother's, which had become such a pleasing component of their home. At this moment, that was about all in the kitchen that was pleasing Pat.

"No, you make love to me," she responded archly, taking the seat next to him.

"And what's that supposed to mean? You're my wife. Of course I make love to you. I do love you."

"Well you didn't that time," she stated flatly, her voice caustic.

Paul looked at her horrified, drawing back in his chair as if to distance himself. "What do you mean?"

"It was as though you were totally impersonal, as though you'd never seen me before, didn't give a damn who I was. I half expected you to slip some money on the bureau when you left."

"Jesus...I didn't..." Now he really was distressed.

"Rape me? No, but it didn't matter who was there with you. You just wanted a woman and I happened to be handy. I don't know if you would have forced me if I hadn't wanted to, but I don't think so. You've never been like that. I mean as big and strong as you are, you really could do anything you wanted with me to be honest, but that's not you. As weird as everything was, you still were careful."

"Oh Christ." Paul looked down at his hands, large and powerful in spite of the long, delicate fingers. They were clenched on the table and she could see he was making an effort to force them open and let the fingers relax. "Oh shit. I didn't hurt you? You're sure?"

She studied him, uncertain; she was having difficulty with her own anxiety, not knowing what next to say. Then picking her words carefully, she answered. "No. It was just like the time before. You wanted me and that was that. I wouldn't have wanted to deny you anyhow...I love you, Paul." And she did, which made this all so painful.

"Deny me, ah shit. You can deny me anytime you want to. This always was supposed to be a two-way street but the time before? What the hell are you talking about?" His voice was getting louder, more agitated, and she could see from the look on his face that he was distraught and bewildered.

"I told you, about two months ago—it was almost the same. I woke up. You screwed me. No, fucked is a better description. Then you disappeared without a word. I nearly went crazy. You were in bed that night but I didn't get to talk to you and then the next day, you came home with flowers and I was crying and you just took me to bed and made love to me. Real love, that time. I figured something bad had occurred at work that you didn't want to discuss and that you were apologizing. But because you didn't actually say anything, I didn't either. And I know it's been a two-way street. If I recall correctly, I've been the aggressor at times and changed your mind. Definitely equal opportunity going on between us."

Pat blushed suddenly, remembering the seduction she had initiated merely a week before—the first such really although there had been plenty of times when she demonstrated her interest. It was another morning that Paul had an early conference call planned for Europe and the alarm clock had gone off well before 6:00, an hour earlier than they usually rose. "Paul," she'd said suggestively, rolling next to him.

"Hey, I've got to be early to work today. You know that," he protested although he didn't push her away.

"Pa...ul," she had repeated drawing out his name seductively, her left leg sliding over his thigh as she pulled herself closer, fitting them together more comfortably. Her left arm had slowly stretched its way across his torso and her fingers began playing with his shoulder, then working down his arm, tenderly stroking the soft hair as they progressed.

"Not enough time," Paul murmured but he trembled a little as she continued to press against him and then he reached down a hand and begin moving it up and down her leg. "Nice leg...such nice legs," he said. "I saw that right at the start."

But to belabor his statement, she moved her leg up closer to his torso, just barely touching his crotch, and whispered in an enticing tone, "How could you? I was sprawled on the ice and I was wearing jeans."

"When I helped you take off the skates and put on your boots. I could tell right away. Good legs, I've always liked good legs." He was breathing heavier and clearly was becoming aroused as she ascertained by rubbing her leg gently against him.

"I knew it," she scolded lightly. "You knocked me over on purpose." It was their continuing quarrel, non-serious, unreal. It had become one of the on-going jokes in their relationship.

"No way," he refuted. "Absolutely, no way." His hand moved up now to softly grasp and manipulate her small but shapely breast. "Nice tits too. I like them also."

"Crude, counselor. Crude, but effective." Her lips were soft against his nipple and she had begun to lick, her tongue making little patterns on the surrounding skin.

"Hmm...," he sighed shivering slightly as he pulled her even tighter, well aware of her warm, pubic area pressed tantalizingly to him. "Nice puss, too."

"So eloquent, counselor," she whispered breathlessly, feeling herself starting to throb as her leg moved still gently but more forcefully against him, feeling him hardened against the lascivious limb.

"Eloquent, sm'eloquent," Paul moaned and he rolled over, facing her. "Beautiful, beautiful brown eyes," he hummed, peering up into hers, and he pressed her even more tightly to his body. "Beautiful everything, beautiful feeling," he muttered as he entered her. "*Magnifique, ma petite.*"

"Yes," she readily agreed as they rolled further over with him now positioned above her. She pulled her legs up to tighten around him, to hold him close, to let him penetrate her even deeper. "Oh yes, perfect, that's it."

"Perfect like you," he managed to gasp out.

"And you."

"Right, us, a perfect pair."

"Oh yes," she murmured exhaling. "And I really feel perfect now. It couldn't be more perfect."

"Hmm," he mumbled, thrusting harder and harder until he had pushed her from that so nearly painful yet so satisfying plateau into the pinnacle of pure pleasure and joined her there.

"Perfect...perfection from small packages," he sighed after, obviously releasing his hold on her with reluctance and at last getting up begrudging but dutifully. "Pretty, precious, petite packages," he added, leaning over to give her a final kiss.

"Helped by powerful, potent..." she answered pertly.

He put his finger gently to her lips, smiling. "Naughty, naughty—who's the one that's been censuring the other about being vulgar!"

"...patient practitioners," she'd finished and he burst out laughing. It had been perfect even though he'd barely gotten to work on time. That night, he'd arrived home with more flowers and through dinner, been uncharacteristically quiet but smiling besotted every time she looked at him, when he'd silently mouth the words, 'perfect seductress.' Now she looked at him wondering if he remembered. He stared at her seriously, nodding his head slightly, and she knew he had. Their last truly perfect day.

Suddenly Pat jerked back to the present where things weren't perfect, anything but. "This time, this time you were gone for two days, Paul, two whole days! I told you I was nearly crazy! Perfectly crazy!" She shouted the last statement, realizing how upset she was, had been.

"Two days," he half whispered, shaking his head. "And this is the second time. Ah shit. Shit, shit, shit!" Eyes lowered, he started beating his fists on the kitchen table and their glasses and the wine bottle began rattling. Startled, Pat snatched up her glass and the bottle but oblivious, Paul kept pounding savagely and she was afraid he was going to crack the table top and hurt himself. Suddenly, his glass slid off the side, crashing to the floor, shards flying all over and the wine splashing blemishing purple stains across the nearby cabinets like angry defacing birthmarks. Shocked, he stopped, looked down at his hands, now reddened from the brutal exertion, and then back up at her. The look on his face was full of despair, his eyes haunted like her imagined portrait of the tortured poet. "Ah shit," he said quietly.

Astounded by his action, she put her glass and bottle back down and moved her chair next to him. Putting her arms around him, she drew his head to her breast in an effort to sooth—all her own resentment now gone. His breathing was gasping and agonized and she could feel his body trembling. "Paul, Boytoy, tell me where you've been.

What's the matter? Is it drugs? Do you use?" Or worse, deal, she suddenly thought, again considering that unsavory possible explanation for all his money, which she had discarded earlier.

He jerked away and looked up at her stunned, his eyes wide again, affronted. "Hell, no! I had a hard enough time giving up smoking. I did, you know, started as a teenager. It was the in thing over there..." he stopped, a pained smile crossing his lips, "in thing in my crowd, in college. Christ, I can practically tell you to the second when I stopped and sometimes when we have sex, I think how great it would be to have a cigarette after. That was enough addiction for me. No, no drugs, not knowingly."

"What then? I love you but I'm afraid."

"You're afraid," he mumbled, remote and sounding devoid of emotion. His voice was toneless now, sounding far off as though not part of him. "You. Well, Pat, to be utterly frank, I don't have the slightest idea."

Now it was her turn to be shocked. "You didn't realize this was happening?"

"No."

"But how did you explain to yourself that you weren't here this weekend?"

"Pat, I thought I was here this weekend. I wanted to be here this weekend. I hoped I was here this weekend. I woke up in our bed and I admit I didn't have any real idea that anything had occurred. You were there. I saw the Sunday paper when I went down to make the coffee this morning along with the remains of one of your disgusting peanut butter and something sandwiches. If I thought about anything else, it was to wonder why we'd had sandwiches last night. I admit I wasn't clear that I'd lost some time but I was home, with you, safe, period."

"This has happened before...I don't mean just two months ago, but before, hasn't it?"

He looked at her woefully, his face pale and anxious, as if deciding what to say. "Yes. But not for a long time and not for long times, if you know what I mean."

"No, not really."

"I've lost time before in my mind. When I was a little boy..." He stopped abruptly for a moment. Then nervously licking his lips, he started speaking again and Pat realized she was truly staggered, almost more so than by his loss of control. Paul was never nervous. He was one of the most self-assured individuals she'd ever known—not arrogant or conceited, but confident—a real take charge kind of guy. It had been one of the traits that had attracted her. Now she was frightened by the misery in his voice.

"It happened to me a few times then but after the first time, only for minutes or maybe even seconds, never long. Apparently I kept functioning normally, if we could call it normal, so I don't think others noticed. I was so little that if they did, it was probably marked down to day dreaming or just being inattentive the way a small kid is." Pat nodded her head; she knew all about that sort of thing. Her Mittying had annoyed her teachers when she was in grammar school and been the bane of her parents. But in Paul's case, it must have been like having nightmares in the daytime. Instinctively, she wanted to say something of comfort, but his piteous look and the genuine pain of the moment froze the words on her lips. She felt her heart beating faster and was afraid she was going to have trouble breathing—hyperventilating like her childhood pal, Marsha, whose always practical mother kept stacks of paper bags in readiness for the frequent attacks.

"I used to pretend that was something that happened to everyone but then when I got older, I realized it didn't. I think technically it's called a fugue state. I've done some reading about it, but I was scared to tell anyone, scared they'd think I was crazy but then, when I came back to..." He stopped again and she waited patiently, fighting to breathe normally, hiding her own anxiety. "Then when I was ready for college, it stopped and I just assumed it was something I outgrew."

Pat stared at him, puzzled, aware of something that had been bothering her at least subconsciously since they'd met. "Paul, you're always starting to tell me something and then you stop. You just plain stop! I never noticed at first, but you do, don't you?" she interjected excitedly. "I didn't realize at first that you were doing that. You're usually so precise, a real word smith, but you start to make a remark and then you'll hesitate and change the subject and it's always about something that happened when you were young."

Ignoring what she'd said, which as far as she was concerned proved her point, he continued in a dry, pedantic tone. "I had a full medical when I went into the Air Force, you know. There was no indication that I might have epilepsy, not even petit mal—nothing like that; and, no one ever mentioned that I just sort of dropped out mentally so I never made a big deal of it. But a few months ago, just after we got married, it happened again, damn it. Just minutes, I was able to figure that out, but it was happening again. What you tell me happened two months ago and this weekend—actual days, a weekend disappearing, that I can't remember."

"Paul, you didn't answer what I was asking," Pat persisted disturbed. Her hand was gripping his now, as if by holding on tightly, he'd not be able to get away or change the subject again. "What is it that happened? If you can't talk to me, you've got to talk to someone. You have no idea where you were or what transpired?"

"No. I figured I must have been here. I hoped I was here for goodness sake, safe here with you at home." Clearly crestfallen, he looked directly at her. His eyes were large, haunted, the green murky, cloudy. "You're going to leave me now?"

Pat was so visibly shocked at the mere suggestion that she gave him a long dumb stare, not fully comprehending. Marriage was for keeps like her parents'. How could Paul say something like this? More frightening, was this something she had been hoping to hear, an out for them both? No, never; she'd married him because she loved him. Marriages were for better or worse just the way the ceremony read. "Paul, Boytoy, how can you say that. I love you. I married you. I've been so scared. But you've got to talk to me." She felt like crying, but was afraid if she began, she'd never stop.

From the tormented look in those sad green eyes, she knew he probably did too.

"I'm sorry, Pat. I'm scared too." He took her hands. "I'm scared...really scared. Scared I might hurt you, do something. Ah shit, Pat. Maybe you should leave," he said softly, clearly having trouble articulating the words.

"Don't be ridiculous," she snapped back determined that she wasn't going to be the one to quit because times were suddenly rough, their idyllic beginning lost. "You've got to see someone. Your medical insurance covers that, doesn't it? If not, mine does partially. Maybe these blackouts are caused by something physical and if you tell the doctors, they'll look. If not, it's nothing to be ashamed of, Paul. As long as we know there's a problem, we can do something. We'll find someone."

"I can't, darlin'."

"What do you mean?"

"I can't," he repeated dully but she detected a fleeting look of alarm cross his face. "I had to talk to someone when I was a kid at the very beginning and they couldn't figure this out or at least they weren't willing to talk to me about it then."

"You told people about these time losses?" She hesitated, not wanting to say seizures.

"Take my word for it. I've seen shrinks since I was five, no four, I guess, and nothing helped. I can't remember. I just can't remember anything." Paul's voice was rising again and his hands were tightening on hers, beginning to shake from agitation before at last he let go. "Jesus, I tried to. I really did, Pat, but I can't. Maybe they were right. Maybe I didn't want to because then I'd have to tell them."

"Tell them?" Pat pulled a hand loose to rub her temples, feeling the knotty pressure building. She couldn't remember when she'd felt so tense.

"About my father and my mother and what happened."

"Paul," she spoke softly, gently in a light and almost cheery voice that at the same time was soothing and tender, even though she didn't feel that way in the least—certainly not the cheery bit. "You haven't told me the truth about your family, have you?"

"You didn't like them?" he asked sadly, looking at her as beguiling as a child, his eyes bewildered but innocent. "It was the kind of family I was supposed to have. They just didn't stay around long enough."

She stared at him strangely, a chill capturing her spine. "What's that supposed to mean?"

"The father who took me fishing and hunting and played baseball. That's what he told me we'd do when I was older. It's what my grandfather had done with him. Then of course when I was older, he couldn't. The mother who'd taught and liked science? She did, you know—like science. She'd studied botany in college but she just never got the chance to teach although my grandmother had. Neither of my parents got the chance—me either."

"What do you mean?"

"They weren't around, Pat. They were gone."

"I know you told me they died, but you were a teenager when your father died."

"Yes, but he wasn't around and neither was I."

"I don't understand. I don't understand any of this. Oh, Boytoy," Pat moaned in fright. "What is it? What's happening? I've been so scared, so worried that something happened to you when you were gone and now you tell me something like this."

"Come on." Standing, Paul took her hand and pulled her up. Wrapping an arm around her, he softly said, "Come down to the basement with me. I've got to show you something."

CHAPTER 10

Paul turned on the stair light and they made their way carefully down the steps to the unfinished basement area. He still had tight hold of her hand as though this time he was the one who was afraid she might disappear. Perhaps he's right, thought Pat, her apprehension growing as they descended. Their basement, usually so ordinary, suddenly seemed to be an ominous place and Pat wondered if she was afraid of what she was about to learn or of Paul himself. Trust, she thought, I have to trust him. This was the man she loved; he wouldn't hurt her. He hadn't even when he didn't know who she was.

To one side, the last few unpacked boxes from Pat's old apartment and the ones belonging to Paul remained neatly stacked, another of the projects both had avoided. Pat wondered to herself why she hadn't thought of going down there during the weekend to continue her search for clues about Paul. Then she realized that she'd continued repressing in spite of her strong resolutions, that she'd been afraid of what she might find. Well, now apparently was the time for that discovery.

Get a hold of yourself, she thought, the basement is innocuous. Nothing was going to happen. It was just the same as it had been when she'd shown nosy Mr. Beck and been so embarrassed. Aside from taking their wash down on a weekly basis, she rarely came down now that gardening season was over. Although Paul had asked just last week if they weren't supposed to be putting in bulbs or something. It was another project she'd planned for the lost weekend and then completely forgotten after the Saturday morning episode. Yet how much Paul had enjoyed the couple weekends in April when he'd strategically placed the potted plants from the party around their small back patio. Then they'd put in spring bulbs and a couple of azalea bushes because those had surrounded his grandmother's Alabama home. That is if the grandmother really had existed or any of the childhood stories about the woman were true. At this point, Pat wasn't sure of anything but Paul's love of flowers.

Yes, he did love flowers. In fact, when it had been azalea time, they'd made a special trip to the National Arboretum and walked and picnicked amid the myriad colors that covered the hillsides and lined the walkways. To her surprise, Paul had even told her the scientific names.

"There was a place near Montgomery, when I was a kid, called Jasmine Hill Gardens. It had all sorts of flowers and classical statuary—a replica of the Temple of Hera even. But to my mother it was really famous for the azaleas, flowering cherry trees, and jasmine of course. I remember her taking me there once when I was little. She liked azaleas so much and she started teaching me the names—nudiflorum for the pink and calendulaceum for the flames which were also yellow and orange, not just scarlet. She made it a game, chanting out the names, so I'd remember. Nu...di...flor...um," he hummed softly, a distant but content look on his face. "She was a great teacher, Pix, and I've never forgotten her love for them."

"So do you...all flowers, don't you?"

"Oh yah," he agreed, looking pensive. "My dad brought some home every week even if my mother did have a garden. She used to let me dig out there although I'm not sure anything I planted ever really grew. We spent a lot of time in the garden when the weather was warm."

"I thought it was always warm in Alabama," remarked Pat, but actually thinking of all the times Paul had brought her flowers. Were they an attempt to emulate his father?

"Hmm? Oh no, they get winter too and then of course sometimes it's too hot. But when it was nice, in the late spring and early autumn, my mother would fix me little picnics or tea parties and we'd sit outside and she'd read to me or tell me wonderful fairy tales."

Pat had been brought up on tea parties too when GG would give her some special treat to eat on a tray, consumed while hidden under the kitchen table. She knew her other grandmothers thought that outrageous, but Mary Patton Lind knew the way to a child's heart—food and a 'secret' place of one's own. Pat could therefore easily envision the lovely, laughing blonde woman from the little picture, holding her small dark son on her lap and whispering stories into his ear while the two snacked companionably. How tragic that those experiences had lasted such a short time. Paul, by now, was staring vacantly at the flowers, no doubt lost in time somewhere in a sunny, fragrant Alabama garden—magic to a little boy. Gently, she touched his elbow, "Well let's hope your gardening efforts are successful this year."

Half-laughing, he had looked at her cheerfully, returned to the then present. "Definitely. If not, I'll just set you out here in your Jamaican straw hat with all those pretty posies."

"You were the one who picked the hat and only if you ply me with rum punch and play reggae music."

"Then you'd probably make me do contortions to get under the hoe handle or something. I think I'd better concentrate on my planting."

Yet for all his talk of gardening, it was later apparent that Paul really hadn't had much experience and Pat ended up showing him what to do, making sure it was only weeds he pulled. "I guess your dad eventually gave up on the garden, huh?"

"What do you mean?" He was perplexed and strangely tense at her comment.

"You said he'd garden and fish with you."

"Oh...well, after a while he just got busier at work and I guess I lost interest."

"Too much soccer?"

"Yah, boy stuff, but I still like flowers."

"Well, we can sit out here and have cocktails if you've outgrown tea parties," she said.

"Either would be nice," Paul replied, a fleeting, dreamy smile crossing his face and she knew he was still remembering. But somehow, although they'd occasionally cook outside on the grill or sit there and have a drink during the summer evenings, they never had a tea party in their new garden. Perceptively, she was able to intuit that it was something too special, one of his rare memories of his mother, and she never suggested it again.

Now Pat could only wonder how much of that narration had been real—how much, for that matter, anything was that he had told her. The garden tools and empty pots along with her happy summer memories were neatly stacked near the glass doors leading to the tiny rear patio. Turning the area into a comfortable den or rec room had also been on their list of future projects—a growing list meant for a lifelong relationship, she'd believed. Would it have been a den such as her father craved? Or a place where small children could play and Paul would install a toy train as she'd sometimes dreamed but been unable to articulate to her husband. Her secret list.

But for now, there was only a small workbench with a peg board where Paul had hung his various indoor tools. The card table, removed from the kitchen, and some folding chairs were placed to one side and there, almost accusing her, were the two wingback chairs. The happy planned project for this past weekend lost when Paul once again turned into Mr. Hyde.

"Why don't you sit down," he said, gesturing at one of the offending chairs. "This is going to take me a few minutes. I've got to dig out my footlocker."

Complying, she sank down, thinking inconsequentially how elegant it and its twin would be if Paul ever did do the promised refinishing. He definitely appeared to have a flair for carpentry—a real tool time guy like the old *Home Improvement* reruns. And in Paul's case, just as her father's, a competent one— Al not Tim; although who had taught him the skill she couldn't imagine if the father had been another romantic figment of Paul's fertile mind. Still, certainly the kitchen wrought iron was a success and rather pettily she was glad he hadn't broken the glass in his rage and frustration. The wine she was sure could be wiped off.

God, what was wrong with her? Her husband had just

gone through an emotional crisis and apparently constructed a whole imaginary world far surpassing her feeble Mittying while here she was worried about having to clean a mess and his breaking some cheap wine glass mass-produced for Dollar Tree. Worse yet, not because he might hurt himself, but because of the inconvenience! And musing over a couple of old chairs!

Trying to relax, she leaned against the high back, and touched the chair's arm tentatively. In actuality, she felt like pounding her fist against it, but forced herself to remain calm. So instead, nervously her fingers caressed it as she concentrated on remembering the pleasure of their day's outing when they had found the pair, trying to recapture a last happy day they'd spent together before she had reason to worry about Paul's mental health. There were so many things she and he were going to do and now she wondered if they ever would and she held back a sob that she knew was building in her throat.

Painstakingly as was his nature, Paul removed boxes and stacked them meticulously to one side. Then he uncovered the small footlocker that had been at the bottom of the pile. This he pulled out and dragged over to where Pat was sitting. Lowering himself to the floor, silently and single mindedly, he worked at its combination lock.

Pat was staggered at the sight: Paul actually sitting on the floor in one of his expensive business suits. Like her, he usually changed into something comfortable once he got home although he paid a small fortune for his entire wardrobe or maybe because he had. Items from The Gap definitely being more expendable than his office apparel. Certainly he also took great care in maintaining all his clothes and his appearance in general—not so much due to vanity, she thought, but because he had a certain pride. Never, never in ordinary circumstances would he consider subjecting one of his suits to contact with the basement floor. Yet here he was, perfectly groomed in a custom tailored charcoal-grey, three-piece suit squatting on the cold, unfinished and no doubt uncomfortable damp cement. If anything showed her the seriousness of what was happening, that did!

When the lock popped open, Paul lifted the lid and she held her breath, not knowing what to expect. It was almost with relief that she saw there were photo albums and file folders stuffed with old newspapers, not some fragmented bones or other horror. Yet at the same time, she realized that whatever the little trunk did contain was in affect her husband's family skeleton.

Rummaging through the folders, he finally selected one and passed it up to her without saying a word. Then he sat back, waiting for her to read the contents. His countenance was pale and strained and his eyes looked stormy—dark green now like the Atlantic on a turbulent winter day. His large but shapely hands were tightly grasping his knees and she could see that his knuckles were white. Worse, he was obviously more than a little lost and, nervously, had begun slightly rocking back and forth like a small boy sitting at the feet of his kindergarten teacher.

Opening the folder, she started to pull out the clippings, not understanding at first what she was seeing. The headlines were lurid: *French Multi-Millionaire's Daughter Murdered, Senator's Son Arrested, Prominent Attorney Criminally Charged, Jury Convicts, Life Imprisonment, Wolfe Child Disappears.*

"Paul Wolfe," she said reading and glanced over at Paul. His face had turned ashen. "Oh God, the poems. The pacing wolf, that was your father in prison and all that stuff about death, it was them, wasn't it?"

"Yah, maybe...yah and me and just everything."

"And the W," she said slowly feeling like she was Lois Lane finally recognizing Superman, "Paul W—W for Wolfe. You're little Paul, the boy who was kidnapped."

"Naturally. Paul Wolfe, son of Paul Wolfe, Jr., grandson of Paul Wolfe, Sr. Crazy Paul, Murderer Paul, Senator Paul. But not so little now," he murmured despondently, eyes downcast, face grimacing.

Traumatized, not crazy, thought Pat in sudden relief. "Your mother was the daughter of that French banking family and your grandfather was the U.S. Senator from Alabama. Your father was supposed to be some hot shot lawyer in international banking. I remember now. It was all over the TV and newspapers and my mother wouldn't let me watch the news because the crime was so shocking—kind of like the Lindbergh kidnapping, or..." Pat stopped herself just in time from referring to the Manson murders with their frightening similarities. A beautiful pregnant woman slashed to death by her husband and her baby dying shortly after— Paul's mother and brother. Lamely, Pat finished, "Little children shouldn't know things like that but of course the big kids talked at school. The case and trail lasted for ages, daily news and you were there." She looked at him, her eyes full of pity, tears now brimming.

"I wasn't supposed to be," he admitted, his eyes still downcast. "I had a slight cold but they were going to send me to school anyhow. At the last moment, after my dad left—he was driving over to Baltimore for some meeting—I threw up or something and my mother put me back in bed. That was a point the prosecution made a big deal of—that my father thought I was out of the house."

Pat looked puzzled. "But surely that proved he couldn't have been the killer?"

"It should have but he never got to Baltimore. He apparently had a flat tire on the parkway and was caught in the rain. Then when he finally got to a phone to call that he'd be late, he discovered the meeting was canceled. At the trial the people in Baltimore said they'd called his office the day before and spoken to him. The prosecution said the flat tire was a fake and that he'd just left later. My father's lawyers offered a reward for anyone who might have seen him changing the tire, but no one ever came forth. Then there were so many other inconsistencies in his story...that and the fact that a neighbor heard my mother screaming his name when she was being stabbed." Paul continued to look down, his head bent over as if he felt like throwing up right then.

"She'd given me some cough syrup or a hot toddy or

something that must have had some alcohol in it that morning after I was sick. In any case, I fell asleep, I guess, and then I heard screams and a man shouting. At first I thought it was a dream and then when I realized I was awake, I thought it was TV or maybe the radio. I just didn't pay attention at first—still groggy, I suppose. Finally I understood it was my mother screaming."

Paul glanced up at Pat and she saw that a tear had started down his cheek. His fists were tightly clinched again. She couldn't tell for sure if it were anguish or frustration or, she assumed, both, for his voice had become harsh and jagged. "I knew it was her but I was afraid to go and see. I knew something bad was happening and I guess I just got into this little toy house my father had built for me and tried to hide but I heard her keep screaming. She was stabbed over a dozen times, Pix, and she was calling for help and I didn't do anything."

Pat reached over to touch him sympathetically but he was so distressed, he jerked away. Gently she said, "You were only a little boy, Paul. What? Four? Five? I don't remember exactly how old I was when it happened— kindergarten too I guess."

He stared at her, trembling, his speech breathy, becoming more shrill—all that soft, smooth cadence, which so contributed to his professional demeanor, gone. "She was my mother and she was calling for help and I didn't do anything. I loved her, Pix, and I didn't do anything! She was so beautiful and good and kind and I hid when someone was killing her."

"Paul, they would have hurt you too," Pat said reasonably but she could see that wasn't assuaging his guilt and she felt such pity. It was as though her own stomach was contracting in pain and nausea and she wondered what he must feel...had felt.

"Not if it were my father," he asserted and he looked at her sadly. "I've never known. I loved him too but everyone tried to make me say it was him but I didn't see. I didn't see, Pix. I don't know. They said at the trial that she'd had a lover and that the baby wasn't my father's, that he'd found out and gone berserk but I didn't want to believe that. I loved them both and we'd all been so happy. I don't know if she had a lover." He was crying again, tears now streaming down his face. "I just didn't know. Hell, at that age, I didn't know what a lover was, but even after I grew up, I didn't know. They made me testify, but I couldn't tell anyone anything and I never got to spend any time with my father again once the trial started.

"Later, my French grandfather ended up taking me to Europe and he eventually stuck me in a Swiss boarding school. I hated it and I hated him. Louis Martin of Martin Internationale. He thought he was Louis the Fourteenth, the Sun King himself. Actually he was more like Louis the Eleventh, the Spider King," Paul hissed, his voice sibilant and raw with anger—a bitter, sarcastic voice Pat had not heard before nor ever expected.

"The Martin family had been important for decades. They made their pile in the mid-nineteenth century after the Revolution of 1848 but Louis was the one who turned the family bank and all its tentacles into an international conglomerate. He had been furious when my parents got married even though my dad's father was a senator. It just wasn't the kind of marriage he expected his daughter, his only child, to make—to an insignificant law student, worse yet an American, instead of some rich European business scion who would further the family empire. Love was never supposed to be part of the equation but my folks met that summer at Oxford when my father arrived over there for his Fulbright. My mother was taking some special program in English literature and I guess for them it was love at first sight, like you were for me," he said softly.

Paul's voice was calmer again, that of the Paul she knew and Pat felt a little jerk to her heart. He'd never said that to her and she'd assumed his love was something that had happened gradually over the weeks they'd spent together. Certainly until he'd asked her to go to New York, she really had had no clue as to where their relationship was going although she had hoped it would intensify.

"When my dad finished his year in England, my mother went back to America with him against her father's wishes and was practically disowned by her family. My parents had kept in touch during the rest of the year he was at Oxford even though she'd returned to France at summer's end to start at the Sorbonne. I think he went over to Paris to see her during holidays, unbeknownst to Louis, which must have been quite a feat." At Pat's puzzled look, Paul explained, "Louis may not be very loving but he is a control freak and my mother had been one of his assets."

Pat's mouth dropped open. It was medieval—financial alliances through real marriages and in the present, not one of her romantic daydreams of being a Venetian Juliet. "Oh," she said, shocked.

Paul merely nodded. "Anyhow, somehow Louis slipped up on my parents' romance, which probably made him even meaner. They got married almost right away once they arrived in Alabama and she was with my father through law school taking some classes at Tulane. No actually, I suppose she was in the liberal arts female part back then—Sophie Newcomb. I don't remember although I guess I arrived before they finished.

"In any case, once there they were just two struggling students living fairly frugally instead of a European heiress on the international marriage mart. Even if Grandpa was a senator, the Wolfes weren't really rich. No one could ever accuse my grandfather of being corrupt and profiting from his senatorial seat," Paul stated proudly. "Both my American grandparents, they were great. I had spent lots of vacations in Alabama from the time I was born so their place was like a second home. We usually went there for Christmas and my mother would sometimes even go in the spring. *Maman* got along so well with them. My grandmother said she was the daughter she'd never had and because *Maman* had lost her own mother, that apparently filled her needs too."

"Your trips to those Jasmine Gardens," Pat commented, "the azaleas."

"Yes, Easter in Alabama, though we'd go to the arboretum here too. That's why I just had to take you there, to see it again. She really did love azaleas—especially the flames and the Asian varieties. Her own grandmother had lived in the south of France and had a country villa with a huge formal garden and of course had all the kinds that grew there although I think they called them rhododendrons. Same species though," he added thoughtfully, one of his mother's lessons recalled.

"After *Maman's* mother died, she'd go there during holidays. Louis had stuck her in a convent boarding school by then and she spent little time with him. He was too busy for her between increasing his empire and auditioning for his next consort—lots of auditioning, I gather. The result of course was that *Maman* was much closer to the grandmother and her best memories were the times with her. Runs in the family, I suppose," he said sadly. Pat nodded her head. She loved her parents, but she'd been especially close to all her grandmothers with GG leading the pack.

"Anyhow *Maman* was a great flower lover. She had all sorts in our garden plus the azaleas. She'd spend hours out there, humming and singing and I'd 'help' her. I probably did more damage than good as you discovered this year. I still don't seem to have weeds down pat although I have an amazing vocabulary of Latin names. I told you she taught science, at least to me. I wasn't too talented as a gardener then either," he added ruefully, "but she passed the love on to me. That's one memory I didn't lose." Pat nodded her head again, recalling once more the hours they'd spent the past spring puttering on their tiny plot.

"My grandparents had gardens too though wild, informal, real American style. They had this lovely old home not too far from Montgomery—classical like out of your *Gone With the Wind* on maybe a hundred acres. Besides all those azaleas, there was wisteria, and camellias and even a magnolia or two for you, sugar," he said with a pained smile. "And the gardenias—my lord, the scent of those flowers in bloom! There were times when they had to shut all the windows and doors because the odor was so overpowering. I remember my grandmother telling me once about a cousin of hers who had a Yankee beau from New York City back in the Depression days. Anyhow, he wanted to make a big impression on Cousin Lucinda and one year for her June birthday, he wired ten dollars to some local florist to send her a gardenia."

Pat looked at him with a fond smile. Gardenias had always been luxury items to her too and Paul had given her some for her own late June birthday. Reading her mind, he said, "Right, I wanted to make an impression too. But even though that was big money back then, the guy assumed it would probably only buy her a dozen gardenias or so. Well let me tell you, apparently it bought a truck full and a big one at that. It was worse than a funeral, Grandma said, and it became the talk of the town. The family laughed about it for years."

"Did Cousin Lucinda marry the man?" asked Pat with lively curiosity, almost pathetically eager for one of Paul's happy but real Alabama tales.

"Nope," he replied, "a fool and his money, you know. That's why I stuck with only a couple for you. But aside from the flowers, what I most recall about the place was that there were big, straggly pine trees—mostly shortleaf and loblolly and a pecan grove and some huge ol' live oaks draped with Spanish moss; I remember once I covered myself with the stuff playing some stupid game and Grandma and Sarah nearly went ballistic." Pat looked at him strangely. "They were afraid I was going to get chiggers," explained Paul with a lopsided but now nearly cheerless grin.

"Anyhow, there was also a pond for fishing and some empty barns. They no longer were doing any farming although they did still run a little cattle. The place was antebellum and for some reason survived although I guess once upon a time, it was a huge plantation with a thousand or more acres. But the war devastated the family and they had to sell off parcels of land over the years. I loved it because there were all sorts of nooks and crannies for a little boy to hide in...just like Christopher Robin and his hundred acre wood. I was good at hiding," he added bitterly.

Pat knew he was referring to the murder and decided to change the subject, "War?"

"Sugar, when you were truly in the South years ago, at least with older folk, there was only one war."

"Civil?"

"Between the States, you damn Yankee as you well know," he half quipped even though it was obvious his heart wasn't in it and he had just reacted from practice in their own personal, pseudo and playful North-South conflict. "Shucks, they even had a little spotted pony for me named Dixie and my dad's pony when he was little was called Rebel. My grandmother had had a riding horse called Bonnie Blue, but I think that's about as far as they went in loyalty to the Stars and Bars. No seditious thoughts there."

A small smile reappeared on his face. "Actually, my grandmother did things like that to 'rile you Yankees.' She loved to tease people. She could really be quite outrageous, which was part of her charm and maybe not the best attribute for a politician's wife, but my grandfather told me he loved her every day of their marriage. 'Some more than others, of course,' was the way he put it. Grandma could be hell on wheels and yet have people eating out of her hand at the same time," laughed Paul.

"A nicer version of Scarlett O'Hara?"

"Oh, definitely, but she would have liked that. I adored her just like you did your GG. She'd put me on good ol' Dixie and walk me around and there was also a goat that they'd hitch up to a little cart, but I was scared of him because he always tried to butt me. I wasn't the bravest kid...kid, no pun intended," he added, looking down at his hands and Pat knew he was thinking again about not helping his mother.

"Me either," she confessed. "I was terrified of going over the old Marshall Avenue Bridge between Saint Paul and Minneapolis. Remember, the new one now near my folks' place? Of course that was also partially due to the height above the water. I hated high places."

Paul looked at her surprised. "I thought you said you'd do some hikes in the mountains with me and learn to ski properly come winter. How the hell did you cope with the ski lift up in Pennsylvania?"

"Hikes, not rock climbing, and there was lots of snow under the lift. I'm from Minnesota as you keep reminding me. Snow is our friend—soft and fluffy, even if it ain't so. Besides, I'm not paranoid. I just avoid looking down and I doubt if I would have ever been able to ski the way you apparently do although I was going to give it a try. But with the old bridge, I always knew it was going to collapse and I'd drown which scared me even more back then. When a bridge did go down a few years ago, I had nightmares, remembering my fears and realizing how awful it was for all those poor people who drowned. And when I was little, I used to drive my folks insane about keeping the car windows closed when we drove across so I wouldn't fall out and tumble over the rails. Once when I was about five or six, I was down by the Mississippi shore with Lyle and I slipped and fell into the water and started screaming my head off. He just stood there and laughed."

"Your brother didn't help?" Paul was open-mouthed.

"It wasn't more than a foot deep where I was," she explained sheepishly. "When I stood up, it didn't even reach my knees. I was just too scared to realize. It was like the winter before when he'd taken me tobogganing at the golf course and we were supposed to shoot over this little creek, which was probably four or five feet wide. Maybe there were too many kids on the toboggan, but somehow we didn't make it across and the toboggan stopped there right on the ice. Then the ice started cracking. The big kids jumped off and I just sat there terrified and managed to get all wet. The creek couldn't have been more than a foot or two deep either but at that time I was practically paranoid about water too. Lyle was furious because he had to take me right home and after my mother bawled him out for letting me get wet. That was the last time he took me sliding that year!"

"You didn't tell me about that when we were walking around there at Easter."

"Too embarrassed," she mumbled, thinking of her own obviously innocuous secrets compared to Paul's. If she'd revealed them, would he have told her about his past then and they could have avoided this anguished weekend?

"And you weren't scared about the water when we were in Jamaica." The softened dreamy look in Paul's eyes revealed how much their island honeymoon had meant.

"I'm a big girl now, Paul," Pat said gently. "I learned to swim a couple of years later and lost all that fear. Little kids are afraid of lots of things." She didn't add that heights still bothered her but that phobia was petty compared to what Paul had had to face. How one would ever get over the terror of being present at a murder, she wasn't sure. Well, maybe she was. He said he couldn't remember things. It wasn't something she wanted to press right now. In fact she was glad they were chatting, reminiscing like this. He was sounding himself again and slowly she was learning his real story, but at what an emotional price for them both. This confession could never be easy.

"Yah, I guess they are," he agreed. "I sure was. Later when I was a teenager, my grandparents were renting that house on Thomas Avenue, the pink brick one which I told you was just a couple blocks from the Huntingdon Campus. That's the small liberal arts college in Montgomery I thought I might attend when Grandma got cancer again. They'd had to sell the family property by then. It was actually her place. Her only brother died in World War I so she inherited it all. Grandpa's family was more modest although his father had been a judge."

There's modest and modest, thought Pat. Even though the Stroms and Linds had been successful farmers at the beginning of the last century, but with all their children the land and wealth had gradually disappeared over the next decades. No, by and large, she and Paul came from different ends of the great Middle Class spectrum just as she'd always suspected. And his poor mother! My God, she'd been a real heiress.

"My grandfather was broke by the time he died. Everything—my folks' house, Grandma's farm, Grandpa's investments—all went for my dad's defense and the continued appeals. Then later there were my grandmother's medical bills too. My grandparents wanted to help me with college but they had next to nothing. Even then they did what they could. But finally, the family antiques, those were all auctioned off before Grandpa had his heart attack to pay some of the expenses. The few things left like his library, memorabilia he'd accumulated as a senator I donated to the state archives. There's a special collection now. I've wanted you to see it someday, but I didn't know when or if I could tell you this. Part of me has always wanted you to know.

"I loved my family so much, Pix. I was so proud of my grandfather and I wanted to share this with you. But, part of me didn't, couldn't tell you. I would have liked to have kept some things, but I had no place for them, no money to rent space, no money for school. All I could keep is here." Paul waved his hand toward a couple of boxes and then brought it down with a slam on the footlocker. "All," he whispered, more to himself than Pat.

"What about your pony and the goat?" she asked and then felt like a fool, realizing they no doubt would probably have been dead by the time Paul had returned from Europe, just like his parents. And when that return had been, she still didn't know but now she understood his need for their hobby, an attempt to replace the furnishings from the home he'd loved and lost, an effort to reconstruct the past he should have had and wanted to share with her.

"Poor old Dixie had gone to equine heaven. Billy Goat Gruff too although I probably wouldn't have cared if they'd turned him into some of that goat curry we had in Jamaica. I've heard the farmhouse became a sort of bed and breakfast or restaurant or something open to the public but I could never bring myself to go and see it. Actually, I've never been back to Alabama since I returned to college after Grandpa died, Pix. That's why I didn't take you," he said bluntly, looking at her poignantly. She nodded, understanding. No hidden wife or six children, just this painful concealed past that had to be so much, much worse and again she felt nauseated in sympathy.

"Of course when all of this first happened, the murder that is, the folks were still up here in D.C. part of the time, at least my grandfather was. What I told you about them is mostly true. My grandmother's cancer just started earlier, but she beat the first bout, and after that she wanted to stay in Alabama most of the time so that was pretty much the way it was. Grandpa of course had to be in D.C. when Congress was in session but he just kept a small apartment near the Senate Office Buildings then. He had been mentioned as a presidential candidate before the murder happened or at least a vice presidential runner, you know."

"Yes, I do. They talked about him in my political science classes. In fact, in high school, my favorite teacher, Mr. Cruz, who taught government, admired him tremendously. He always said that Paul Wolfe was supposed to be brilliant, a real visionary, considering some of the bills he introduced, and a man with genuine compassion for the little guy. A real loss." How insipid of me, thought Pat. What an inadequate thing to say but Paul didn't seem to notice.

"Yah, the scandal ruined him, not that he didn't have some enemies already, especially at home. For one thing, he'd riled the Ku Klux Klan."

Pat looked at him astounded, "I thought..."

"You didn't think they were still around."

"Well, not exactly."

"Pat, they have them or their clones over in Maryland even today. And if people don't call these groups the KKK, you know there are still plenty of white supremacist, hate groups out there, not that a person has to be white to be a racist. Back then there were the Alabama Knights and regardless of what the Invisible Empire was called, Grandpa was vehemently against it. Where our family lived, the local cyclops, that's the president of the klavern or den, especially hated him. When you're not afraid to stand up to people or for a cause, you make enemies. Grandpa was no exception.

"Anyhow, he finished out that term and actually ran for one more because his supporters wanted him to. They were afraid of his opponent, a real reactionary. But his heart wasn't in it. I don't know if it was because of that or the active opposition of the KKK or the fact that the other candidate managed to get hold of a lot of campaign funding, he lost. The election was so damn close and the loss hurt so much after all those years of public service.

"And yes, he was brilliant, no question, and good and he had integrity so he probably wouldn't have gotten to be president even if this hadn't happened," said Paul caustically. "Also, after the kidnapping and before Grandma got sick the last time, he really wasn't interested in continuing a political career, but what he did want was to be a judge. There was talk about the next vacancy on the Supreme Court and that's what he hoped would happen. Grandma said for that, she'd be willing to return to D.C. She never enjoyed being a politician's wife all that much even though she had all the social graces. He would have been great, Pix." Nodding to himself, Paul muttered, "Great, just great. He was a good and wise man but this destroyed him...it destroyed them all...me too, maybe. And us?" He looked at her, his eyes full of despair, a beseeching look, almost like that of a little child. "I don't want to lose you. I hadn't intended to ask you to marry me. I hadn't intended to get married because..."

She realized what he was trying to say and although it pained her, articulated the thought for him. "Because you were afraid you might do something like that yourself? Because you were afraid there was some insanity running in the family?" God, how these mental blackouts must have frightened him. No wonder he'd become so distraught tonight.

"Yes. The other women I ran around with didn't matter. They were all short-term propositions. There were a fair amount even if I didn't talk about them," he added casually.

"I'm not surprised," she murmured, trying to be equally

casual although she was sure she wouldn't have liked a single one.

"But I liked you the second I met you. You were so damn cute when I first saw you. So petite with those big brown eyes, your tiny turned up nose and all that curly dark hair falling out of your stocking cap. With that bright red cap and matching sweater, you looked like a cute little pixie—just the kind my mother had told me about—fragile, delicate, elfin prettiness even though I was surprised later once I got you out of your clothes and discovered how curvaceous you were with that tantalizing neck." Pat blushed and Paul chuckled softly, staring at his perfect little wife, who would never top a hundred pounds but whose figure was as watchable as her face. And what a face, usually so effortlessly bright. Would he see that brightness again, he despaired.

"Well, you are, petite but perfect. And then when you spoke, you had that nice, soft, sweet voice. I was enchanted." Pat almost believed him; she wanted to. So that was why he called her Pixie, not just because of her size. Then he brought her back to reality, "I also liked the fact that you didn't try any come on when I took you back to your room that first night we met."

"Come on? My God, I was practically writhing in pain. What the hell did you expect," Pat snorted indignantly.

"Listen, I've seen all sorts of come-ons. No, it was obvious that you really had gotten hurt but you handled yourself with dignity."

"Dignity! I can't believe I'm hearing this. If I hadn't been dignified or if I'd tried to pick you up or something you would have walked off?"

"Maybe not walked off," he conceded. "You were awfully cute and you writhe quite nicely as I've often told you. I'm sure I would have been tempted although not with any thoughts of more than a fling up there if it had happened."

"I writhe nicely!"

"One of your better traits."

"God, Paul. We're discussing sex at a time like this!"

"Hey, you asked. But no, it was obvious you weren't like your friend Betty the Bimbo."

"Betty is not a bimbo," retorted Pat annoyed, although she well knew she herself had never approved of Betty's overly active sex life.

"Well, she tried to put the moves on me the first time you took me to one of your friends' parties."

"What!" Pat felt the blood rush from her face.

Paul reached up to touch her hand, "Calm down, Pix. She's never tried anything since we got engaged, ok? I guess once the ring is presented, there's some honor among friends involved."

"She put the moves on you?" Pat was still astounded and wanted to ask if any of her other friends had, but this was not the time or place as she had just pointed out with some feeling. Someone propositioning her husband was petty compared to the present problem.

"Anyhow," he continued, obviously not being willing yet to drop the subject entirely. "I really liked you and then we started going out and I was comfortable with you and I wanted to be with you...all the time."

"You didn't exactly rush into anything physical."

"It wasn't because I didn't want you. I told you. I was utterly smitten. I was just afraid if I were too impetuous, I might want to make more of our relationship."

"I don't understand," Pat said perplexed. Hadn't he just remarked it was love at first sight for him? Although maybe she was beginning to fathom what he really meant and then she was thoroughly disgusted with herself. Here she was sparring with him when he was trying to tell her about himself—allowing her finally into that private, hidden place she'd wanted revealed. Obviously, her nerves were shot too.

"If we didn't have a sexual relationship, I figured maybe you could be just a friend. I wanted a friend, someone I could talk to. Men do things with other men; they don't really talk. It's women who do and I needed to talk. Sex I could get elsewhere. I had," he added bluntly, "quite recently in fact, like just before I met you. I was out on the ice that night alone because the other people I knew there were couples and I was really annoyed at having been stood up by..."

"Stood up?" Pat looked at him quizzically, her eyes widened in surprise. "You were supposed to be up there with another woman?"

At her shocked look, he said softly, "You always knew you weren't the first. Neither was I. I never asked you and they weren't important."

"You could have asked me," she replied stoutly, her voice beginning to quiver. She'd always planned to discuss her whole past with Paul, but she'd never visualized its happening like this. "I would have told you. There was the guy I lived with in grad school and a few other shorter relationships although not many, but none of them was really important. Ronnie, my grad school companion, I'd thought he might be, but I was wrong. He was into..." she hesitated, "drugs."

"And that's why you actually thought that might be the matter with me?"

"I considered it, yes, but I decided not," she said looking him squarely in the face.

"And you were also worried that I might be dealing, which would explain the extra money?" he asked ironically.

Slightly flushed, she nodded her head. "But just momentarily. I couldn't believe you were that kind of man."

"Thank you," he said solemnly. "There was a fair amount of pills and some booze when I was in boarding school, which supposedly the staff didn't know although I doubt if they'd worried about the latter. Wine, beer—it's so much a part of the European life style and because of that, not such a big deal. But we did have some guy in the *lycée*, who was supposed to be dealing *blanche* as the milieu called it. Personally I thought that was more rumor unless people were using it during their hols. The school actually ran a pretty tight ship." Pat looked at him quizzically. "Heroin," he explained. "There were lots of drugs in the military too—particularly in Hawaii where you have to watch every step if you're in the jungle areas so you don't trip a wire." Pat's face was now the epitome of puzzlement. "The marijuana growers booby trap their crops—can't let all that nice military expertise from SE Asia be wasted. I rarely was in places where that was a danger though one of my colleagues ran into such an occurrence out at Andersen AFB on Guam. Amazing—so much for security. Of course I did encounter users and dealers when I was with JAG, but no."

Digressing into a lecture on drugs was all very well, but learning about who was supposed to be at the ski resort was more important so Pat persisted. "Paul—the woman who didn't come. I was also beginning to wonder this weekend if there had been anyone special when I met you."

"And? I was your last chance?"

"How can you say that? You knocked me off my feet," she tried to quip, hurt at his remark—a remark so cold, so unlike Paul. He knew it too—she could see.

"That was shitty of me. I'm sorry, Pat. You knocked me over too or I never would have tried to find you afterwards. You were so pretty and I felt so bad when you fell and then you were so tough when we made our way back to the hotel even though I could see you were hurting. I was really worried that you were injured worse than you thought. It was obviously quite a spill, but you just thanked me politely as if I'd brought you back from a date or something and then went into your room."

"Where I promptly gritted my teeth so I wouldn't start screaming. You should have been there when I put the ice on. I thought I was going to scream the place down," she added, bravely attempting to sound the self she was before he had just so callously wounded her.

"Well, you didn't show it. I had to leave the first thing the next morning and I didn't know what else to do. I wanted to apologize and when I found out you were from D.C..."

"The twenty dollars."

"Yes and worth every penny. I would have paid more if I could have gotten your address or better yet, telephone number but the clerk would only sell so much. Anyhow, I hoped I'd get to see you again and even if I didn't, I wanted to make some gesture." His words she knew were an apology and she tried to smile.

"Class, Paul, always class. That's what you have."

"You too," he smiled back, recognizing she'd forgiven him. "I didn't really expect a thanks and with no way to contact you, was afraid that was it. But I had to try so think of the gifts as a true apology for the accident and the twenty as a lottery ticket in hopes you'd get in touch with me."

Remembering her own reaction when she'd decided to call him, she was astonished at how similarly their minds had been working even then. "So, that and putting your fine legal brain to work, you thought up a cover story once I did call to track me down."

"It worked; I was a winner."

"Thank you."

Still he knew he hadn't yet answered her question nor truly apologized sufficiently for the thoughtless comment earlier. He'd never have been Pat's last so-called chance whereas she symbolized his one and only—something he had to tell her. "The woman and the rest of the women I've been with, I guess they were about of the same importance, which isn't saying a lot." Pat's eyes were moist and too bright, but she'd been honest with him about this Ronnie so she deserved to know. "Yes, you met her. I'd known her since I first arrived in D.C."

"Miranda Nicholson," Pat stated flatly, adding quietly and not too graciously, "the lynx."

"That's right. Panther was the way I originally envisioned her, but lynx will do," he agreed. "I hadn't really thought it was that obvious."

"At the charity Valentine party, she had had her hand on your arm when I came back into the room. You didn't say anything after, but I thought she was the most stunning woman there." Pat remembered the incident vividly. As she had approached the two, hearing Miranda's throaty, intense and oh so sexy voice telling Paul to call. His polite almost curt response that she had his office number if it were a business question. Both of them turning to look at her, the woman's hand dropping, and his cool smile as he'd introduced them.

Nicholson's eyes had narrowed slightly upon seeing Pat and her response to the introduction had been borderline polite. The words so correct, but the body language disdainful with arrogance seeping through. Nicholson had turned to Paul then, her hand reaching out to touch his once more, languidly, perhaps possessively. Then with a haughty smile, she had left them standing there. To Pat's eyes, the woman was a creature of wondrous and self-assured beauty and Pat knew she hated her. The proprietary gesture seemed the last straw. And Pat, in spite of herself, had felt inadequate and practically goggle-eyed at the woman's lush resplendence.

"Stunning...another good choice of words," Paul commented acidly. "Yes, she is and yes, she does. And she also wasn't very nice to you."

"You noticed."

"Of course I did," he snapped. "I was furious but you were such a lady that I decided to be a gentleman too."

"You succeeded. That's why I couldn't decide if she really had any holds on you other than her damn hand or if I was mistaken in thinking you and she had been an item."

"Item...yes, you might have been able to call it that. I met her the first week I was in D.C. and she zeroed in on me immediately, God knows why." Pat's eyes told him she did. "I think it was being introduced as Beck and Stringfellow's newest associate plus the fact we were at a very tony affair at the French Embassy."

"You'd attend something there?"

"Pat, it was nearly twenty-five years after the murder. There was no reason to associate me with my mother. Besides, I was there for business reasons. Beck wanted me to go because I'd be dealing with people there over some of our business. You know I have to be present at things like that."

"Like the Valentine party," she interrupted.

"Yes," he admitted. "That was a charity event—one of Beck's favorites so there were quite a few of us from work even if it was by invitation. A very expensive invitation, I might add, and an event I had no idea Miranda would be attending. But, since I had you to escort," he smiled, "it was worth every cent it cost in addition to its being a good cause. Anyhow, regarding Miranda, she was at the embassy party in all her glory with a pedigree to match."

"Pedigree?"

"Philadelphia Main Line, father a banker, mother head of a major charitable trust, which was the reason it turns out she was at the Valentine party too—old girl network there. Add the fact that her older sister is married to a White House top aide and her big brother seems on the fast track to becoming an ambassador himself."

"Not bad credentials for breaking into the Washington scene," Pat murmured and her lips pursed as she thought of how elementary school teacher Joan and computer programmer Lyle stacked up in comparison and then was mortified. Her siblings were wonderful people and they and Paul had hit it off immediately. What was the matter with her? Was she becoming so insecure that she was acting like Ronnie?

"Right," agreed Paul. "Then factor in a B.A. from Smith, Harvard Law, and clerking for one of the Justices and you see what I mean. I'm not sure why she focused on me aside from the job. B and S international... shit, I never thought of that. B...S..., yah we do a lot of that, internal too. Anyhow, it usually pays off and the firm's associates go places. Maybe she figured a potentially top notch corporate lawyer had his strong points."

And maybe she just saw how attractive you are, thought Pat although she knew Paul was right. Attractive wouldn't have been enough for someone like sleek feline Miranda.

"Also, there was the fact that I was having a conversation, *en français*," continued Paul, "with the so enchanting wife of one of our most important Parisian clients when we met at this 'top drawer' soiree. Miranda is very impressed by France and French society. She spent a junior year abroad and was on the borderline of running with the right crowd at the Sorbonne and in fact had met one of them, who was attached to the Embassy, explaining that invitation. But she didn't quite make the cut with the Parisian elite, which was a real blow to someone who had always been 'in' at home. Anyhow, I seemed to be doing just fine and my French obviously passed muster."

At this Paul laughed sardonically, "I never told her that hers isn't as good as she thinks. Actually, her accent is horrible—worse than yours, sweetheart." Pat's hurt look surprised him and he cursed himself again for being inconsiderate although this faux pas was nothing in comparison to his previous thoughtless remark. "Ah sugar, you never even studied the language. Why should yours be good? Whoever taught you the little you do know sounded like someone out of *Fargo*."

Pat blushed, thinking of Ronnie's attempts at being suave and his being the source of her limited French. "And what's wrong with a Midwest accent?" she protested somewhat weakly, refraining from adding a brash 'you betcha.'

"Nothing in English, *mais en français, c'est horrible*! I'll teach you, sweetheart, if you want," Paul assured her. "It is the language of love but even if Miranda had lots of experience there, and I'm sure she did at least the sex part," he added darkly, "she never had the ear. She had the vocabulary and knew a lot of the current jargon, but her ear is truly tin. It was like hearing someone from Brooklyn or the South Bronx trying to do Shakespeare at Stratford on Avon."

"To hell with the French. I can imagine why she was interested," mumbled Pat.

"You're prejudiced."

"No, you were, are stunning yourself, counselor. I've seen you in an evening suit, remember? That very evening I met Marvelous Miranda, as a matter of fact."

"And out of one too," he smiled. "That's better."

"So obviously did she!" Pat added sharply.

"Well, yes," he admitted somewhat chagrined. "In fact that very first night I met her, which is somewhat fast for me." I know, thought Pat coldly, although she wouldn't have wanted to roll over with anyone right away—not even Paul in spite of her fretting for weeks about the pace of their relationship. "Miranda makes up her mind rapidly on things like that," he continued oblivious this time, thank God, to her reaction. "Later I discovered that she'd also been accompanied to the party by someone else—the young French attaché in fact. She just walked out with me, not even bothering to tell the poor bastard, but I learned that weeks later. I never would have left with her if I'd known. Hell, if I'd known, I would have expected what happened next."

"And that was..."

"I just told you, Pat. She was supposed to be with me up in Pennsylvania skiing that weekend you and I met. But suddenly she got a better offer...the Representative from... Shit, never mind, I'll keep that info privileged," he smiled slightly, "in case a modern Larry Flynt or someone else ever puts out another bounty call on Congress and I need some spare change." Pat smiled too, sure she'd learn this information if she really wanted to. "Yah, I didn't know whom she stood me up for then, but I was furious. Still, I had made the reservations, put down the deposit, and I like to ski plus there were others going from the firm so I could have made some moves while I was up there if I'd really wanted to. If fact, if you hadn't twisted your ankle, I probably would have asked you to go up with me there later...just to ski," he added, and then grinned slightly, "well maybe—now I'd want a bit more."

"I'm not sure skis and I were meant to be." And you'd clearly get the bit more, she answered with a sultry glance, receiving a fleeting grin in reply.

"We'll see this winter, honey...I hope."

"Me too, but about Miss Tits..."

"Pat, Pat, Pat. Yes they are spectacular, aren't they? Silicon."

"I don't believe you! She'd do something dumb like that with a body like hers?"

"Pat, when's she's fifty, she's going to have a dimple on her forehead, and you know why?" She looked at him puzzled. "From all the plastic surgery. It will be her belly button after all the face lifts." Pat burst into hysterical laughter. "I'm serious," Paul asserted although he was grinning widely and sounded definitely like the man she knew.

"But she's gorgeous! What is she? Almost as tall as you, thin..."

"Except for the tits," interjected Paul wickedly.

"Stop that! I still don't believe you. Raven hair, flashing black eyes, alabaster skin..."

"And you said you weren't the poet though I was suspicious of that hair too. Women don't just dye on top anymore."

"Paul!"

"Well they don't, honey. There are all sorts of salons nowadays." Pat blushed and Paul grinned at her. "My naive Midwestern waif. Add morals of an alley cat, disposition of a weasel once you find her out, soul of...no, I don't think she has one. She's going to do fine here in D.C. Unfortunately, though, the less than honorable gentleman from the House was spoken for by a lady at home and was just momentarily straying, which he had made quite clear to *nôtre chère* Miranda when all three of us had our memorable meeting. It was quite a blow to her ego, *pauvre enfant*, since she was used to doing the screw job on others."

"Literally as well as figuratively."

"*Mais oui, ma petite.*"

"Cut the French, Paul. You said that was what had turned her on."

"It's helped in most relationships, *ma belle.*"

Ignoring this decided wisecrack, Pat asked, "So why was she making up to you that night and being such a bitch to me?"

"Because that was exactly what she was doing. Her

Valentine's present from the man on the hill was his announcing his engagement to the well-connected lady back home that very same day. It had been quite romantically played up in the press. Anyhow, to show how broken up she was, Miranda was already on the prowl again that night and sighting me, she remembered I had a few positive qualities. She also thought I was at the party by myself. Not that my having a date would have mattered to her," he added matter-of-factly. "It certainly didn't when she realized I'd brought you. You came up just after I'd told her I was there with you and didn't intend to leave without you or even when I did, meet her after. The snobby put-down for you was to show us both you weren't in her, and I guess my, league and then after because she realized I could care less that she wanted to make up. You were the only interesting woman there that night."

"Thank you."

"Hey, you looked like a million dollars that evening. I'd never seen you all dressed up before."

"Paul, the dress was on sale, I'd made the jacket myself, the jewelry was my grandmother's, not something from Cartier like her diamonds."

"They could have been paste, for all I cared. You were spectacular." From the look in his eyes, she knew he meant it and she remembered how excited she'd been when he'd invited her. A holiday charitable function at Kennedy Center followed by a private party at one of the Watergate penthouses, no less. She'd never been invited to anything like that in all her years in D.C. and she had agonized over what to wear.

At Betty's insistence, they'd roamed Georgetown and going to one of the charity consignment stores patronized by some of D.C.'s wealthier women, she'd purchased a long winter-wool sleeveless sheath in white. Somehow, Betty had convinced her that she wasn't going to bump into the original owner at the party and that even if she did, getting clothes that way was the fashionable thing to do as well as a damn good buy. To further convince Pat, Betty had said,

"Remember, it's for charity."

White, that was a summer color, Pat had then argued but her friend assured her that winter white would be spectacular with her fair skin and contrasting dark hair and eyes. Next they'd purchased a pair of long black silk gloves, amazingly fitting her small hand size 'like a glove' they'd both laughed, and after gone out to get black suede shoes—inches higher than Pat had ever worn—and an evening clutch to match. Betty had bemoaned the fact that Pat wouldn't buy or rent a fur jacket, but it wasn't just a matter of money. In principle, Pat didn't believe in wearing something that had been killed just for adornment although she knew as a native Minnesotan, furs could be very comforting during the long frigid winter nights. And, the short days too! As a child, she had often snuggled up to GG on winter excursions, pressing her nose to the old lady's ancient mink coat for that extra warmth.

Further, Pat had no objection to wool or alpaca or anything shorn from an animal. The shoes she figured had once been wrapped around a tasty morsel of beef. So, completing her ensemble had been a short black wool bolero jacket, which she had painstakingly incrusted with glistening black bugle beads and sequins. Her grandmother's jet teardrop earrings and a matching choker had complemented her decor. When Paul had picked her up that evening, dashing himself in black tie, he'd whistled appreciatively and murmured, "*Olé!*" And, until she'd met Miranda Nicholson, tightly encased in a long black velvet gown, which Pat was sure came straight out of *Vogue* with price to match and all those real jewels, she had indeed felt like that million dollars.

Paul seemed to know what she was thinking. "I left with you, Pix. You know I'd never have gone without you but I didn't realize she'd hurt your feelings that much," he apologized.

"She didn't—not for long, and so you did," smiled back Pat.

"You were never in the same class." Pat looked at him surprised. "You are always a lady. She just pretends to be.

And it was that classy lady I had to fight at first. I wanted to be with you so much but if we had an affair, I was afraid I'd fall more in love with you. Shit, I already had, but I didn't want to do that."

"Why? You've just said you would have considered me as a fling—a one night stand, when we met." And love, she thought. You said it was at first sight!

"Yah, but that probably would have been it. Those kind of women never lasted long—something your buddy Betty hasn't figured out. Miranda wouldn't either even if she hadn't dumped me first," he stated bluntly. "And then because once I got to know you, I realized I'd want to marry you, of course," he answered simply. "Marriage was something I shouldn't do even though I knew I loved you."

"But we did start a relationship."

"Of course we did," he said angrily. "It just reached the point that I had to have you. Christ, you obviously wanted me." Pat felt her ears turning red. "Well you did and how the hell was I going to keep you if I didn't satisfy some of your needs?"

"My needs," she said softly, but staring at him with an irritated expression, her eyes hurt again, piercing him.

Everything he was saying seemed to be coming out wrong, Paul realized, angry with himself. "And mine too, damn it. Sweet Jesus, you knew I wanted you. Look what happened when we went to New York!"

She smiled slightly, remembering. "It was wonderful. I thought it would be good with you, but..." she was blushing again.

"Hell yes. It was wonderful and then I knew I couldn't let you get away."

"You hadn't planned to ask me to marry when we went up there? It was an audition or something like your grandfather's?" But better than a rebound, she thought although a small bit of her wondered if Miranda had been more important than Paul would concede.

Now he was the one clearly embarrassed. Floundering, he admitted, "Sort of, I guess, but never like *Grandpère's*. But, well, you were auditioning me too, weren't you?"

"I suppose I was," she acknowledged finally. "I really hadn't thought about that."

"Listen, I told you I was in love with you before we went, before we had sex. I just didn't want to admit it because I couldn't marry you. You weren't some diversion like Miranda."

"But you did marry me."

"I know I did, but I didn't want to!" Her face turned stark white and he thought she was going to faint. "Oh, God," he moaned miserably, "that's not what I meant."

"What did you mean?" she managed to sputter out, feeling like she'd been kicked in the stomach.

"Well, think about it, Pat! I may be a murderer's son but then...then I realized I couldn't let you get away, let anyone else have you. I never knew anyone could fall in love so fast. I'd always thought it was a longer, drawn out process. My grandmother told me it could happen, remember? That it had been that way with my parents."

"Thank you," she said softly, relieved and joyful at his answer and he sighed for finally he had said something right. "I didn't want anyone else to have you either," she replied. "That's one of the reasons I've been so upset by what's been happening. I was afraid there was another woman...Miranda or..."

"No, Pat," he stated firmly. "No other woman, never since I've been with you. I swear. That's why I ended up proposing and asking you to stay the extra day in New York so we could get the ring. I was afraid if I didn't put a ring on your finger then and there, I'd change my mind and forever regret it."

"The fabulous ring. I couldn't find the bill for it." Paul looked at her strangely. "This weekend," she said, "I was worried about so much—another woman, money problems, your work. I just didn't know what was happening and I..." she hesitated, looking at him guiltily, "I snooped."

"You snooped?"

"I went through your file cabinet, Paul."

"Oh...well it wasn't locked."

"I know that but I'd never looked in there unless you asked me to get something and I hadn't asked and I'm sorry. I was just afraid you were in trouble—maybe with finances."

"And if I had been?" he asked with curiosity.

"I would have used my savings, cashed in my bonds, tried to get us on some kind of plan where we could consolidate our debts, work it out."

He looked at her, a kind, sweet smile appearing on his face. "You would have done that?"

"Sure, we're married."

"Nothing up there was a secret, little darlin'. You could have looked at my files any time, whether you asked or not but I appreciate the thought."

"Well, you weren't here and obviously money isn't a problem."

"No..." he sighed, running his fingers through his hair, before adding slowly, "It isn't. Funny, now that I can make it, and have it, I don't need it."

"I'm not sure I understand."

"All my papers aren't up there in that cabinet, Pat, nor down here either for that matter."

"I think I realized that. I was certain you had stuff at work."

"Not there either."

"What? You have gold bars hidden away?"

"Not exactly, but I do have another income."

"From your French grandfather?" she asked surprised.

"Ha," he snorted. "*Grandpère* Martin wouldn't give me a *sou* if he had his way but his mother had left a small trust for my mother, simple spending money by their standards. When I was twenty-five, it came to me. Of course by then I was out of law school and didn't need it but I couldn't touch it before then. In fact, I really hadn't known about it. A friend of my grandfather's—Grandpa Wolfe—sent me the information, including a letter Grandpa had prepared to give me when I reached that age before he died. He'd known, Pat, about his heart but he didn't want me to worry, hoping there'd be time. That was the kind of man he was, but I guess he just couldn't take being without Grandma. It was all so damn ironic—more money than I'd ever had or even needed but not when it really could have helped me or my grandparents. It's invested in some European conglomerates and the income deposited into a Swiss bank now," Paul said with some satisfaction, "not Martin Internationale and I have a European credit card and checking account. I have a French passport too. *Mon cher grandpère* saw to that as well and to be honest, as I got older, it made sense to me too. I rarely use any of those items but for your ring, the expenses were a bit more than I wanted to show up on my Master Card, ok?"

"I wondered about that. I saw the honeymoon expenses and our party. God, Paul, you paid a fortune. We could have practically had a regular wedding."

He laughed dryly. "We did as far as I'm concerned. I couldn't feel more married, but you were trying to be thorough in your little search. I wish some of my current paralegals excelled in that trait. If I ever get to hire one, I'm going to find someone from Tulane."

"Isn't that a bit chauvinistic?"

"No and not old school ties either. The university has one of the best programs in the country for training them. But it's just as well that I had used the other card. I've got a safe deposit box down in D.C. near the office. I keep all my European stuff there. And Pat, there is some jewelry in that box too—including a diamond choker better than Miranda's by far. It belonged to my mother. Next time we play dress-up, you can have it if you want. It's been yours since I asked you to marry me. Those items were just something else I didn't know how to mention or when to present."

"Not the bracelet you gave me?"

"No, that really was my grandmother's. It was the only piece of jewelry she had left when she died beside her wedding ring and Grandpa made sure that stayed on her finger when she was buried. Even her engagement ring had to go," he said softly, his face pained and Pat now really knew why he had insisted on buying her the diamond. "If only I'd known about the trust and everything then. The bracelet had been her mother's and she couldn't bear to sell it like her other things. I never knew I had this other jewelry until I got Grandpa's letter. My grandparents could have sold it too, but they didn't think that was right even though, lord knows, they must have been tempted when money became so tight. But they felt I should have it as a remembrance of my mother. That I'd want it for the woman I was going to marry. *Maman* was wearing that choker the night before she was murdered. She and my father were going to a party at the French Embassy and she was spectacular. You'll be too."

"Oh Paul," Pat wrapped her arms around him, doubting that she'd ever rival the beauty of the woman in his prized photo, but thankful that to him, love was blind.

"I guess I'd better get a card for you to sign so your name is on the safe deposit box now... in case anything happens."

"Don't say that!" she sputtered, clearly upset.

"Sugar, we're married," he soothed. "It's not just this. I should have done it before. I've signed my insurance and pension rights over to you at work and changed the deed so the house is in both our names but I've been lax about other things like the trust proceeds and I'm supposed to be the lawyer. An updated will, living trust...all of that. Those are the proper instruments for transferring assets to you if..." he stopped. "I'll have to get that done. The last thing I'd ever want would be for any of that money in Switzerland or anything else to go back to my grandfather because he was my last blood relative; and I want you to have a durable power of attorney in case..." Again he stopped.

Pat winced, wills naturally meant considering death. She knew it was illogical on her part. They were too young to have wills, but then she'd never really had anything of value before and like Paul had assigned her insurance and other savings to him and her parents. People her parents' age had wills and probably people with children like Joan and Lyle, but her and Paul? Also, a power of attorney that could be used if he were...to mean in case...in case he was unable to make decisions of his own. No, that was too painful even though she knew he was right. It had been more of her own stupid procrastination and denial—mostly the denial. And if his French grandparent was still around, who knew what a powerful man might do particularly since Paul had dual citizenship. So instead of arguing, she queried, "He's still alive?"

"Hell, yes. The old bastard will hit a hundred or more probably. He's only in his early eighties. And yes, I...we're fine financially. Not filthy rich. My mother's legacy was nothing compared to what the Martins consider money and she did use some of it. Christ, she was just twenty-five when she died so she'd just gotten it. I hope she had a little fun with it even though by then my dad was doing ok financially. It had a chance to regenerate a bit, minus some unexpected costs later," Paul added darkly, "but aside from your ring, I haven't used it since it reverted to me. I'm no multimillionaire, sweetheart, just very well to do and that I've kept. With the Martin money, I'd feel it was filthy. Louis Martin is the kind of person who'd cheerfully made deals with anyone, terrorists included. He doesn't give a damn about anything except his precious bank and getting richer. No wonder my mother ran off with my father."

"Tell me about your parents."

"I did."

"No, tell me really."

"Really? That's a hard one. What I did tell you was real. They did love each other. I'm sure of that, and that's why I could never understand people saying she was having an affair or that my father killed her because she was."

"You were just a little kid, Paul."

"Yah, but little kids can see and feel too. They loved each other, Pix. My home was filled with love. One can't fake that. It was the way I feel about you. I couldn't cheat on you. I'm sure I'd know if you did on me."

"I wouldn't."

He looked at her, studying her earnest face, her big brown eyes wide and totally sincere. "I don't think you would either, but even if you did, I don't think I'd want to hurt you. Hell, I know I wouldn't! Jesus, you scared the shit out of me when you were telling me what happened in bed this weekend, how I..."

"I swear, Paul. You didn't hurt me. It was strange, almost inhuman, so impersonal, but you didn't hurt me. You even made sure I came."

He smiled cynically. "A gentleman in spite of myself? Weight on the elbows, opening doors, remembering to put down the toilet seat..."

"Yes," she agreed, smiling. "Class, that was the first thing I learned about you too, remember? You'd never hurt me." Not on purpose, she thought.

"Christ, I hope I never will," he answered fervently.

"So what do we do?"

"I don't know, Pix. I honestly don't know. I suppose I will have to see someone, but I don't want to." He looked at her pained. "After the murder—the police, the prosecution, the defense, everyone was hassling me to know what happened. I must have had to talk to someone every day at first and I was terrified. I couldn't remember anything and I was afraid if I did that I'd know my dad had done it once I understood what had happened. I've always been afraid to know which is the problem and no doubt why I was having the blackouts. And that makes me think I would see him stabbing her if I remembered which is even worse." He sighed, a long despondent sound. "Catch 22—I've gone round and round on it, wondering if I should undergo hypnotism or something and find out definitely. That was something *Grandpère* wanted and lord knows I came close to it in Switzerland."

"Paul...that poster upstairs? The framed one from Switzerland?"

"You make a great detective. Yes, that's where the school was—just outside the village at the foot of that mountain. The photo it was made from was taken when I was in high school of a race I was in. I'll even point out which dot I am," he quipped. "It had been a big race with skiers from all over Europe and the town commune used it as a souvenir poster after. I actually was fairly good— probably the best skier in the school, which was why they entered me. Anyhow, I came in second that day, and I think the staff had some idea about my becoming a regular competitor thereafter but of course when I returned to the States, I just gave it up. After all, where could I pursue it then, particularly since I had no money to run off to places like Aspen. Maybe that's why I kidded about becoming a surfer dude out in California. It wasn't until I was stationed in Germany that I took the sport up again.

"It was one of the good memories I've retained of my life over there. At first I hated it and then as I got older, I just hated the beginnings. I still do, my memories of what happened after the murder. All those people, they pretended to be my friends and then they'd push and wheedle and it was awful. Even Grandpa and Grandma Wolfe pressured me somewhat after my father was arrested. They kept hoping I'd remember so it would clear him. And then *Grandpère* Martin when he arrived—that was really awful. He was practically threatening me. Hell, he did. The whole damn time I was in Switzerland, I had to see a shrink every month or so the first few years and it was always the same. What had I seen? What had I heard? They were almost putting words in my mouth," Paul said bitterly. Pat winced; his pain was again so evident.

"Trying to force those memories that kids are supposed to have repressed and then miraculously remember years later. I refused to play and the few times I did see *Louis le Magnifique*, he'd accuse me of lying. I wasn't. I just couldn't remember and I also refused to lie although lord knows, it would have made life easier for me and wouldn't have made any difference to what had happened to my father. No, that's not true; people would have believed for sure that he'd done it and he never admitted it. Louis would have been delighted. One time the two of us had such a fight that I was afraid that he was going to put me in an asylum or have them drug me or something. Thank God I was at the school then or he might have."

Pat looked at him, feeling sick. "Oh Paul."

"Yah, it was pretty awful and that's why I got out of Switzerland the second I hit eighteen. I never even finished *lycée* because I was a year behind due to my shaky start at not knowing the languages when I arrived. Guess I had to finish college," he said half facetiously. "Otherwise I'd have been just another high school dropout. Anyhow, I'd become friendly with one of the school staff and he felt sorry for me. He ended up getting in touch with Grandpa Wolfe, who arranged the paper work, and even lent me enough money to buy a ticket back to the States. Once I arrived, Louis couldn't touch me. After all, I had an American birth certificate and I was legally an adult. Fortunately for my friend, the old bastard didn't figure out how I got the fare either or he probably would have seen to it that Mario was fired and then blackballed everywhere else." Pat shook her head in disgust.

"Right, that's the kind of man Louis is. Anyhow, eventually I was able to pay him back.

"But when I got to Alabama, Grandma was fighting cancer again, just like I said. Grandpa by then had been out of politics for years and was working at a law firm...shit, working, not even a partner. Still he was able to pull some strings as an alum and get me into Tulane as an undergraduate at the last minute. After that, it was just the way I told you, more or less. I at least got to know my Alabama grandparents as an adult, to have a little time with them. They were wonderful people and they never believed my father did it. He loved my mother and they loved her too. They also couldn't believe she'd cheated on him but I hurt them because I couldn't remember for them either," he said sadly. "I couldn't lie for them, Pat, not even them.

"The only one who never pressured me was my dad," Paul finally said thoughtfully. "I didn't get to see him after I was five and of course Louis wouldn't let me have any contact with any of my American family once he'd taken me. No mail, nothing. Dad asked me once after the murder, just once, if I'd seen anything. I said I hadn't, and then he said it was probably just as well. When I was growing up, I sometimes thought that proved he had done it and didn't want me to tell, but later I think he meant it would have been too awful if I had seen. The trouble is I'm just not sure, Pat." He looked at her with an agonized expression. "No one wants to think his father murdered his mother."

She leaned over in the chair and drew him to her, burying her face in his thick, soft hair. His head was on her lap and he was leaning against her leg. He felt her warm breath against his ear as she said softly, "Oh Paul. Let's go upstairs now. Do you want anything to eat?"

"No," he said. "I probably should clean up that mess I made in the kitchen."

"I'll get it tomorrow. I'm not hungry either. We've talked enough. Tomorrow, we'll think about this tomorrow. Let's just go lie down."

"You still want to sleep with me?"

She drew back and looked at him shocked. "You're my husband. I love you."

"You're not afraid?"

"No," Pat said hesitantly, diplomatically choosing her words. "I was scared about you, that something might happen to you, but I haven't been scared about me. I never was." She realized she meant what she was saying.

"You're absolutely sure?" Paul looked at her intently, a trial lawyer examining her credibility.

"You think I'd lie to you?"

"No...no. That's probably another reason why I knew I had to marry you." Paul got up and took her hand and the two walked upstairs. There they undressed slowly. Once in bed, he turned to her, holding her tightly as though she were his lifeline, but he made no effort to initiate sex. Neither did she, realizing that it was comfort and security that they both wished.

Later though, Pat awoke and knew Paul was crying again. Gently, she reached over and gently she started to woo him and then they did make love. Not the wild, unreal, intense act of the past Saturday morning, but slowly and tenderly, a therapeutic act and healing. When it was over, he continued to hold her, playing with her silky hair, allowing the unruly curls to slip and slide through his fingers. He pressed his face to her drinking in the odor of her perfume, the scent of her body, and whispered huskily, "Don't leave me, Pix. Please don't leave me."

In answer, she squeezed him tightly, giving him a gentle kiss. "Never, it's all right, Boytoy," she cooed. "It's all right. We'll make it all right." She felt his body begin to relax in relief. They lay there—she with her head on his breast. She could hear his heart beating rapidly and thought how she'd never seen him cry before this sad, unreal night, realizing how vulnerable he too could be—how vulnerable he'd always been and how well he'd hidden it. And, how embarrassed in fact he had been by his emotional release, mentioning he hadn't cried since he was a child and trying to joke with a quip about what do you expect from a man who not only likes quiche, but can make it. At last he fell back asleep and the beat of his heart became steady and familiar. Oh, Boytoy, she thought, but her arms continued to hold him protectively and she cleaved to him, afraid to let go, afraid she'd wake up and he'd be gone again or once more metamorphose into that strange, lost being.

CHAPTER 11

The next morning, both of them awoke early, apprehensive and nervous. Pat's relief that it was Paul in her arms, really her Paul, was monumental for she still was upset by what had happened. He, himself, appeared not much better, still feeling the strain of the last few hours. They lay there for a few minutes, just cuddling, giving each other emotional support and at last she asked, "What now? Besides calling in sick or something?"

"I don't know," he answered truthfully. "I honestly don't know and you're probably right. I can't go into the office this morning as if nothing happened. Will you stay home with me today?" His voice was calm, that reassuring sound she'd grown to love, but she could see his face was tense and his eyes silently pleading.

"Of course," she nodded her head. There was no way she could leave him to face the day alone and there was still too much to discuss.

"I was awake some last night."

"I know you were," she said, giving him a reassuring little kiss.

"That's not what I meant," he smiled shyly, "but that too. That definitely too, my little darlin'. No, I suppose I will have to speak to someone, but good lord...I don't want to. I can't stand to go through this again. I thought it was over...as much as it could be over. When I married you, I thought I had a new start if only that damn program..."

She looked at him, clearly puzzled. "Program?"

"*Crimes of the Past Century*," he said by explanation, shutting his eyes wearily.

And then suddenly, she remembered. "The night you cut your finger."

"Hell, yes. I was lucky I didn't cut off my hand," he declared with feeling. "I had no idea they were going to put the damn thing on TV. I never watch crap like that but I suppose I should have realized the case would come up again and be featured on one of those pseudo sensationalisms they pretend are true interpretations of actual cases. The Wolfe murder has been highlighted every few years, but this was going to be special since the twenty-fifth anniversary was almost there. Jesus, Pix, she's been gone all those years, a quarter of a century. She was hardly that herself. It should have been the first third of her life, not the entirety. She was like a ray of light—blonde, shining, laughing all the time although the last months it was different. Then she'd become quiet and sometimes she'd cry. I remember asking her why she was so sad and she'd said *'Pas triste, mon petit, fatigué.'* But before then she was Claire—bright and clear—*Clair de lune*, my father used to whistle that all the time.

"More charming than 'Five Foot Two, Eyes of...'," Pat murmured.

"Not to me."

"But I'm not five two," she suddenly confessed, her face reddening. Paul looked at her surprised. "Only five one. I had some secrets too."

"Oh Pix," he laughed. "I would have loved you if you were six two and I had to look up to you. My mother never specified the correct size for a fairy princess. Anyhow, I guess when she became pregnant again, she changed. But before, she made every day an adventure for me and the stories she used to read me."

"Those French children's books you have? They really weren't something you picked up to learn the language."

"No. They were gifts from *le bon Père Noël*—Father Christmas, Santa Claus, you know. They're among the few things that my grandparents kept for me—just like the diamonds for the woman I'd love and marry," he remarked gently and she pressed a kiss to his cheek and squeezed him tighter. "She also made up the most wonderful tales about fairies and pixies and would show me where they lived."

"During your garden sessions."

"Yes," he said smiling. "That was when she told me

once that everybody had some magical little creature, an elf or pixie, that watched out for them but after she died and I was taken away, I didn't believe it." He looked sadly at Pat. "I wanted to but when I got to Europe I couldn't believe a good fairy would let something like that happen. I hadn't thought of those stories for years after and then I saw you sprawled under those twinkling Christmas lights and I swear to God, Mary Patton Strom, that was my first reaction. I'd found my very own, special pixie and one as cute as a button."

"Oh Paul," she said embarrassed. "I...I just figured you were teasing me because I'm small. Joan and Lyle, especially Lyle, always did. Everyone did. I just never grew up to be a big blond Scandinavian like the rest of the family."

"You weren't supposed to," he said seriously. "You were what my mother promised me. I just didn't know it was going to take so long to find you. But it still would have been you, even if you'd been blonde or that towering six foot plus giant. Pixies are very good at camouflage."

Still embarrassed, Pat returned to the subject. "You were telling me about when we were in the kitchen, remember, the TV program?"

"Oh yah. They had a lead in about the fact they were going to feature the case that night..."

"And you were chopping vegetables for the ratatouille." Yes the ratatouille, she remembered. It had been such a surprise to her when she discovered that Paul enjoyed cooking almost as much as eating and then even more so when he told her that he'd worked in a New Orleans restaurant while in college.

Her mind drifted even further back as she recalled his teasingly asking her why she was amazed. "After all, aren't men the best chefs?"

"You won't get a rise out of me," she had chuckled in response. "But Dad and Lyle would rather be caught dead before they cooked over anything but a camp fire and poor Tom," referring to Joan's husband, "he can't even cope with a can opener."

"And I by contrast, would like you to know I can even make a mean quiche." At this boast, Pat giggled. "What, you believe the propaganda that real men don't like quiche, much less eat it?" She shook her head violently. "Good, I'll fix you one. Anyhow, working there meant great free meals for me, plus some needed cash."

"Somehow I never thought you had to work during college—I mean the Air Force scholarship for law school, that was one thing, but during your undergrad years."

"You thought I was independently wealthy? Didn't you work?" he asked, turning the question.

"Sure, I told you that. I started during high school in an insurance agency belonging to a friend of my brother-in-law. I guess being good at numbers made them think I might go into that line of work. What it did show me was the last thing I wanted to be was an actuary. But you...I've always had the idea that with being a lawyer's son there was plenty of money."

"Corrupt, big-time litigators?" he smiled gently, shaking his head slightly. "Think more of one step above legal aid. My dad really felt for the little guy...so did my grandfather. Besides, there was no real insurance for me when Dad died and my grandmother had so many medical expenses that ate up the rest of our so-called great wealth. No, Pix, I was thankful to have a job and more than thankful for loans and scholarships."

Well, thought Pat, she should have listened back then to what he was telling her besides his personal take on cooking. She should have also realized with that restaurant experience, he wouldn't have cut himself that way. Paul was always so exceptionally careful. Slowly she said, "There was blood all over the place and you were stark white. I thought you were going into shock."

"I was," he said, "but not from the damn cut."

"Well, you did fairly well on that. I was sick when I saw it."

"You were Florence Nightingale herself. You didn't show a thing."

"At least we could stop the bleeding but I was so afraid you'd need surgery."

"The emergency ward doctor said if the cut had been a little deeper, I would have. At least I only nicked the tendon."

"You didn't tell me that."

"I didn't want you to worry," he replied simply.

"Paul, you didn't do it on purpose, did you?" She looked at him horrified as she suddenly considered that prospect.

"Hell no. I was just so shocked when they flashed the picture up on the screen."

"The picture?"

"Well, obviously one you didn't see. It showed me and my folks in our garden. It was taken at the same time as the one in the study and I was terrified you'd see it and recognize it."

"Is that the reason you kept pacing at the emergency ward, to keep me away from the television?"

"Yes and at least that worked. I didn't know what I would have done if you'd seen the photo and recognized me and them. Hell, you have anyhow and I still don't know what to do. Mary Patton," he said to her seriously, "I'm scared, really scared. I haven't felt this way since I was a little kid." And just by the use of her real name, she knew he was since Pix, for whatever reason, had become his pet appellation for her in bed and sometimes out.

"But you didn't know anything, Paul."

"I was there. I must know something to act this way and I don't want to. I don't want to remember my father killing my mother. And worse yet, I'm not sure what I've been doing now during these memory lapses. Am I dangerous when I'm out there somewhere?" His intense stare revealed valid concern and she knew the question was genuine.

"There's been no sign that anything happened while you were gone—I mean no marks on you and your clothes weren't torn or bloody or anything when you come back.

The Miata was fine...I looked," she confessed hesitantly but he only nodded his head as if confirming it was the only logical thing to do. "Nothing shows that you've been in any trouble and how do you know your father did commit the murder if you can't remember?" she now asked reasonably, but certain this wouldn't appease him. If only she could truly answer.

"He must have, damn it. They convicted him. Contrary to what a lot of people want to believe, most people who go to prison are guilty."

"But he never confessed. Stop being the devil's advocate, Paul! He always said he was innocent. Your grandparents believed he was."

"He was their son and I told you, it's the norm for prisoners to say they're innocent."

"Your grandfather had too much integrity for accepting something like that if it weren't true. You told me so yourself."

"Listen, sugar, when you love someone, you don't want to believe things like that. I obviously still don't or I wouldn't be acting like this."

"But why are you and why now?"

"I told you. The damn documentary, I suppose. Publicity for it was going to be all over the place the next few days. I look like my dad, if you haven't noticed. I'm Paul Wolfe too. I thought I told you that Louis had my name changed for the new passport when he snatched me."

"Snatched you? You said he took you to Europe but I just thought that it was called a kidnapping because your Alabama grandparents didn't give permission for you to go or know at first that you'd gone with him."

"Take my word for it, sugar, I was properly snatched. It wasn't just being taken for a joy ride by *Grandpère*. Hell, Louis wasn't even along. I was christened Paul Martin Wolfe, though lord knows why my mother did that. Maybe in spite of all her father's meanness, she hoped he'd speak to her again or maybe just because it was her last name. Anyhow, Louis had the last name dropped. When I came back to the

States, I even considered retaliating by dropping the Martin entirely or at least taking back my original name but Grandpa Wolfe counseled me to leave the name as it was so there'd be no immediate association—no stigma," Paul added reflectively. "Poor Grandpa, he'd learned the hard way what association meant after the trial. No more talk of being part of a presidential ticket or the Supreme Court—all federal courts lost forever. I still put the W back in although I never spelled the name out. I guess I was too chicken. Ah shit, shit, shit. That's me, chicken and crazy."

"Neither, Paul, especially not crazy. You're not crazy."

"Not crazy? After the way I've been acting? How the hell can you say that? I'm apparently missing days for Christ's sake, Pat. Actual days!"

"Disturbed, scared—your word. I can see that, but not crazy, honey. You're not crazy," she insisted stoutly and her eyes were pleading that he believe her as she said this, while working to re-convince herself. His doubts were eating at her.

"Thanks for the vote of confidence," he said softly, tightly hugging her small warm form, "but what am I doing when I go into these little episodes, aside from fucking you?"

Pat shuddered. Even though Paul could be charmingly risqué, he really wasn't vulgar and until last night, she'd rarely heard him use such language or swear. Kindly Sarah's religious training had obviously taken but now he was sounding like Ronnie always had in private.

"Hey, I'm sorry. But that's what you told me I was doing and that's as scary as anything else. You mean so much to me and to think I'd used you like that. I've never believed in using a woman just as a sex object and you of all people. Oh lord, I'm sorry, sugar, I truly am sorry." He was stroking her hair softly and looking at her sadly.

"Double the pleasure," she quipped to cheer him up, "not everyone gets a mysterious stranger." And not everyone wants one and what if he was right and she was wrong and he was crazy? No, she had to stop thinking that way, but then even if he was, there had to be some way to help him.

Oh Paul, she thought, I love you so much, we've got to fix this. Out loud, she said calmly, "You have to talk to someone. You've started with me finally."

"And there's more."

"So tell me," she urged gently, lifting her hand to smooth his brow. "Tell me what it really was like for you."

Slowly, fitfully he began. In no time she realized how terrible the experience had been for him, how disrupting to his young life—a little boy, scarcely more than a baby. To lose in slightly over a year's period everything he loved and to be torn away from everyone he knew, literally. She agonized as he told her about his sparse memories of the day his mother was killed and of the bewildering days after. "My grandmother came up from Alabama and for a while we were back in the house but then the police arrested my father," he started.

From there on, it was obvious that life for them all had become a nightmare. Although his grandparents tried to comfort and protect him, even their efforts could not shelter him from the prying questions of the police or exposure to the press. He'd wake up at night, he told her, crying because he was plagued by dreams of longing for the mother he adored, never fully understanding why she'd left him. Or equally, bad memories of big, loud, demanding people who kept shouting at him and poking cameras or microphones in his face when he had to go to the court or even left the house. From then on, he had to be kept in the darkened house with the curtains drawn, not even having the escape of playing in the beloved garden.

Then more frightening, his Grandfather Martin arrived and the man complained formally to his ambassador that he should have custody of his grandson, who was a registered French citizen. As a result, there had been a first angry meeting with this unknown French grandfather. His grandmother had taken Paul to the hotel where the man and his present wife were staying to spend an afternoon alone with them. This turned into a bona fide nightmare. To a small child, Louis Martin seemed towering in his anger—an absolute ogre. In reality, Martin was probably only five foot six or seven but he was a bulky, solid man with an enraged beet-red face who had shouted at Paul in French and then been furious when the child wouldn't reply. Switching to a heavily accented English, he'd called his grandson an imbecile, murderer's spawn and other insults, which even a four-year old could comprehend in tone if not content.

Paul had been terrified and refused to answer anything so the man had grabbed him, shaking him, demanding that he tell what he had witnessed, that in effect he reveal how he'd seen his father stab his mother. Paul remembered staring at him vacantly, retreating into his mind, and this strange, unknown grandfather had become even more incensed and struck him. It was Louis's much younger second wife—suave, aristocratic Isobel—who finally pried the traumatized child from his hands. At first Paul thought he might have an ally in the woman, but later she too had been indifferent. At least though, she was not as snide and belittling as her successor, pulchritudinous and greedy Matilde, who had been born only a year or two before Claire, but who was as selfish as Paul's mother had been generous.

When his Grandfather Wolfe returned to get him, Paul refused to talk, unable to tell him about the horrific introduction to his mother's parent. Louis Martin had then informed his in-law that he intended to take the child and a heated argument ensued between the two men, another bitter memory for the child especially since Paul had never seen his beloved Grandfather Wolfe angry.

Pat shook her head in miserable wonder as she listened to Paul's tragic recital. How anyone could be so mean to a tiny anguished boy was beyond her comprehension. At last Paul wound down, unable to continue. Knowing he had reached an emotional impasse, she reached over and took his hand, intertwining his long, slender fingers with hers. Gently she said, "This has been a start, Paul. But now you have to see someone professionally."

"Maybe I'll talk to my boss."

"Your boss? Mr. Beck?" Pat was astonished that he

would even consider that peculiar man.

"He was my father's best friend."

"What!"

"Sure, the firm originally was Beck, Stringfellow and Wolfe. Alphabetic, my dad told me. Didn't you know that?"

"Why would I?"

"I suppose there's no reason you should. My dad started it with the other two and it was just beginning to take off when all this happened. Stringfellow is dead now but they didn't take his name off the door," declared Paul caustically. "Hell, think of what a great advertisement we could have been for criminal law. Hire Paul Wolfe—takes a murderer to defend one," he laughed cynically, a totally cheerless sound that tore at Pat's heart. "Beck actually was one of my dad's lawyers for the appeals although he never specialized in criminal law. He was also my godfather."

"Does he know who you are?" Pat asked amazed, but saddened by Paul's flippant sarcasm and astounded at the thought that Wesley Beck would be anyone's godfather. A less avuncular man, she couldn't imagine. Godfathers were supposed to be personal Santas, jolly, loving.

"To be honest? I'm not sure. I mean once *Grandpère* Louis took me back to Europe and had my name changed legally, how would he know and even when I ended up sticking the W back in, there was no obvious connection, at least on paper. When I returned to the States as a teenager, I never contacted Mr. Beck. For one thing, I'm not sure he really liked me."

"A godfather who didn't like his godchild! Well, he does now."

"Now, my dear wife, I am supposedly a competent rising attorney with a whole array of valuable attributes," commented Paul snidely. "Most associates work their asses off, not that I don't devote a lot of hours as you've no doubt noticed. By comparison, I'm given great latitude. None of my contemporaries there get the time off I do. I told you before. It's the languages, plain and simple. I'm about the only one they have who is truly fluent; the others use translators except for a Chicano guy and a Puerto Rican but they were hired more to fill minority quotas. Actually they got three for the price of one with González as the lady's also black, not that I've noticed Puerto Ricans seeming to make that distinction. Maybe that should be our next island holiday," Paul interjected somewhat optimistically and Pat nodded her head enthusiastically. Anything to encourage him about the future, she reflected. They had to think positively.

"Anyhow, at the time of the murder, I was a snotty-nosed little kid who was too loud and was always interrupting my elders or trying to get their attention. Mr. Beck has never married. I doubt if he'd know what to do with a kid. I've sometimes wondered if he knew what to do with a woman." This Paul added as an afterthought.

"Paul!" Although after the strange way the man had acted the time he'd visited them, Pat wasn't sure her husband was wrong. House tours, for God's sake! Still, sexual preferences were a moot point whether Paul was right or wrong in his speculation. If she'd thought about it, she would have said asexual herself or just narcissist or an egoist in the purest sense; but, a man as politically savvy and astute in his business practices as Wesley Beck would have to be a strong ally.

"Well, it's true. He never had one around when he visited my parents and they did a lot of things together when I was really little. The last year or so—just before the murder happened—he wasn't there much unless he'd drop by to bring something to the house. Of course I'd still see him sometimes when my dad would take me to the office."

"Where you played with the magic markers and decided to be a lawyer when you grew up?" Pat interrupted.

Paul smiled fleetingly at her. "Right, but now I play mostly on the phone or with my computer or attend meetings when I'm not reading stacks of papers in my spare time. Sometimes I wish it were still with magic markers," he added wistfully.

"Me too," she agreed. A safe, safe world with magic markers, she thought, and tea parties in the garden for Paul and going tobogganing with Lyle for me but then I wouldn't have Paul and surely he's been worth it all.

Paul continued, "My mother didn't seem to like him much, I remember. Odd, I hadn't thought about that for years. But he'd been my father's roommate at Oxford and I guess the two hit it off right from the start in spite of the fact they were so different. In a curious way, they complimented each other—Beck so staid and my dad outgoing. Oh, Pix, I wish you could have met my father. Everyone liked him. He was so kind and funny."

"Like you," she interrupted.

"Not lately. But maybe Dad was a murderer too," Paul added despondently, gazing away, not able to look at her as he uttered these harsh words.

"No, that's not how you remember him," asserted Pat strongly. Hearing Paul cycling up and down in his memories was heartbreaking. "Tell me more—the way you do remember him. That has to be the truth," she encouraged.

"Well, both were headed for law school. They kept up though Beck was at the University of Maryland at the law school in Baltimore, while my folks were at Tulane. Eventually over the years, he and my dad thought they'd go into partnership. Beck didn't come from any money or anything. He had scholarships all the way through, the way I ended up doing, but he was supposed to be just brilliant and really was thorough at what he did. That's one reason Grandpa was so discouraged by the outcome of the appeals. He figured Beck would be able to ferret out anything if it could be found.

"My dad was smart too and he had the connections when the two started their firm but he wasn't as obsessive. I mean he went into the kind of law he did I think because he wanted to prove something to Louis; but, he didn't have the same kind of ambition and he just wasn't interested in politics. If Beck and he could have traded places, I'm sure Beck would have ended up a presidential candidate. As it was, he just carved out a legal empire."

"What about Stringfellow?"

"Oh, he was a good ol' boy, a little older, some political connections, more money than Beck or my father, and a nice guy. He was actually the son of one of my grandfather's friends, a congressman from Virginia. I guess he and my dad had known each other since they were kids."

"Capitol Hill brat packs?" Pat laughed.

"Something like that," agreed Paul smiling. "In those days, D.C. was relatively small and Congress was like a large family. Grandpa told me people might argue—debate he said—during the day, but after work, people would socialize or at least be polite."

"Kind of like company picnics and office Christmas parties?"

"A bit more than that considering the unique bond. It was far from the cut-throat atmosphere of rampant partisanship they have now. Simply, congressional families were friends. Anyhow Stringfellow had been practicing in the D.C. area after he got out of UVA Law and he and Dad kept up too. When my father decided he wanted to go into international law up here, they started talking and struck a deal. Beck kind of tagged along and Dad convinced Stringfellow he should be included.

"I always wondered when I was little why Stringfellow wasn't the one to be my godfather. Certainly my mother and I liked him better. He used to remember my birthdays and Christmas and if he was in the office when I went with my dad, he'd always produce something—a chocolate bar, a new pencil, just something. And magic tricks! My lord, he'd pull a quarter out of my ear when that was real money and better yet, give it to me...stuff like that," smiled Paul in memory. "Still, it's not that Beck didn't come through with the loot too. I mean how could he avoid it but it was always something ostentatious and not necessarily something I liked or was old enough to use. A chemistry set the Christmas I turned four. You can bet my mother had that poked away where I couldn't get it!

"Stringfellow, though, he was a nice man, Pix, genuinely nice—a real southern gentleman. It wasn't just the little gifts.

He always had time to say something to me and treat me as if I were a real person. Most people don't do that with kids. They see them as pets or ignore them. If he were here, I'd go to him immediately," said Paul thoughtfully. "He'd know what to do and he'd have some compassion."

"And you don't think Beck will? So why him instead of someone else?"

"Oh, because I suppose he does know who I really am and I've just been kidding myself," sighed Paul resigned. "He's never said anything but then hell, I did apply for the job when I was getting out of the Air Force and I'm sure the firm did their share of snooping."

"But you said you have a different name, records, everything."

"Ah, Pix. Martin, for Christ's sake. If I hadn't applied for the job here, there never would have been any reason to know. But that was my mother's name, my middle name when I was christened and you know who was probably holding me. All my folks' friends knew she was related to Martin of Martin Internationale. I told you Beck was at Oxford with my parents. I think he even may have introduced them. He would have met her then when she was single, *la belle demoiselle* Martin.

"And having Paul as a first name and supposedly coming from Alabama and going to Tulane like my father and grandfather. The only change in the pattern was going out West to law school instead of staying at Tulane and my serving in the Air Force but I still ended up a lawyer and gravitated back to the East coast to get involved in international law—European not Pacific Rim. That's me, a nearly thirty-year old lawyer named Paul who looks like his father. My dad was my age when the murder happened. He was dead before he was forty, Pat. Good Lord, I never thought of that. It was the same date as when I spaced out this weekend."

Pat and Paul looked at each other, the identical thought occurring. "And two months ago?" she finally asked. "When they were going to show the TV program?"

"That was the anniversary of the murder," Paul answered flatly. "July 15, just after Bastille Day. They'd gone to that party at the French Embassy the night before. That was when she was wearing the diamond choker—your choker. I remember..." Pat could see by his eyes that he did. "*Maman* came down the stairs in this white gown. It was Empire Style. You know, tucked up under the breasts—very *décolletage* with a high waist line. Then it flowed down, straight and loose, to help cover the pregnancy. She was over seven months *enceinte* then—enclosed, with child. God, French has a nice sound for that. Her blonde hair was up in a sophisticated chignon but she looked *comme un ange*. She should have been on top of a Christmas tree. Hell, no, she looked like Louis Napoleon's empress. Eugenie never would have held a candle to her. Louis...," he mumbled in an abstract manner, "another opportunistic Louis—probably who *Grandpère* modeled himself on."

Ignoring the digression, Pat felt as though she could see the scene through his eyes. Poor, poor woman, only in her mid-twenties, pregnant, and obviously so beautiful that her son, a little four-year old, remembered every detail of that last night. And God, she thought almost as a prayer, Paul was reverting to more and more French expressions now that he'd told her who he was. Before these had been used in intimacy or jest and light asides, but not *de rigueur*, as he'd probably say. The comments actually were overtaking his English. Almost everything mumbled in bed last night had been French, language of love or not, and she'd just held him, not caring if she really understood or not.

"Yes," Paul said, "that was the anniversary and this second time was the date of my father's death."

"He died in prison, didn't he?"

"Yes." Paul's eyes turned cold, dark, and almost without emotion, he said, "He was in the wrong place at the wrong time. A fight broke out between a couple of the inmates and it accelerated into a free-for-all brawl. He was stabbed. No one knew who did it, nor why. He apparently had become known as the Lone Wolfe." There was a despondent laugh, which chilled Pat. "And usually, people did just that—left him alone. He also had a reputation for being willing to give the other inmates legal advice so if anything, he was protected from some of the nastier aspects of prison life, not that it really mattered in the end. That made the stabbing even more of a mystery apparently. He died and I never got to see him again."

Paul leaned back, looking up at the ceiling. "I never got to talk to him all those years. He lived for seven years in that damn prison and I never saw him after they took him out of that fucking D.C. courtroom. I'd just turned twelve when he died, Pat, and when he was gone, they, Louis and Matilde— Isobel had been given her walking papers by then—never bothered to tell me nor did anyone at the school. It was something I saw in an old copy of *Newsweek* in the school library. I was just glancing through and there it was, short and simple, the headline, Pat, that's how I found out. *Paul Wolfe, Jr. Stabbed in Prison Riot.* That was his obituary, a sensational little column detailing the whole story. I didn't handle that too well. He had lived a couple days, like my baby brother, but he didn't recover consciousness and of course they never found out who did it. There are never witnesses in prison, Pix," Paul added dryly and then mumbled under his breath, "Stabbed—all three of them. What a shitty way to go."

Pat reached out to squeeze his hand, "I'm sorry, so sorry," she murmured ineffectually but he really wasn't listening.

"I've got Xeroxes of everything I could locate on him from libraries in one of those files downstairs. And I dredged up everything I could find on the internet once I got to law school plus I started looking up the old court transcripts last autumn after I came out here. Then there were the obits with a few details about *Maman's* background and murder and the fact that my father never confessed and was working on another appeal."

"And that's why you really came back here?" she asked softly.

"Yah, I guess so…besides wanting to join Dad's firm. In fact I went to the Library of Congress and dug out all the news clippings I hadn't been able to locate before. I got hold of some of the foreign ones too—those I could read; pretty sensational compared to the *Post* and *Times*, but those were bad enough. I'd started searching even when I was at Tulane, kind of my adult hobby," he added dryly. "That's how I spent any free weekend time before I met you. Part of me always wanted to research the court transcripts here and part…well, I lived here in Washington until it all happened."

Pat felt as though she had had a revelation. Slowly she asked, "The house in Georgetown? Is that why we used to take the walks there? It was the one we stopped in front of that time and you got the stomach cramps."

It had been a sunny afternoon in spring, just after they returned from the Twin Cities. She'd thought they were going to drive out into the country but suddenly Paul had suggested lunch at a little French cafe on Wisconsin Avenue. After, they'd strolled a few blocks down the avenue and turned into a side street—a part of Georgetown they'd not visited previously. The fruit trees were in bloom and azaleas flowering. One house, a white two story, was surrounded by the huge blossom-laden bushes, which had to be decades old from their size. Pat had exclaimed at their beauty and stopped to admire them when she realized Paul was a few paces behind her.

Bent over, he was pale, sweating and looked as if he wanted to throw up right there on the sidewalk. Concerned, she'd rejoined him and they'd returned to his car, going immediately home, for once his allowing her to drive the prized Miata. He'd been silent and remote the rest of the afternoon, ending what had been a happy weekend and although she hadn't realized it then, that was their last trip to Georgetown and the beginning of the excursions outside the city.

"My sudden food poisoning? Yes, that was it—my parents' happy home. I had tried to see if I could go by there for months after I arrived in D.C. but I could never steel myself to even walk down the street. I guess I thought once I had you with me, after we were married, I could face seeing it but I was wrong. I wanted to scream when I saw the place, to turn around and run or find a dark little space and hide again the way I did when it happened."

"Oh, Paul, I'm so sorry."

"Not very manly, I'm afraid," he commented wryly.

"To feel sick when you see the place where someone stabbed your mother to death? How manly is someone supposed to be?" she demanded angrily. "You were a little boy for God's sake. Just a little boy—hardly more than a baby!" Her voice was rising in anguish for what he must have felt. "And then what? All that news coverage, having to go to court, not getting to see your father afterwards? What the hell did they do with you?"

"I told you, Pix, they isolated me. I wasn't even able to get mail from my dad's folks...or my dad." Paul's eyes were moist. "He wrote to me, you know. He was allowed to do that. Grandma Wolfe told me and so did she and Grandpa but none of the letters were returned. Louis kept or destroyed them all. I lost even that—my father's only words."

At this cruelty, Pat burst into tears, sobbing so hard she couldn't say anything. Paul reached for her, hugging her again until she had stopped.

"Oh Pat, I'm sorry. Don't cry again, please," he begged, going to his knees and grasping her hands. "I know my father and my grandparents loved me. Louis couldn't change that. And what else could the school do? As far as they were concerned, he was my guardian and there were orders to return anything for me, not that the Wolfes even knew where I was at first, which is why I'm sure Louis was the one to keep the mail. And I was so little when I went over, I didn't know how to contact them. When I reached majority, I said to hell with it and I came back to the States but by then my grandmother was dying. The Martin family gave me nothing to help then. It was my Grandfather Wolfe and then student aid, summer jobs, and a couple small scholarships that financed Tulane. That and the job in the restaurant that surprised you." Pat nodded her head, ashamed that she hadn't realized the efforts he had made to achieve his education, thinking he was probably just seeking extra spending money.

"I needed that help," Paul said earnestly. "There was no real money left in the Wolfe family because they'd spent it all on appeals for my dad. They never stopped believing he was innocent. I've told you everything I remember, Pix, and now it's time to find out what's happening to me. And yes, sure, I fooled myself at first about being unknown up here, but Beck knows. He'd have to unless he was blind."

"So you'll go to him?"

"Yah, I guess so." Paul stared back up at the ceiling, his lips tight.

"But you don't want to."

"To be honest, no."

"Why then?"

"Why? Because he's the only one left from then. Because he's my boss and if I'm losing it mentally or just emotionally, he should know. For being here only a year, I really have been given considerable responsibilities with the firm. That's all true. It may have been who I was that got me the job, but it has been my work performance that's kept me," he suddenly said fiercely.

"I believe you."

"Do you, do you really?"

She could see he was getting upset again. In all their relationship, she realized now that if there had really been a dominant partner, it had been he. It wasn't that they didn't discuss things and make mutual decisions, but just as with the finances, he had slowly taken charge and she had let it happen. It was almost the way it had been at home with her as the baby of the family. Lyle and Joan both bossing her around, lovingly to be sure, but still being the ones in charge until she had almost reached her teens. It was natural of course, since her parents had practically patterned her to follow her siblings' lead, not out of any malice but rather to protect her since she was so much younger.

Lyle probably had had the same sort of patterning when he was little and was told to mind his big sister, two years his elder. Odd, she'd never thought of that. And in her relationship with Ronnie, it had been his idea that they cohabit. It wasn't that she was a push over. She certainly was assertive enough as a student and in her present job or she wouldn't have been as successful. But with Paul, she had followed his lead. Automatically deferring to his wishes like rushing into their quick marriage. Would, though, it have made any difference if she had waited? Would she have learned more? Probably not, considering the fact that he'd spent a decade or more hiding, repressing his tragic history.

Paul had been such a sure, capable individual, just the kind of person she felt she could depend upon, a real contrast to Ronnie, who turned out to be more talk than action. It was a trait that probably had also been lacking in the other men she'd considered and eventually rejected. Of course, to be honest, they may have already rejected her too as a potential partner. In any case, there'd been something important missing with Paul's predecessors as far as she was concerned. So, being with him wasn't taking a subservient position. She had followed him out of love, because she wanted to, because she'd known he'd be there for her. Now, it was very apparent that he needed someone to give him support in his crisis. All that repression had finally come to a head and in part, marrying her, giving in to his emotions and being willing finally to love might also have caused this calamity. Calmly and assertively, she now asked, "Paul, what is it? You're going through a work predicament as well as an identity one? You're smart, personable, hard- working. You earned those degrees and had that experience, didn't you?"

"Yes."

"You could have gotten a decent job somewhere else with that background, right?"

"I suppose so, yes—of course. I did get other offers—most more lucrative."

"Then why are you doing this? Beck himself told me

how much they prized your linguistic abilities as well as your work in general." Paul snorted. "Well, he did and he was trying to find out if you were thinking of leaving, remember?"

"Yes, you're right. You did tell me that," he finally agreed, almost pathetically relieved.

"So, don't you think they value you for what you're doing? I also got a peek at your salary statement. Even if you didn't have a secret Swiss account, or whatever, you're pulling down a hefty sum."

"Ah, my sweet little fortune hunter," he squeezed her, trying to lighten the conversation, a touch of his old bravado resurfacing.

"Cut it out! You know what I'm saying." She was not going to be sidetracked. This was one time she'd face something that might prove unpleasant, not be delinquent in her duty. No procrastination this time.

"Yes," he answered frankly. "I do and I think I honestly earn the money and my European investments and Swiss account are legal. They're not going to drag me off to Leavenworth or wherever for tax evasion or defrauding the government. I just hope they aren't going to drag me off anywhere..." he ended dejectedly.

"Well so do I and let's both hope not. I thought we'd signed up for life as in together and certainly not in a cell." Nor an asylum, she left unsaid.

"Oh lord," he sighed dejectedly, but she was sure he was visualizing that nightmare replete with padded rooms and body restraints out of some horror-show depiction of a mental hospital dating to a previous century.

"So you're going to start with Mr. Beck. Then maybe we can find where you've been disappearing to, what you've been doing."

"Yes. I'll try to see him this week."

"And you'll tell him everything?"

"Not exactly. I'll tell him who I am and apologize for not having said so at the start. I'll mention that damn TV program this summer and how it's been bothering me ever since and I'll say that...shit, I'll say that I've been very upset and think maybe I'm going to have to talk to someone, possibly get some counseling, and that I'm worried I may be less attentive to my professional obligations than I should be. Will I tell him I'm spacing out? Not likely, but what the hell I did the two weekends, I haven't the slightest idea. Sweet Jesus, I wish I knew what I've been doing those times I was away!"

Paul's pathos was so evident that Pat reached out and touched him lightly, stroking his cheek soothingly with her fingertips. He nodded appreciatively and grabbed her hand, squeezing it gently. "I'll try to look at my office files before the meeting to see if I may have been doing something strange at work. Oh lord, I hope not. It isn't just that this was my dad's firm that made me want to come here. It's one of the best in the country for what it does and I wanted to make the grade—to show I could do it too, just like he and Beck had."

"Me too, I mean hope that everything is ok at work," she remarked quietly, but then the thought of what else Paul might have been doing frightened her even more. Where had he been? How had he been spending all those hours he had been missing? He looked fine each time he came back. She hadn't lied to him about that. There were no signs of violence—no torn, bloody garments or anything awful like that. No signs of anything in fact. He'd been just Paul, her Paul, how she hoped her Paul, but she knew she still was missing some important information. Something Paul hadn't wanted to discuss, but she felt she must know. "Paul," she said softly, "what happened when your French grandfather took you?"

"Well, after the fiasco at the hotel..." started Paul slowly and then stopped, and she knew he was still having a hard time, but she waited. "Ok," he said finally and taking a deep breath, laboriously he told her. "Once Grandpa got me home from that disastrous visit to the hotel, he and Grandma decided she would take me back to Alabama. Within days, the two of us were living at the family home on the farm. I can't tell you how great those few months were—healing, I guess. Grandma gave me a small garden and when Grandpa arrived, he'd take me fishing at the farm's pond—all the things I pretended I'd done with my dad.

"The other person to show me love was Sarah, the family housekeeper. She would demonstrate her affection in simple, every day, practical ways. For instance, she'd take my small catch of fish to fry along with the hush puppies I adored. Needed lots of batter to pretend I'd really caught something," Paul told Pat, shaking his head still bemused at the effort. "Dear Sarah. It was like having two grandmothers. She always found an extra cookie for me or some little treat and once when I brought her some puny little apples, she actually made them into a pie for me. Between the worms and spots, I doubt that she was able to get off more than a bite per apple, but she did it. Tons of sugar do wonders for a little kid," he smiled remembering. "When they took me away, I missed her as much as Grandma and Grandpa."

"Did you get to see her again?"

"No," he sighed. "She had a stroke several years later so I never did. I thought about her a lot though. She was a tiny little woman—a mere slip, but perky and lively like you—not at all the profile of a stroke victim, but she'd lived with lots of stress and disappointments. In looks, she was chocolate brown and she had a gold tooth with a heart to match. For some reason, I thought that tooth was just wonderful and wanted one too. She'd stayed in the country all her life and was almost a stereotype but my lord she was a good woman with a warm and generous nature. She'd married some 'no account' when she was young, who'd beaten her. Grandpa had seen he was arrested and taken care of her medical bills but she lost a baby and couldn't have another one so she'd loved my dad and me as though we were her own. Anyhow, she'd worked for our family for years and although I know it's not politically correct nowadays, she was part of the family and we were part of hers and I guess she felt guilty when I was taken even though they tried to tell her it wasn't her fault."

"What happened? I remember that was on the TV too."
Of course Pat did: reports of the missing child, which had
scared her and her little friends. To be stolen from one's
family, every normal child's nightmare. Later there was a
court case or something. That was in the news and yes she
had seen pictures of Paul then but not the happy, laughing
child shown in the small photo on his desk. These were
shots of the frightened boy, taken no doubt from his
appearance at his father's trial. Images of a little boy she
never would have recognized as that earlier child or as the
man she married.

"Oh, I was in a country school—one of those
consolidated ones so we rode buses instead of walking the
way my dad did as a kid when they were in Alabama. He
went there before Grandpa got in the Senate although the
schools weren't merged then and I guess he started in
practically a one-room school house. I don't remember
much about the place, but I guess it was all right. I did have a
pretty teacher, blonde like my mother, which made her
probably seem more special than she was, but she was kind
to me and she didn't let the other kids tease me though most
of them had heard something about my parents. Anyhow,
one afternoon when the school bus let me off at our lane—
that was maybe a quarter mile from the house—there was a
car waiting and a woman and a man grabbed me. Usually
Sarah or Grandma came to meet me at the bus, but one day
a week my grandma helped at the hospital and that was the
day. She was a Grey Lady," Paul smiled but Pat looked
puzzled. "Women volunteers like Candy Strippers were the
girl ones. Anyhow, I thought that meant it was because she
had grey hair and couldn't understand why everyone thought
that was so funny.

"As my grandfather told me later, it obviously was all so
carefully planned. Someone phoned just about the time that
Sarah would have walked down to get me and gave her some
cock and bull story about my having missed the school bus
and that she should go directly to the school. Of course
when she did arrive, I was nowhere to be found and nobody

knew anything. Then they had to track down the school bus driver and discovered I'd really been on the bus. After there were calls to my grandmother and she called my grandfather but by the time the police were finally alerted, I was long gone."

"Oh, Paul, you must have been so scared."

"I probably would have been if I'd known what was happening."

"What do you mean?"

"They gave me a shot or something once they had me in the car."

"They drugged you—a little boy? Your own grandfather had you drugged?" Pat was outraged. She couldn't believe what she was hearing.

"Yes. I guess then they drove right into Montgomery, which was about an hour away. There was a small private plane waiting and it flew directly to Atlanta. By the time there was an actual bulletin out on me, we were well out over the Atlantic. I was on the corporate jet of one of Louis's friends—business associate actually; *Grandpère* isn't the kind of man who has friends. I didn't wake up for hours and the woman from the car was there. She was English—very proper, my dear, and dressed by then like a nurse so maybe she really was one. She looked like someone from a PBS mystery, one of those imported from the BBC. I remember she was tall, thin, with hair pulled back—prim, I guess is the word. Definitely not the ordinary profile of a kidnapper. More like Mary Poppins though from the book, not Julie Andrews." He smiled, "No, indeed. Julie Andrews' Mary Poppins wouldn't have been so bad."

"And the man?"

"Oh, nondescript—taller, dark, foreign—non-English speaking that is, nor French, but nothing villainous. Very ordinary in fact but he was the one who grabbed me and although the woman was the one who gave me the shot, he held me. I was most scared of him. Anyhow, when I woke up, the woman told me I'd been sick but not to worry. To say I was confused is an understatement. Terrified probably but I was so doped up at that point that I was drifting in and out of sleep." Paul's cadence had slowed down, and to Pat's surprise, he was taking on a deep southern accent, the element missing, she had thought. With the recitation, he seemed to be reverting, at least in speech, to how he must have sounded as a little Alabama boy.

"They ended up taking me to the villa of another of *Grandpère's* associates on Crete of all the remote, unlikely places and no doubt why it was chosen. The English nurse, if she was one, disappeared and nobody there would speak any English to me. You know the expression, 'it's Greek to me', well it sure as hell was though they actually say 'it's Chinese to them'." At Pat's look of puzzlement, he explained, "That was something I learned when I went back to Greece as an adult, a much more pleasant trip, I can assure you. In any case, I was scared stiff though everyone was nice to me...I mean they took good care of me, fed me even though it wasn't stuff I was used to—lamb, seafood, odd vegetable dishes, probably like mousaka or the spanikopita that I thrive on now. Hmm," he said reflectively, "I wonder if that's why I used to dislike spinach. Anyhow, they also gave me lots of toys, took me to the beach, and in general were decent to me even if I was terrified. The Greeks by nature are very nice to children; I was lucky that way but I had no idea what had happened or where I was. It must have been like what people talk about when they say alien abduction," he added bemused.

"Oh Paul," Pat had her arms around him again. "Oh Paul, I'm so sorry. What happened then?"

"Oh I guess I was there a week or two, crying my heart out, and then Louis showed up, being his usual bastard self. He took me back to France to one of his vacation houses down near Cannes and settled me in with a tutor so I'd be prepared for a proper school—French speaking of course," declared Paul nastily, "since my mother hadn't taught me properly."

"Oh, Paul," mewed Pat again, pity permeating each word.

"Well, that was the kind of person he was. I really doubt if he was upset about her death per se. To someone like him, I think it was the affront that it would be his daughter who was murdered. I mean obviously he hadn't given a damn about her once she'd run off with my dad. No efforts were ever made by him to reconcile with a beloved only child. Grandma Wolfe told me my mother had tried to contract him a few times, but he'd ignored her approaches. I think her final effort was naming me Martin, but she heard nothing in response to that overture and I guess gave up."

"What a truly terrible man he must be."

"He is. That was when he also told me my name was Paul Martin only and not to forget it and that I was French and not to forget that either! It was a beautiful reunion, let me tell you, utterly touching." Paul's sarcasm was bitingly acid.

"But how, how could he do that?" Pat asked, gripping him tightly as if he might even at this late date again disappear. She felt her stomach turn at the cruelty shown a little boy, any little boy but especially her husband. It must have been a terrorizing experience for him. It wasn't as though his grandfather had taken Paul because he loved the child. Clearly, it was spite, plain and simple.

"Oh it was a done deal, sugar. I told you my mother registered me with the French Embassy when I was born. I had dual citizenship and Louis knew how to pull all the strings. Martin Internationale is mega business, as big if not bigger than D E Inc. What *mon cher Grandpère* couldn't do legally, he could easily buy if he had to, but it apparently was all pretty straight forward. The French judicial system had named him my legal guardian, the name change was complete, everything had been taken care of."

"But the Wolfes?"

"They knew or at least guessed, of course, almost immediately. I mean there was no ransom request and there was a lead to the car so the police were able to track down the rental fairly rapidly. When they learned that, they picked up on the planes but they couldn't prove it was kidnapping.

The plane from Montgomery was an ordinary charter. No one had paid any attention to a couple with a sleeping child, a little girl at that. I guess they put me in a dress and stuck on a wig—blonde and curly, although I doubt that I'd have passed for Shirley Temple." He touched his nose gingerly. "Had a bit of a beak even then.

"Once they...we got to Atlanta, we went right onto the private jet belonging to the first Greek businessman, hence showing up on Crete; but then the trail ended since I was handed over to someone else. It wouldn't have mattered even if it had been one of the Martin planes. Everyone on board was European including some French citizens and they even had what appeared to be a legal passport for a little boy on that flight named Paul Martin since by then the dress and wig were gone. Of course once my grandparents heard that they knew immediately who the child was and who had to be responsible, but that meant nothing to the authorities.

"Grandpa Wolfe started pulling in any favors he could as a senator but we were safely in Europe before it was substantiated that I was the child on the passport. I was out of the country and they didn't know exactly where. Then by the time they formally protested to the French government, it all bogged down in appeals and those dragged on. Actual possession counts in law, little sweetheart, and Louis had me. More than that, remember I wasn't in Greece or even France any longer. He'd shipped me off to the school in Switzerland within months."

"Oh....," moaned Pat. As pained as she felt on hearing his story, she was sure that the actual experience had to have been hundreds, no thousands of times worse for him.

As if knowing what she was thinking, he said gently, "Hey, it wasn't as bad as I made out, Pix, though I admit life with Louis was no picnic. I told you he thought I was a little brat and I was living up to his expectations. *Chère* Isobel didn't like me much better although she didn't hit me or yell at me all the time the way he did. No, that wasn't ladylike."

Matilde, by contrast—no, he wouldn't mention sly Matilde now. Pat was upset enough. Ah yes, dear Matilde who pinched and slapped and had once pushed him so hard that he'd fallen, cracking a rib. He was eight then and on one of the last holidays to Louis's home. He'd never told his grandfather, not just out of fear of further retaliation, but because he already knew he'd never be believed. Matilde's complaints about Paul's clumsiness and general insolence stopped the yearly visit. Paul, in retrospect, felt a cracked rib had been a small price for such relief but he'd later had even greater satisfaction when Louis divorced the bitch and he eventually heard she'd received little settlement. That's what happens when the lady of the house dallies with the chauffeur.

Instead Paul said, "In the first school—the one in France, no one was unkind but all I kept hearing from Louis, the times he bothered to notice me, was that my father was a damn murderer and that I was to tell everyone that. That part was awful." Paul looked away, not wanting her to see the expression on his face, knowing he could never hide how truly painful that had been. "It must have gone on for weeks until finally he gave up in disgust. That's when he took me out of the country and dumped me in the boarding school not too far from Geneva. And there, ah yes, I learned German and proper French as well as my smattering of Italian."

"Your restaurant language."

"Right," he nodded in agreement. "It's supposed to be one of the official Swiss languages but the others and English were what we really studied. Switzerland's odd that way. A canton may be mostly German or French, but there can be a whole village that uses the other language. That was certainly true where I was; it was in one of the sixteen German-speaking cantons but most people near the school spoke French even though the surrounding villages were predominantly German. Of course the school founder, Dr. Henri Foshée, had been French from a Huguenot family that emigrated during the religious persecution of Protestants in France. I guess a whole group of the refugees settled there. I think the country's actual ratio is something like seventy-percent native German speakers, about nineteen-percent French, and ten-percent Italian."

"That's ninety-nine percent."

"*Mon Dieu*, always worried about numbers, aren't you? One percent are Romansch."

"Romansch?"

"Right, a kind of corruption of Latin."

"Aside from the German, they all are."

"Swell, now you're a linguistics specialist too." Paul was smiling slightly, taking the sting out of his remark. "Anyhow, all I was trying to say was that my gym instructor was Italian from the Ticinio Canton down in the Lepontine Alps.'

"Mario?"

Paul nodded his head. "Yes, my friend. He's also the one who taught me to ski and skate." He looked at her pointedly, adding, "The latter fairly well, I might mention. You really were the one who bumped into me the night we met." Paul's countenance was so sad now that Pat realized the playful little in-joke, a small illusion of their own marriage, had just been lost. How much more of their own small world would change, be sacrificed, she wondered.

"I know you were unhappy in Switzerland at first but were they nice to you there over all?" she asked hesitantly.

"Well, that school was actually fairly decent—good thing as I spent almost eleven years growing up there." Pat winced at the thought of her husband staying practically half his life in a boarding school, but Paul appeared not to notice. "The majority of the teachers and the matron were ok. Plus the head master was really decent and I think kept *Grandpère* in line somewhat," and saved me from some asylum, he added mentally, thanking stern though fair Dr. Gerrard for probably the thousandth time. "This was a prestigious school, Pat, and the head, not the parents, was truly in charge. If *Grandpère* had caused problems, I would have been out *tout de suite*."

"But he could have sent you to another school."

"Not with the same reputation. *L'École Foshée* is a continental version of Eton and means something later.

Grandpère did have some plans for me ultimately so he wouldn't have wanted to lose that advantage."

"Oh," murmured Pat, wondering what they were.

"Anyhow, we were in group houses—kind of like small dormitories with maybe eight to ten boys and a master. By *lycée*, when there were more boarders, there'd be two to a room in an actual dorm. We always had good food and plenty—the Gallic touch," laughed Paul, "and there were lots of sports, some excursions, and very good instruction aside from a few notable exceptions, unfortunately."

"Meaning?" Pat asked apprehensively.

"Oh, I learned all sorts of things that proper little European boys learn at proper boarding schools besides my proper French. Maybe it was a little worse for me. Hell it was. Unfortunately, I wasn't a proper little European boy and the others, particularly the older ones, let me know that distinction. I was a murderer's child. That news got out fairly rapidly, and I couldn't even speak a real language correctly but what else would one expect from an American? They let me know that too," he said bitterly. "English wasn't commonly studied until later in the curriculum and then that was the British version so I was damned again since I was too stubborn to convert and fought to keep my accent. On the writing they caught me since I wasn't old enough to have started that much beyond the alphabet. Consequently, I still use *ou* in a lot of my spelling or *re* instead of *er* but that may have been the French influence too. I know it ended up driving the JAG secretary out in Hawaii crazy and certainly missed up the spell-checks.

"Still, even if the older boys gave me a hard time at first—and they did, they did that to all the newcomers. It was a matter of degree but I had turned into such a stubborn little shit that they eventually gave up. I'd learned that trait from *cher* Louis," he added with satisfaction. "They couldn't even begin to compete with what he dished out. Also the school as a policy never let hazing get out of hand, particularly for the little kids.

"Where I was less fortunate was to have one of the

more unenlightened teachers at first. They canned him a couple of years later but that didn't help me. For example, he'd make me read something in German and then force me to try to translate it into French to amuse the class and of course I didn't have the slightest idea of what I was doing. My accent apparently was a laugh a minute even though my mother had spoken some to me in French and I'd had those months in France, but at that point my so-called linguistic skills weren't exactly the best. I'm amazed I ever did want to speak a foreign language after that."

"But Mr. Beck says you're a wonder."

"You would have been too if you'd have had to learn it to survive. If I hadn't met a pretty Cajun girl at Tulane and then had some nice German girlfriends when I was in the Air Force, I probably never would have wanted to use either language again."

"But you were such a baby then," Pat commiserated, wondering if she as a child could have survived total emersion in a foreign culture much less language.

"Well, I grew up fast," Paul stated pragmatically. "Think of it as a boot camp or a military academy."

"And that's why you went into the Air Force?" Pat asked. No wonder with his Alabama family gone, he'd considered the life of a career officer and a return to the regimentation of his youth.

"Partially. It was kind of like going home again—male bonding, that sort of thing," he added poignantly. "I mean there was no one at my real home by that point and I sure as hell wasn't going back to France. Still, over all, the adolescent years could have been worse."

Pat wondered how until he said gently, "Believe me, Pix, I could have ended up in lots worse situations than that school. I mean I might have had to stay with Louis. As it was, I was sure he had to pay a pretty penny to keep me there, which was giving me some satisfaction, and at least by the time I was a teenager I didn't have to see him more than once a year when he came to bully me for a day or two. He just didn't want to give up on the tantalizing prospect of my testifying against my father in the press if nowhere else; but, my mind was just blank on that and fortunately, the shrinks I saw were ethical even if they were overly persistent. Again I think the head master, Dr. Gerrard, had some say, thank God."

Paul sighed, a long heartfelt sigh, and Pat felt as though she could read his mind, almost intuiting what he might have become. Paul, her Paul as a brow-beaten, insecure man or worse, a clone of the hated grandfather—a son who had betrayed his father or much worse, a man driven to madness. Yet, wasn't some of this madness?

"Yes, thank God indeed, they were that," Paul confirmed. "No hypnotism, no drug therapy. Like good Freudians, they just encouraged me to talk, not that I did much. I think ultimately they convinced Louis I really hadn't seen anything, that I'd just gone and hid when the murder was taking place. After that he started calling me a little coward and the last couple years I was over there, I didn't even see him."

"Coward, my ass," snarled Pat, furious at the insinuation. No wonder Paul was so upset about not coming to his mother's defense as if a four-year old could. That bastard, his grandfather, was probably the one who put the idea of cowardice into his head as if Paul could have been some big hero when he was hardly out of diapers.

"Pix, such language, but a pretty ass," he said pulling her over to his lap and patting hers, more for comfort than any other purpose.

Ignoring the compliment, she asked, "I wonder how brave your bullying Louis would have been when he was four."

"Probably mean as hell. He sure looked like a pit bull though I believe they have better dispositions. In any case, we'll never know, fortunately. I haven't seen him for several years."

"You saw him again after you left Switzerland?" Pat was surprised. From what Paul had just told her, she couldn't imagine his making any effort to see the man. If anything, Paul probably would have done anything he could to avoid such an encounter.

"Oh yes, he was able to keep tabs on me. When I was in Germany on tour, I was surprised at the BOQ one day to discover I had a visitor. It was a fairly stormy meeting. This time I wasn't an immature little kid or a callow adolescent and he wasn't able to intimidate me. I don't think the arrogant bastard really believed I'd ever grow up enough to face him off. Our meeting didn't even last ten minutes and I just walked off and left him, something else he wasn't used to having happen. I've never heard from him since and quite frankly, I hope the next time I hear about him, he's dead."

"Paul..."

"Well, it's true. He destroyed any chance I had for a loving childhood. I'll never forgive him for that. I think he thought when he came to see me that I'd jump at an opportunity to join Martin Internationale. Can you believe that? That was his big back-up plan and the reason for the solid schooling. He had come to offer me his forgiveness, with strings of course, and give me the opportunity to see if I'd measure up to his standards as heir apparent. His lovely young third wife—Matilde the one I remember so kindly—never gave him a child, nor had Isobel, his second. He had ended up divorcing again and marrying someone even younger, practically an adolescent, to get another heir. Of course my mother was never good enough to be considered for that position. It was supposed to be the man she married."

"Sexist pig," murmured Pat fervently.

"That too, sugar, but then my mother also didn't do what he wanted when she ran off with my father. Louis was such an arrogant asshole. I doubt that he even considered that perhaps he was the one who no longer could father a child. *Merde alors*, maybe my French grandmother cuckolded the old bastard. Certainly my mother looked nothing like any of the Martin side of the family." Paul smiled and then added reflectively, "I never thought of that. Hell, Louis was in his fifties when he took me and then he was close to seventy when he married the fourth wife although I never could figure why he kept Matilde so long. Still, her mind had as many curves as her body so she probably kept him satisfied. I've never had the dubious pleasure of meeting this last one, but there was no better luck with her either.

"Anyhow, suddenly he had renewed interest in me—the sole blood heir. I guess he thought I'd fall all over myself to join his illustrious organization. He practically told me I'd be as rich as Croesus, as if I needed his money then. But where was all that filthy lucre when I did need it? It was because of him I couldn't even touch *Maman's* trust. And you know the really rotten part of that?" Pat shook her head.

"The cheap SOB actually paid for most of my schooling with it! I found out about that when I was over there in the Air Force and got Grandpa's letter from his friend. I immediately contacted the bank about my trust and they in turn notified Louis, as trustee, that the account would be transferred to me and the trust terminated. It actually should have been turned over to me sooner, but it took a while for Grandpa's friend to track me down and of course Louis never had any intention of my getting it, or even knowing it existed, if he could help it. Anyhow, that's how he located me again."

Pat gasped, her eyes wide. "He could do that—keep you from your inheritance?"

"Could, would. When *Maman* died, he automatically became the trustee for any heirs she might have until the eldest reached twenty-five. Grandpa Wolfe had contacted him about my needing money for college but the bastard didn't even answer him just like he ignored my mother's attempts to reestablish contact. Grandpa never told me, of course, but a copy of his letter was in the box of correspondence, which was also waiting for me with his friend when I turned twenty five; I guess both of them figured I'd be old enough to handle some of this knowledge then. To think Grandpa had to beg, Pix, beg that shit to give me access to my own money. For education, no less, after that filthy rich bastard had been using my mother's trust fund for my tuition at the Swiss school. Even the payment for all those shrinks was coming out of it too! I was sick when I found that out. Poor Grandpa. Fortunately Louis could use only a portion of that money for my 'wellbeing', i.e. legal talk meaning he couldn't deplete the trust," said Paul sarcastically.

"In any case, in my most eloquent French, I told Louis to fuck off and then I repeated it loudly in German and even louder in English in case anyone near us hadn't gotten the gist of the conversation. I thought he was going to have a fit," said Paul with a self-satisfied smile. "Small of me, I know, and not what I really would have liked to have done or said to him, but better than nothing and such a blow to his mega-ego. I don't think, sugar, that you'll ever have the opportunity to meet the man."

"I wouldn't want to," Pat said with feeling, outraged at all she had heard. How lucky, truly lucky she, the blue collar child, had been. And, while she had been Mittying away with dreams of wealth, Paul—who had actually been born to it—would no doubt have given anything to trade places. "You told me you had no family when we met. As far as I'm concerned, that still is true. But you do have family now: me and mine. You know that." She looked at him solemnly, her eyes staring deeply into his, making a pledge.

He stared back, his green eyes warm and loving now, the ocean storm dispersed, and answered equally seriously, "Yes and I like that. I just wish I could have shared mine, the good part, with you." Then he gave her a tender kiss as if to seal a pact.

CHAPTER 12

It was Pat's flex Monday and she was doubly thankful to have a day away from the office. From her perspective, it was well worth working nine hour shifts in order to have each tenth day free. The last week since she had learned the truth about Paul had been stressful and emotional as well as exhausting—physically as well as mentally. She'd barely noticed his departure this morning, only to groan at the sound of the alarm, roll over, and grab a pillow to stuff over her head. Not even the smell of fresh coffee had enticed her out of bed and she was shocked to discover it was almost noon when she did awake.

Now up and moving, albeit languidly, her mind by contrast was racing once more. As of yet, Paul's missing hours remained a mystery, which worried them both. Then there had been the additional burden of trying to act normally at work, worse no doubt for Paul. In their free time, they spent hours talking about what to do next, which meant little sleep for either. This no doubt explained her marathon snooze.

Paul still didn't want to see a doctor, which distressed her greatly, and so far had not had his appointment with Wesley Beck since the man had been called out of town. This delay she knew was intensifying her anxiety. The dreaded meeting though was to take place this afternoon and the strain of waiting to hear what would transpire had kept her on pins and needles, not that she didn't have other concerns. Still, Mr. Beck might convince Paul to see a doctor. In fact, there might be no choice as a stipulation for his keeping his job. Yet much as she wanted the medical advice, this was not the way she wanted it to happen. Particularly now, Paul needed to make his own choices.

Slowly she began to tackle tasks around the house and had just gotten off the phone when she heard the doorbell ring. That's odd, she thought, we're not expecting anyone.

Glancing through the peephole, she was astounded to see the short and slightly stocky figure of Mr. Beck, himself, dressed per usual impeccably in a suit that probably cost twice the amount of what she considered to be Paul's extravagant wardrobe purchases.

Opening the door, she exclaimed, "Mr. Beck, what a surprise." And wasn't that the truth. This was the last person she wanted to see, certainly now.

"Such a pleasure to see you, Mrs. Martin. Is Paul here?"

"Why no. I thought he said he was going to meet you at the office today."

"Isn't that strange. I was so sure he said to meet him here at the house, that he had something so confidential to discuss that he preferred to talk about it away from work. Would you happen to know anything about that, my dear child?"

My dear child, thought Pat, who in God's name uses expressions like that nowadays? She thought when GG died she'd never hear that phrase again and certainly not from someone like Wesley Beck. But homey axiom or not and although she hated to admit it, she did not feel at ease around the unctuous man and never had. Besides what Paul had to discuss with him was Paul's business. Oh why the hell couldn't her stubborn husband have gone to a doctor instead? As diplomatically as possible, she answered, "Not really. Paul was the one who requested the interview."

Beck laughed, but it was a dry and un-amusing sound. "Protecting confidentiality. Very good. Perhaps you should have been a lawyer too." He didn't repeat the condescending 'my dear child' but Pat felt as though he had and half expected an equally condescending pat on the head. Get hold of yourself, she thought, this was Paul's boss and his father's friend. Paul was going to him for help.

Politely she asked, "Won't you come in? We can call and try to locate him."

"That would be fine, my dear. You're looking very well. Marriage obviously agrees with you."

"It does," she smiled good humored for a moment until

the thought flashed through her mind that at least it had until this mess started. Still smiling, she indicated the futon couch.

"Well, you have a fine young man there. We think very highly of him. He should go far."

"I'm happy you think so. He works very hard."

"Oh, I know he does. In fact, I've been rather worried about him lately. He has acted distracted."

Had Paul spoken to him some already and not told her? Or had Paul been acting peculiarly at work too, Pat wondered. No, she knew that the earlier appointment with Beck had been canceled when the man left town so Paul would be talking to him for the first time today. But then hadn't Paul's father maintained there was a meeting he was supposed to attend in Baltimore when beautiful Claire was murdered—a meeting that had already been canceled, much less an appointment no one else knew about? Had the elder Paul believed there really was such a meeting and that had been another sign of his insanity? God, what if her Paul was doing the same thing? But Pat couldn't ask that so instead, she equivocated. "Tired, I think. He's been a bit under the weather."

"I'm sorry to hear that. Has he been to a doctor?"

Paul can answer that one too, she decided. "I'm really not sure if it's that serious."

"Of course not although one doesn't like to let things go, especially when one is worried."

What has Paul already said to him, she wondered, but she kept her face neutral. "Certainly not," she agreed. "Would you like to call the office now to see if he's there?"

"Excellent idea, my dear child."

"Why don't you use the phone in here." Trying not to cringe at the annoying phrase—one which she'd loved on GG's lips, she pointed to the antique instrument by the futon—another of Paul's whimsical purchases. Made of white porcelain with the metal portions gold-plated, it was an old French model with a rotary dial and Paul prized it for the sound of a European ring. "I'm afraid we still haven't completed decorating the place. We get something when we see and like it so who knows how long the process will take."

"Who knows indeed," Beck agreed, but his look as he glanced around the room was coldly detached.

This was so different from the avid curiosity of the party guest who'd wanted a private tour. Nosiness, that's all that had been, thought Pat. But then what could one expect from a man whose house looked like a museum. God knows how long it took him! Instead, politely she inquired, "May I get you coffee or something while you wait?"

"That's very kind of you. A cup of tea perhaps."

"Certainly." Pat found herself backing out of the room almost like a suppliant at the Chinese Imperial court, feeling quite discomforted. How on earth could Paul have messed up an appointment with his boss—particularly this all important one? Was he, God forbid, losing time again? And why, as pleasant as Mr. Beck was acting, did she feel this way? Probably the unexpectedness of having the big boss show up on the doorstep and the fact she couldn't warm to the man. Then too, someone as meticulous—she had after all seen his office and home—no doubt would be disdainful of their meager efforts to date. The only other time he'd come to their home was to the open house and then the area had been crowded with people, an impressive buffet, the artfully arranged spring flowers, live musicians—in other words a party setting, even if followed by the embarrassing house tour. It wasn't either that the place was a mess now. Quite frankly, there wasn't enough in it to mess and maybe that was the problem.   For all her explanation of their shopping habits, Pat was still upset that they hadn't completely furnished the town house. This also was a strange sensation since her own apartment in reality had never been more than comfortably furnished. The difference between a place to live and home?

Yet aside from that one big function, they hadn't had many guests; but never before had she felt as though someone was actually surveying and criticizing and maybe giving them marks or even gold stars on some invisible tally sheet. A former classmate currently working with a major pharmaceutical company once told her his company did just that and that he had fourteen stars. When she'd asked how he got them, her usually erudite friend responded, "Kiss ass." Later she'd wondered who'd been the supervisor to only give him four since usually one could get up to five at a time. Then she decided maybe it was just as well she hadn't inquired since possibly her friend had never gotten full marks.

That was it, the reason for her unrest. She felt as though she was being judged every time she was in Wesley Beck's company. Paul probably got demerits if her hair was messy, which too often it was, she thought ruefully for her waves and curls had wills of their own. Gamin, Paul would say as he twirled the rowdy locks.

Or maybe there was a wrinkle in her skirt and she hadn't polished her shoes to the required brilliance. Then looking down she realized she hadn't as she woefully regarded the pair of trusty old penny loafers, which dated back to high school and were repaired year after year.

I've got to stop thinking this way, my imagination is out of control, Pat tried rationalizing. It must be everything that had been happening. I'm getting paranoid, she decided, but she made an extra effort to make the tea tray look attractive, not that she was using the elaborate set presented by Paul's office. Hell, she thought, that would be pretentious at this point plus she probably had allowed it to tarnish and Wesley Beck would give them ten demerits extra. No, today's special was a serviceable rattan number, one of a set that she had picked up at a Pier 1 sale and which she and Paul used when sitting outside or in front of the TV. Then, she added a recently purchased bright blue dish towel to match the cups and saucers, hoping that might spruce up her effort. This of course was provided Mr. Beck didn't fondle the material and realize its true function, detecting practical Indian cotton rather than an Irish linen tray cloth.

"I'll be there," Beck was saying into the phone as Pat came back into the living room with the covered tray holding the sugar, milk, a tiny dish of lemon slices, and the pottery cups of steaming tea.

Beck wanted to know how his lowly employees live, Pat thought a bit snidely. Let him use their everyday stoneware. "I'm sorry. I forgot to ask what you might like."

"Milk and sugar, English style. I learned to enjoy it that way at Oxford. Over there they'd steep it in a pot of course, so civilized."

"So did my great grandmother," she replied politely but inwardly gritting her teeth and hoping for Mary Patton's strength. What was it GG used to say to her? She could almost remember sitting in the kitchen with the old lady as a little girl and affectionately, Pat remembered her grandmother's homey lessons on the importance of responsibility and self-dignity. It wasn't important that Pat merely had mundane, convenient, inexpensive tea bags; what was important was the courtesy and hospitality according to GG and Mother too, not the specific content of the offering. So even though the daunting Mr. Beck definitely had the ability to make her hostile, she would rise above that. With the same aplomb that GG would have shown, Pat remarked, "How interesting about Oxford. Paul's parents met there." Then she felt like biting her tongue. What if Paul hadn't told him yet?

"Yes, I know," Beck answered, reaching for his cup and staring down at the now caramel-colored tea. "I was there. Big Paul, your Paul's father, and I met Claire at about the same time. In fact I'd begun to squire her about a bit myself but then I introduced her to him at a party..." Momentarily the man's face seemed to twist with distress but it was fleeting. Pat was so shocked at the revelation that Beck knew who Paul was that she wondered if she'd really seen this. As it was, her rattling cup nearly tipped off the saucer. Then calmly, Beck added, "Radiant—a ray of light—that's how she looked."

"Oh," said Pat, thinking again of what Paul had told her, her cup once more stable with only a drop or two of tea sloshing in the saucer. What a vibrant woman his mother must have been that even someone like Wesley Beck would remember that luminous quality. But perhaps if what she thought she'd seen was true, the seemingly cold and distant man had loved and lost all those years ago.

"Don't look shocked, my dear. I've known who Paul was from the moment he arrived to work for me—intellect, personality, breeding, looks—definitely his father's son. In fact, if he hadn't contacted us, I would have tried to find him once I knew he was back in the States. Very tragic, the whole situation."

"Yes," agreed Pat, relieved that she hadn't said something out of turn but wondering how Beck would have tracked Paul down. Moreover, since the man recognized him, why he hadn't said anything? Then she rebuked herself; for goodness sake, Wesley Beck made a special trip here. Just because she was uneasy with the man, didn't mean he wasn't concerned. Stop this. Beck just didn't want to embarrass Paul and was only waiting for Paul to approach him.

"He's handled it quite well, you know. An exceptional young man but then his father was considered to be so as well. The whole family in fact. Paul Wolfe, Sr., Statesman Senator they used to call him, and Paul's father, well that was a true loss."

"Paul thought highly of his father."

"I'm sure he did and we can discuss everything when we meet him."

"Meet him?" Pat looked perplexed.

"Why yes, Paul, your Paul. Apparently he thought we were going to talk at my house and according to the office had just left for there. I spoke to his secretary, who said he was uncharacteristically troubled—enough so that she in fact sounded much the same. He seems to be acting so unusual that I think it would be wise for you to come with me. Silly mistake of Paul's really, but since there are some things I want to show him from his childhood, we'll still go to my place. After all, it would take twice as long for him to get back here and at least I'll be home. Anyhow, I left a message there that he pour a drink and wait until we arrive. But since you'd gone to the trouble to start the tea, I thought we might have a cup first and then you could accompany me. As if she had affirmed, he started to chit chat. "And you, Pat, you're an economist I understand."

Pat couldn't help but wonder why the man had time for tea if he really was concerned about Paul's mental state. Then she realized that to a person like Wesley Beck, the fact he'd accepted the offer of tea meant he had to drink it—not merely gulp it down, but accept the social aspect as well, which entailed civilized conversation. Well, she'd do her best. "Yes. I'm with the Department of Agriculture. I've been there for six years now," she answered by rote, thinking, and I know I told you this at that dinner party at your house as well as every other time we've met. Was she so unimportant that he wouldn't remember? Somehow Pat didn't believe that. Wesley Beck had a mind like a steel trap according to Paul. Actually what Paul had said was that Beck had the reputation of being a cunning man who always was a step ahead and that if he'd been a prosecutor, he'd know how to set a trap, the better to catch one in.

"My, my. Women are so professional nowadays. Claire had the education but I doubt that she ever would have used it."

Irritated at this slur aimed at Paul's beloved mother, Pat retorted, "Paul said she would have made a good teacher."

"Now that's interesting. Claire as a teacher. No, somehow I can't visualize that." Beck was looking very somber as if considering the possibility before rejecting the idea. Pat thought this was probably how he acted in legal situations: ponderous, analytic, making a good show.

"Paul thought she was a wonderful teacher. She taught him lots of things when he was little."

"No doubt," Beck said with a slight laugh. "Paul was always an inquisitive little chap, into everything—a true harbinger of the future."

Somehow to Pat, the words didn't sound quite right but then Paul had said he'd been a pushy child—'obnoxious really' though she found that hard to believe. Still it probably seemed that way to a man like Beck who clearly was uninterested in children. No, the part about being obnoxious Pat didn't believe for a moment. Precocious yes, but never obnoxious except perhaps around Louis Martin and then in self-defense. "Yes, he does have an inquiring mind."

"No question," concurred Beck. "Still inquisitive. Very much so. Well, my dear, I think probably now that I've about finished this delicious tea—Lipton's?"

"Yes," Pat replied, thinking cynically, I'm sorry, I wish I'd had Earl Grey or oolong or something exceptional and very costly but we rarely drink the damn stuff! If he'd asked for coffee, she could have ground one of those gourmet blends Paul bought. But hell, the only reason they had any tea was because Paul liked it iced in the summer. In fact, the first and last time she'd allowed him to make it, she'd nearly spat it out when he'd given her a glass.

"This is sweet," she'd accused.

"Of course, it's ice tea," he'd readily agreed.

"Of course! It's sugar flavored with tea. You must have poured in a whole pound."

"How else do you make it?" he'd asked innocently.

"Are you serious?"

"That's the way they always serve it in Alabama."

"We're not in Alabama! Normal people add the sugar after! Next time I'll make it," she'd admonished, continuing their North-South tussle but now she too was being put on the defensive by her efforts.

"I thought so," Beck commented, taking a final sip. "I usually have China Congou myself. A nice black tea always seems to have that extra something."

Figures, thought Pat, but she kept her mouth shut as she stared back at Beck's piercing gaze, willing herself not to be browbeaten. Be GG, be great, she thought. This man wouldn't intimidate her!

"Well, my dear, we should be going now."

"Going? I still don't understand why I should go."

"Ah yes, I forgot to say. Paul apparently mentioned you to the secretary. Something about wishing you were along as a little support, I believe, for what he wants to discuss."

That's so strange, thought Pat. Paul was going to handle this himself but maybe with someone like Beck, he'd changed his mind. She could certainly see why. "Well, sure...if that's what you think he wants. Maybe we should try his cell phone first," she answered slowly, deciding that perhaps she should be present at the meeting but she wondered then why Paul just didn't return home.

"Oh, my secretary tried while I was speaking to her. No answer."

"That's odd," said Pat. Paul usually had his cell on, if muted—or at least had. Well maybe he felt the all-important conversation should be in a neutral setting, rather than their home, while still wanting Pat's moral support. And maybe Beck realized that and this talk had been an attempt to put her at ease as well as brace himself for the meeting with Paul. And as to Paul, himself, a meeting like this with someone like Beck—actually with anyone, would be fairly harrowing.

"Good. We'll go in my car so you can come back with him after we have our talk. I can assure you the secretary really was upset by the way he was acting when he left the office otherwise I wouldn't insist. Are you sure you don't know what all this is about?"

"Not really, Mr. Beck. This is Paul's story," she answered politely, while adding mentally, I'll be damned if I tell you what I do know. But Beck had said Paul was going to his house to see something there? How would he have known Beck was with her? No, that wasn't right. Paul must have just mentioned wishing Pat were along. This was beginning to be too complicated especially with so much now on her mind.

Beck laughed, that stodgy sound she found so disconcerting as well as patronizing. "Definitely you would have made a good lawyer too. Confidentiality again. It's so important."

Once in Beck's luxurious BMW, Pat sank not only into the soft rich, leather upholstery, but also into a lengthening silence, disturbed only by the intermittent sound of wipers for a slight mist had begun. Staring morosely out the window, she watched the rain intensify as the car sped down the expressway. She was surprised though when they turned off Route 66, catching Spout Run and then the George Washington Parkway towards Alexandria. "I thought you said we were going to your house? You live in Bethesda."

"We are going to my house—my country place. I don't believe you've been there. It's out in Calvert County, Maryland. Do you know the area?"

Yes, Mr. Beck, I do, thought Pat. I've lived here for years and you know that too. I just told you when you asked me what I did. Do you always patronize people? Still, she kept quiet, merely nodding her head, but she was becoming more and more puzzled. Especially by the non-functioning cell phone. Still Paul refused to use it when he was driving and he had taken the car today, planning to go over to the Wisconsin Avenue wine shop after work to select a special gift for their neighbors' fast-approaching anniversary party.

"Paul used to go there as a child. I thought he'd feel more at ease there," the man explained.

"Oh," she was quiet again and then felt guilty for her initial reaction since Beck was obviously making a considerate gesture. This was becoming stranger and stranger but then her whole world had turned strange and she had even more now to consider.

The car passed by National Airport and then through crowded Old Town Alexandria, where for once the usually endless row of traffic lights seemed all in their favor. Next they swung on to the outer loop of the Beltway, crossing nightmarish Wilson Bridge into Maryland and becoming just one more vehicle on the multi-lane highway. Pat gazed ahead, unseeing, as they continued to speed by trucks, buses and other vehicles. Beck obviously was heavy of foot, but he was a precise driver, calculating his moves from lane to lane.

She didn't feel uneasy at his driving...just his personality. What if people really did have auras as Betty maintained. What color would his be, Pat speculated. Somehow, she didn't think she wanted to know and she was sure her own was looking more and more sickly as her agitation over the upcoming meeting increased. Accompanying the man didn't appear to be as good an idea after all, much as she wanted to support Paul.

If only she could have spoken to him, she thought, fingers starting to reach inside her purse for the phone, then stopping as if they had a mind of their own. It was senseless to try calling again. She and Martin Beck were now well on their way.

When they turned down Route 4 heading east, the traffic had gotten heavier for some reason. It was still mid-afternoon, not yet time for the early shift from the government to begin their homeward commute but greater D.C. traffic was always like playing roulette. She'd been so thankful that Paul's house...that their town house was near the metro. Like Paul, she preferred to leave the driving to that nebulous 'us' of public transportation and had considered the half mile or so hike to the station a bit of needed exercise. At worse, with inclement weather, she could always hop a bus which stopped less than a block away from their place.

She continued staring out the window, her thoughts rushing. For Paul to have changed his mind and want her to join him must mean that he was under even greater stress. Stress, she had finally concluded, was what was causing the strange blackouts and she worried about what her husband would be like when they got to Beck's country place. If Paul had gotten this meeting with his boss muddled when it was so important, he must be deteriorating mentally. Would he even recognize them or would he have retreated back into his strange, lonely persona? If so, what would she tell the officious Mr. Beck and how would he react?

Paul was clearly terrified at the prospect of long term analyses or worse yet being hospitalized, and she couldn't blame him. The mention of hypnosis further troubled him for fear of what might be revealed. He really didn't want to know if his father was a murderer, Pat realized, and she had been wondering if she too would have preferred to have

remained in limbo in a similar situation. A similar situation—
there was no way that Donald Strom could ever have done
something like that! Yet to Paul, the thought that his father
was a murderer was equally abhorrent and clearly the reason
he'd fought treatment, preferring the mental anguish of
uncertainty to definitive knowledge of his father's guilt. But
what a cost that had been. Yet, at the same time, something
had to be done about these strange episodes. They'd both
hoped once he'd begun relating his past to her that those
would stop but this behavior today, as related by Beck, was
entirely out of character.

Of course they were only talking about a short time
frame here—simply a week since the twenty-four hours of
self-interrogation and confession, which was how Paul
referred to the traumatic night and day during which he'd
bared his family history. Still, it had been over two months
between the first time he had retreated into that lost past and
the second episode now just the week before. Moreover, he
had mentioned some momentary lapses of memory, hadn't
he? How often were those and did he even realize when they
were happening, which could mean there were more than
the two major ones. Then also, there was still the troubling
question of where he'd gone and what he'd done. Though,
thank God, apparently nothing illegal. No, the police had
never arrived nor called during her fretful waits.

Shortly after crossing the deep, dark Patuxent River,
they turned off the main highway and started heading
southeast towards the Chesapeake. It had been some time
since Pat had been in the area, in spite of her remarks to the
obtrusive Mr. Beck, but she saw that development continued
to encroach on what had been rural lands. Surveyors' flags
and tattered cloth strips, now hanging wet and sodden,
appeared at regular intervals. Worse, there were barren,
ravished spaces with stacks of fallen trees showing land
being made ready for more construction.

The wet, grey weather intensified the feeling of
desolation. Rainy autumn days always depressed Pat in
contrast to the almost euphoria she felt when the leaves first

began to turn. She remembered as a child kicking at the gathered piles of fallen leaves as she walked home from school, pretending she was seeing treasure hoards of copper and gold. And once when one of her friends told her she was moving to a Pacific island, Pat had shaken her head in dismay. To visit perhaps, but miss the seasons? Never. Yet now as she stared out at the gloomy scenery, she wondered if she'd been wrong. Would Paul and she be happier on one of his beloved tropical isles? Should they have run off to Mr. Cruz's Guam?

This should have been a happy day and now all she could think of was that sooner or later, from Boston to Norfolk, all these lovely rural lands would be a component of one giant urban sprawl. Would there be any green left for her grandchildren, she mused? Had GG wondered the same as she watched Minnesota's agrarian population gradually urbanize and farms like hers and the Gramps' become outmoded? But farms killed trees too although at least there remained space and natural growth not rows of cement houses sprouting between asphalt strips, fertilized by gas-combustion engines hastily speeding by.

Beck made another turn and they started bouncing down a narrow, twisting country road, the asphalt soon changing to gravel. What a bizarre place to have a meeting and yet considering the mental anguish Paul had been feeling, perhaps the return to some spot where he had once had happy childhood experiences was the correct selection. Odd, Pat never would have thought that Wesley Beck could have such sensitivity but then just because she was ill at ease around the man didn't mean that he wasn't considerate.

He'd been an extravagantly gracious host the first time they'd gone to dinner at his Bethesda home. Cocktails and hors d'oeuvres, six courses, three kinds of wine, followed by coffee and liquors, all flawlessly served by his houseman. Certainly, aside from Paul's lavish open house and the unsettling Valentine party when she'd first been introduced to this man as well as Marauding Miranda, she'd never encountered such opulent hospitality.

Halfway through Beck's sumptuous dinner party, she and Paul had eyed one another and becoming the designated driver, she'd ended up putting her hand over her wine glasses—a faux pas as she had later read in Miss Manners and probably earning the first demerit in Wesley Beck's tally book. Maybe Paul was right, partners in firms like Beck and Stringfellow did live high on the hog to quote Grandpa Strom. So why the hell couldn't the meeting have taken place at the Bethesda manse—back in civilization rather than this godforsaken area. So much for her worries about urbanization. How antsy she was. Ordinarily she enjoyed being in the country, but not today.

It had to be that the man unnerved her, but again she chided herself. It was Paul too and everything that had happened. Moreover, Paul respected him and wanted to work for Beck the lawyer, not just because the firm was also his father's. Beck had been fair and generous to them both. Heavens, he had to have had input on the wedding gift— solid silver in this day and age, which showed exquisite taste much less extreme generosity. And, certainly Wesley Beck always seemed to say the right things. It was just the way he said them. But damn it all, he was Paul's godfather and his parents' friend and he was making an effort to be kind and supportive. Be fair, Pat reproached herself.

Turning up a dirt lane—this scarcely wider than a wrinkle, they made their way slowly past strands of pines, today ominous against the darkening grey sky with even more rain imminent. At this point, all the trees looked foreboding and intensified Pat's feeling of gloom and complete isolation. Yet here and there she saw a mailbox so someone must live near—probably in weekend retreats for affluent folk from D.C. or Baltimore. Still, she'd hate to be out on this road after dark and hoped that Paul and Beck would say whatever had to be said and get it over with so she and Paul could then drive back home, to their own little den.

Finally they arrived at a clearing where a little stucco country bungalow, dating perhaps to the early 1930s, stood. In some ways, it was like a smaller version of her family home although far from welcoming, but that again had to be her mood. Beyond she could see the embankment of a stream and hear the water, no doubt rushing to the bay. Paul's Miata was parked by the entrance to a screened porch—a jaunty touch of red against the otherwise bleak background.

"Good," murmured Beck as he opened the car door, "he had no problem finding the place." Then Beck came around the car and helped her out. To her surprise though, he didn't release his hold on her arm and was escorting her into the house practically by force. Further, the servant he had mentioned or at least implied wasn't at the door to greet them. In fact, aside from Paul, it looked as though no one else were there.

When they entered the foyer, Pat saw that the main floor of the house had been remodeled. Part of a wall had been knocked out resulting in one large room with a kitchen alcove and bar to one side. The bedrooms like those at home, she supposed, were on the second floor and she was willing to bet there was a basement unless they were too close to the water. Across the main floor expanse were sliding glass doors disclosing the view of a small river and the trees across, thus giving the sensation of being part of the natural setting. There was a large deck or balcony running parallel to the room overlooking the water. All the modifications had to have cost a small fortune, she reflected, but then as senior partner, the man probably took in millions considering how much Paul, as a lowly first year associate, was earning.

One of the doors leading onto that structure was open, in spite of the damp and chill, and Paul was outside, hunched over the balcony railing, staring down at the nearby stream, which appeared to be fast moving since Pat had heard it from the moment she had gotten out of the car. This no doubt was a manifestation of the unusually heavy rains they'd had in the last few days. The same rains that had contributed to her depression. Snow, that was one thing, but continuous rain always dampened her spirits as her father liked to quip. Said spirits though were low enough with her worries about Paul and his mental state.

Her husband turned, hearing them enter the house, and looked surprised. "Pat?" he said in a puzzled tone as he stepped into the room. "What are you doing here?"

Had he forgotten he wanted her there? Worried, Pat started to walk over to assure him when suddenly Beck's hand tightened its hold on her arm so she was unable to cross the room.

"I see you had no problem finding the cottage, Paul. Why don't you just take a chair over there. Pat will sit with me," stated the man bluntly.

Paul's eyes widened and suddenly Pat realized that Wesley Beck was holding a small gun in his other hand. "Sit here on the couch with me, dear child," the man ordered, his words patently false as he literally shoved her down.

"What the hell?" Paul stood tensely, indecisive as to what to do, but clearly furious.

"I told you to take that chair by the balcony. It would be a shame if your little Miss Pixie were hurt." Both looked at him shocked. "And you, my dear, don't want your Boytoy harmed, do you?"

"You bastard," snarled Paul vehemently, "you've been listening to my calls."

"Such touching ones too," Beck remarked condescendingly, a smirk making his ordinarily rotund face smug and even more unappealing. Porcine, Pat decided, although she liked pigs. Turning his head slightly to Pat, Beck confided in his unctuous tone, "He obviously adores you, my dear. And I agree, you certainly are a cute little girl—not the beauty his mother was, but definitely charming. The elfin analogy was most appropriate, but Boytoy?"

"You wouldn't understand," articulated Pat coldly, not sure that she did either. What was happening? Was the man insane or just afraid of Paul, knowing the family history.

"What, was my office bugged or something?" Paul asked angrily. His face was flushed and she could see him tightening his hands into fists, his body rigid. Pat was afraid he'd try to come and get the gun. She stared frantically at him, shaking her head slightly, hoping he knew what she was thinking. Stay calm, she tried to communicate with her anxious eyes and drawn countenance.

"Oh goodness no, nothing that complicated," Beck continued smugly. "I had your phone extension wired onto mine with a special button that lit up when you were talking. I merely had to push it and you wouldn't even hear a click. Amazing what technology is like now. I even had a recorder added, again in my office of course, so I could listen randomly to see if I'd missed anything when I wasn't there. The same with your computer. Every time you used it, I was able to read what you were writing or check later. I had to get someone special in during a holiday late at night to have the work done so no one would know, but that was fine. I have acquaintances, shall we say, capable of that kind of technology. So once in a while I'd just pick the phone up when you were on the line to hear what you were doing. Sometimes it turned out you'd be having an intimate conversation with your lovely little wife. Charming, really charming. I quite enjoyed listening. You never revealed that part of your character in the office, but then you've always been so reticent and proper in your business dealings."

"You're not exactly the sort of person I'd share intimacy with much less joke," snarled Paul glowering.

"Too bad...neither did your father ultimately although I do have a sense of humor. But you were going to share something else with me, weren't you?" Beck asked mildly.

"I don't understand what's happening here," stated Pat, thinking the man's sense of humor probably consisted of pulling wings off flies or pouring gasoline on a cat and tossing a match. Right now she wished she had something to toss and she started casting her eyes surreptitiously around the room, which was stark and harsh in its furnishings just like her enforced captivity. Here was none of the opulence of the luxurious Bethesda residence, presenting a far different side of Wesley Beck's taste and character.

"Are you sure?" Beck asked, smiling to himself as

though enjoying some malicious joke.

"Please, Mr. Beck. Why are we here?" Pat asked in a small voice as calmly and ingratiatingly as possible. The perfect, dear child, she hoped.

"I told you. Paul used to visit here, isn't that right, Paul?"

Paul looked around, his eyes perplexed but with vague awareness. Slowly he answered, "Yes, I do know this place."

"Certainly you do," agreed Beck in his pseudo unctuous tone. "Your mother brought you out here once for a picnic. Your father was away and I'd told him I'd take you fishing. I think he thought I'd invited a whole party. I know your mother did."

"But there wasn't a party and we didn't fish, did we?" Paul asked, confused, his head turning back towards the view of the river.

"No, actually, I find that sport rather boring and never could understand your father's fascination. I let you go in a boat though."

"Oh Jesus," Paul gasped, his eyes widening and his expression turning sickly. "I do remember. There was a rope attached to the boat. You let me get in and then you started releasing the rope so the boat would drift out into the current before you'd jerk it partially back and you were laughing then. It was a day like today—fast running water. I was all alone and you told my mother, you told her you were going to let go."

Beck smiled. "You do have a good memory."

"I was terrified. I couldn't swim yet and I was screaming my head off and she was pleading with you. She said she'd do anything."

"Dear Claire and she did."

"You bastard. I do remember. You finally pulled me back to shore and we went up to the house where you pushed me into one of the bedrooms upstairs 'to watch TV' and locked the door. I started screaming again and beating on the door and you were laughing and then I heard *Maman* screaming. After, she told me it had been a bad trick you'd played and not to tell Dad or anyone else but she was crying. She made me promise. I didn't know then what you were doing but I do now. You took her and raped her, didn't you?"

Beck smiled. "She said she'd do anything. Besides we'd been lovers before."

"I don't believe you."

"Oh but we were. I met her before your father did. She was supposed to be mine, but then when she met him, she told me it was over. I don't know if she ever told him that she'd been with me. I promised her I wouldn't. That was me, always loyal. God, how I hated your father."

"I still don't believe you, you SOB! He thought you were his friend."

"Well, I needed him and that fool Stringfellow. Poor silly, stupid Stringfellow, he had the money."

"He wasn't a fool," retorted Paul. "He was just a nice guy who didn't believe in going for the throat. My grandfather really liked him."

"I rest my case. But, he'd do anything your father wanted. Most people would. Everything came so easy to Paul—school, women, work."

"You were supposed to be brilliant at school and work too. My grandfather described you as being ferociously competitive."

"Of course, I had to make an effort. Your father didn't and I hated him and your grandfather. So patronizing."

"I don't believe that."

"That your grandfather could be patronizing? I assure you that under that gracious southern gentleman exterior, he was as calculating as any successful politician. For that I could have almost admired him, but he never liked me."

"He never said that," Paul stated coolly.

"He didn't have to, I knew."

"But why are we here now?" Pat broke in. "I still don't understand."

"Paul has been inquisitive again, my dear. It was a failure when he was a child and now, alas, it appears to be so once more. He started coming into the office at odd hours, rummaging through old files. Someone saw him a couple of months ago and mentioned it to me so I checked with the guard downstairs to see who had signed in." From the startled expression on Paul's face, Pat realized that this was a revelation and in part answered the question of some of his missing time. The man looked at her sadly. "Such a shame about all this. You're such a pretty young woman and apparently so smart, but then Claire was too."

She looked at him in horror, suddenly realizing why this was happening. "It was you...not his father. You were the man and he saw you. That's what he couldn't remember." Paul was staring at them both, speechless. His eyes had a vacant, dazed expression now as if he was trying to recall the traumatic event.

"Yes, I'm afraid you're correct. I'd hoped he never would but I had to be sure. Such a shame really," Beck commented with manifest insincerity. "Actually, I've liked Paul much better since he's grown up...so much more than his father or arrogant grandfather." Beck spoke as if Paul was no longer in the room and as Pat glanced over to her husband, she wondered if he were right. Paul still had that shocked, lost look.

"But they were your friends. Paul told me. You were his godfather even." She glanced back across the room and saw that Paul's face was now stark white, his fists had re-clinched and he was teetering slightly, back and forth in the chair. He looked like he wanted to cry again or start to hyperventilate, the vulnerable little boy look he'd had when he'd told her the whole tragic story. Pat started to rise, feeling compelled to go to comfort him, but was tugged back down on the sofa forcefully.

"I should have been his father," Beck snapped, his hand tightening painfully on her arm.

"Oh..." she couldn't think of anything else to say.

At that, Paul looked up, once more among them mentally. "I'd rather be dead," he snarled.

"Well," said Beck, "you might have your wish. In

fact..." he stopped abruptly.

Pat asked hesitantly, she couldn't help it. "What are you going to do?" She was terrified she already knew the answer and she could feel the bile rising from her stomach. Even if Beck were to release his hold on her arm, could she run fast enough? Faster than a speeding bullet? Somehow she doubted it.

"Do? Be distressed that young Paul was so unstable. That he killed his young wife and then committed suicide. There must have been something hereditary after all. Such a loss—another brilliant mind. Actually two since the young wife had also been a rising young professional. But...instability is so common nowadays and of course he had his father as a role model at such a tender age." Beck spoke as though he were narrating a case study, a deed done, one of little importance save for its academic interest.

"You're crazy," accused Pat as she listened to Beck's callously indifferent account and knowing that the man truly was impervious as well as remorseless. Paul just stared coldly, seemingly back in control but she could see how unsettled he still was. If he were to move, could they stop Beck, but then Beck might just shoot him too! Their options didn't appear the greatest.

"Not really," the older man answered frowning. "I just don't like the Wolfes—any of the family, the whole pack so to speak," he laughed, amused at his own humor. The only one present who was.

"But why Paul, why me? What have we ever done to you?" Pat was pleading now, scared silly as her father would say. This couldn't be happening. She was only thirty and Paul not even that. Why she hadn't even finished his birthday sweater! How stupid, as if an unfinished sweater would protect them—like one of those nettle cloaks the fairy tale princess made for her twelve swan brothers. Hell, his mother, along with her poor little baby, had died long ago, years before reaching thirty, and at the hands of this mad, evil man. Pat felt frenzied, her stomach churning and contracting in fear. This was a mistake or a bad, bad dream.

It had to be!

"I told you. Your husband was too inquisitive, my dear, and he had begun to remember. When he asked me for this interview, I knew it was only a matter of time. That's one reason I always kept tabs on you over the years, Paul. I bet you didn't know that."

"No," was the hissed response. Paul was staring at him with utter hatred, his eyes a turbulent green, a tidal wave of rage ready to engulf.

"Oh, yes, I even corresponded with your grandfather."

"My grandfather? He never said anything."

"Trust me and you had two grandfathers."

"Louis Martin. I might have known," Paul rasped harshly, his voice now completely devoid of its usual soft speech pattern. "You two are birds of a feather. Vultures, pure and simple."

"Vultures don't kill," Beck stated mildly. "But I'll take it as a compliment that you've grouped us together. The firm—or at least I—have done some especially sensitive work for Martin Internationale. I gather you didn't know that either." The man's superior smugness was nasty to behold.

"Hell, no. I never would have applied for the job if I had," retorted Paul frigidly.

"I didn't think you would. No, your Grandfather Martin found me most helpful and sympathetic when the tragedy took place. He didn't forget later."

"You fucking bastard. You messed up my father's defense and appeals too, didn't you? Grandpa Wolfe—my real grandfather, you shit, always wondered about that. He said you could be so damn combative on legal issues, but that you just didn't seem to have the flair for the criminal aspect."

"Oh, I had the flair, but I didn't have to jeopardize the case," replied Beck. "There was so much circumstantial evidence and besides, I was just a friend of the defense at the actual trial."

"Evidence provided by you?"

"Let's say your Grandfather Martin believed in revenge and rendered the money to see that certain things were done, evidence produced or perhaps not, tips slipped anonymously to the prosecution."

"And you helped see that he knew which. What was it: suppressed information, false witnesses, bribed jurors?"

"Paul, I was devastated by what happened. Louis Martin knew my feelings about your mother—a rejected suitor who had remained a loyal friend. Of course he'd listen to my advice."

"And meanwhile you were part of my father's defense team for the appeals too. You miserable excuse for a human being. I'm surprised you didn't plant the knife on his person."

"Actually, I thought of it but I'm afraid I panicked a little that day. I'd come for reconciliation. I'd even made sure your father wasn't going to be there."

"You knew about the Baltimore trip?"

"That was never a secret, Paul. It was the meeting's cancellation, remember? I'd gone into your father's office when the phone rang. The caller assumed I was Paul and I never bothered to enlighten her or tell him."

"Snoop—even then, you bastard, and after, you set him up besides!"

"Oh don't be a little boy, Paul. Of course I wanted to know what your father was doing. We were partners after all. The rest was just circumstance."

"Circumstance! Some partner."

"In any case, it gave me an opportunity to be alone with your mother when your father wasn't there. She wouldn't see me alone any more, but I thought it would give us a chance to have a reconciliation."

"Well what did you expect? Be alone with a rapist?"

"Rape, don't be so crude. I loved Claire. Naturally I wanted to make love to her."

"Love," derided Paul, his eyes narrowing. "You don't know the meaning of the word."

"Paul, Paul, you're harsh the way she'd become. She

made me quite angry, taunted me even. And the noise. I
hadn't realized you were home. It was quite a shock to see
you in her bedroom door."

"Oh sweet Jesus, I did go to her!" cried Paul in anguish.
"Oh shit, I am remembering. I slipped around the corner
and there you were with her." His countenance was grey and
Pat could almost see the scene unfolding before his eyes.

"Indeed, and wasn't that a surprise. You were supposed
to be at your nursery school or kindergarten or whatever. I
never expected to see you there and of course your father
was off on his wild goose chase to Baltimore."

"Which you had arranged."

"Naturally. No one but your mother was supposed to
be there. She rarely went out any more and I knew after a big
reception like the Bastille Day celebration, she'd be home
resting. I thought it would be my one chance to reason with
her but she was so...so French!"

"You still wanted her to go away with you?" The
disbelief in Paul's voice was chilling.

"I'd come to beg her to go away with me," Beck
laughed harshly, for once showing emotion. "To beg! And
she laughed and taunted me and even screamed at me. But it
was my baby. I wanted both of them. I was even willing to
take you."

"You wouldn't have known what to do with a baby,
much less me!" snarled Paul. "If there had been the slightest
chance it was yours, there is no way you could have done
something like that."

"I wasn't going to let your father bring it up. If Claire
wasn't going to be with me the way she was supposed to be,
he couldn't keep her or the child either."

"You really were...are insane."

"Oh no, Paul, not I. Your father and now you. I think I
knew all along this was going to happen. I knew the second I
saw you standing in that doorway."

"You had the knife and you were..." Paul stopped, not
wanting to complete his sentence, not wanting to relive the
horrible event. But Pat could see from his face that he truly

was there again, a little boy watching the dreaded scene, hearing his mother's screams, first of anger, than terror, and then agony. "Jesus, one bit of the circumstantial evidence was the fact that a neighbor kept hearing her scream Paul, but of course I was the Paul she was screaming at. *Paul chez toi, chez toi*, hide in your little house. That was what she was trying to tell me."

Paul shook his head, his eyes misting as he recalled himself as the small terrified boy. *Maman* was screaming and how he'd gotten out of bed. He'd forgotten to put on his slippers the way she told him so he was afraid she might be angry but she was making such ghastly sounds. He'd hurried down the hallway to her room and then carefully peeked in and there she was with Uncle Wesley and the two were fighting. She was saying terrible things to Uncle Wesley, but it didn't seem to matter for he was smiling but it wasn't a nice smile. And then little Paul...the Paul he was remembering...realized that his beautiful mother was bleeding and Uncle Wesley had raised his arm and something was shining in his hand. And then he struck *Maman* and she let out a terrible shriek and Paul realized that Uncle Wesley was cutting her with a knife. People were supposed to be careful with knifes. That's what Daddy had told him, but Uncle Wesley was poking holes in his mother and she was screaming and screaming and he'd wanted to cover his eyes but he'd started screaming too and had started towards her until she saw him and yelled for him to run and hide and be as quiet as a little mouse.

Uncle Wesley had seen him too and the smile on his face had become truly terrible and he—little Paul—didn't know what to do. He wanted to help *Maman* but she was holding on to Uncle Wesley and trying to keep him from catching that little Paul so he'd run as fast as he could. When he got into his room, he slid into his little house and had hunched down and put his hands over his mouth so he wouldn't scream too, but he wanted to so much and he was so afraid.

Maman was hurt. Uncle Wesley was hurting her and

maybe the new baby and then maybe him and he didn't know what to do. He just sat there, shutting his eyes as tight as he could but he still saw *Maman* bleeding and he knew he was crying but he couldn't make any noise. *Maman* had told him not to so there he sat and when he heard Uncle Wesley stop by his door, he remained huddled and paralyzed, afraid Uncle Wesley would come in and find him. Then there was pounding and shouting from outside and he heard Uncle Wesley's footsteps running down the stairs.

After he waited for his mother. He heard other noises and voices but not *Maman*, so he waited quietly as she'd told him to and kept his eyes shut and his hands over his mouth and he cried and cried silently, screaming inside, until at last his father came so everything would be all right. But it wasn't.

Finally Paul managed to gasp out, "You stabbed and kept slashing her and there was blood all over and she was screaming and trying to cover her stomach, to protect the baby. Why, why the fuck didn't you kill me too?"

"You ran out of the room. I was going to catch you, but your mother had seen you and was still hanging on to me and calling to you. When I got loose, I couldn't find you. You were hiding in your room in that damn secret house your father had made for you—the one they made such an issue of at the trial. Such a clever little construction that I didn't understand what it was. The lid was open and I saw the toys and never realized there was a crawl space underneath. Then too you remained such a quiet little boy, I wouldn't have believed it of a four-year old."

Beck shook his head and then said half admiringly, "Really, Paul, you did surprise me. But before I could search further for you, there was someone beating on the front door. I had to run out the back. I worried about that a lot, Paul, about what you would tell them but you were apparently practically catatonic when they found you. Then the Wolfes took you to Alabama and after that Martin got you. I figured since you hadn't remembered by then, you probably wouldn't. Besides, Martin was so obsessed by his belief that your father had committed the murder. He never would have believed you. He was kind enough to keep me posted about your progress though. If there'd been the slightest hint of your recovering your memory, I would have done something."

"I'm sure," said Paul sarcastically, "an accident? Oh shit, you killed him too, didn't you?"

"Him?"

"My father!"

"I, Paul? Now really."

"It wasn't enough for you to mess up his defense, you bastard. Why the hell did you have to have him killed?"

"He read and reread everything from the trial over and over. He had lots of time, of course. Jailhouse lawyers, you know," laughed Beck at his little joke—a small and totally cheerless laugh. "Actually, Big Paul discovered something...a small slip, actually. He was beginning to start another appeal and he noticed something he hadn't before. And then he asked to see me and began to produce questions. I realized he hadn't discussed his suspicions with your grandfather yet. He was such a fool. He believed in giving someone the chance to defend himself before making accusations. Well that of course was an error."

"Of course," agreed Paul sourly but the poignancy in his face made Pat want to burst into tears. Yes, Paul's father would have been fair and open-minded, just as Paul had remembered, and those very qualities had killed him.

"I knew you'd agree. For an intelligent man, your father was basically naive. He wanted to believe in the innocence of others, in honor and inconsequential things like that—especially friendship. You now, you're much more realistic than he ever was—even a touch cynical I've noticed at work although you're usually too polite or prudent to make that overly apparent."

"I had a different background."

"Well, yes, but those are such useful attributes. If you hadn't been his son, I think I might have been able to make use of you on some of my, shall we say, private ventures."

"Never, you bastard," snapped Paul. "Was that the real reason this all happened? Not just your so-called love for my mother but because my father discovered some of your shaky deals, swindles and skimming like the Foshée estate?"

"Oh my indeed, Paul. You have been a busy little boy; I never realized. I thought you were just looking for information about your parents. You're much more clever than your father. I have been underestimating you. But yes, I'm afraid so; there was that also. If he'd somehow managed to be released, that might have come out too. I really would have preferred that he'd stay in jail so he could relive the whole event and have his hopes of release dashed time after time."

"God, what a sadist," snarled Paul while Pat shivered in agreement.

"No, just a realist so I did have to arrange a little accident, even if it curtailed my pleasure."

"So you really did have him killed. Was Louis part of that too?"

"Only peripherally. He supplied the cash, but I never gave him all the details and possibly he never actually realized, not that I think it would have mattered."

"Yah," said Paul, "only if there could have been some connection."

"Your grandfather is a realist too."

"And I walked right back into your web," growled Paul bitterly.

"Ah yes, and that's when I began to worry. At first I assumed that you just wanted to be a continuation of your father's efforts—the second generation so to speak, but even there too, I'm the one who has brought the firm forward to its preeminent position," Beck asserted proudly, his voice becoming strident. "We're constantly sought out by ambitious young lawyers. We never have to recruit, never! Still I might have made an exception in your case if you hadn't come to us. If it's any satisfaction, you would have made the grade even if I hadn't wanted to keep tabs on you. Your work, Paul, really is quite excellent."

"You expect me to thank you, you smug SOB," asked Paul coldly. "Modest, aren't you."

"No, just pragmatic. As you pointed out, I am a very good lawyer. That was one reason your father wanted to work with me. We both were good. And, it's apparent that you have the talent too. You're probably one of the best young men we've hired." Paul just stared, his lips curled in distaste as though he'd bitten into something rotten. "What? No thanks either for such a nice compliment?" Beck asked with a sardonic smile.

"What do you think?" Paul countered acidly.

"Well, you are good. This way I've had your capable services and I could observe you. I was fairly certain you had no intention of telling me who you were since you hadn't already and that made our relationship easier. Of course I didn't know what to do when it came time to give you your bonuses or to consider making you a partner. The former, yes, but I really didn't want to reward you with the latter. You might say it was against my religion to advance a Wolfe," he laughed nastily.

"You shit," snapped Paul and Pat wasn't sure if he was referring to everything that had had happened or to the perfidy of a man who would use his talents but withhold well-earned rewards. Probably both, she decided and then further decided she was a little crazy too to be reasoning like that. Maybe she was less panicky now. Maybe there was some way she and Paul could get out of this mess. Beck was certainly taking his time, enjoying taunting Paul. She started to move slightly to her left, to get some distance, but the man's hand re-tightened on her arm, making her wince. His eyes though remained on Paul, who had started to half rise at Pat's obvious discomfort and she shook her head slightly.

"Don't Paul, and oh no, my dear Pixie," admonished Beck. "You stay here with me, safe by my side, until I have the opportunity to finish my conversation with your young husband." Safe, Pat screamed in her head, shuttering. "I've thought about this for months now—ever since your beloved Paul reappeared, and I intend to enjoy myself. And you too, Paul, I'm sure you're happy to finally sort all this out. Obviously it's been quite a strain on you trying to remember all these years or, is it to forget?" Beck inquired with interest. "If you hadn't remembered anything after being here a year or so, there was no need to have you around even if I would have lost your considerable abilities."

"Thanks," replied Paul dryly.

"Gratitude at last and you're entirely welcome." Pat couldn't believe the man hadn't caught Paul's deep sarcasm. Was he that egotistical? "And then too, people would have wondered why I let you go, which of course would have affected the rest of your career," added Beck with a slight smile. Paul's eyes narrowed again and Pat could see he was fighting to hold his tongue. "But you were starting to remember, weren't you? I noticed how you were changing at work—getting distracted. I thought at first it might have something to do with your precious little Miss Pixie here." Pat shivered again and Paul just stared stoically. "But it wasn't, alas. Then I discovered you had been spending extra time at the office without even billing the hours, which of course no eager young associate would do. When you asked for this interview, I knew you must be close to knowing."

"But I didn't—not about the murder," interrupted Paul agitatedly. "This didn't have to happen."

"Well, I'm sorry about that," Beck commented with that obvious insincerity. "Just the way I am sometimes about your father. Until he took your mother from me, I actually liked the man or at least saw his potential. Together I knew we could go places. We had a lot in common."

"You had nothing in common. He was decent, honest, genuine. You're despicable, you asshole."

"Names calling and such crude language. Really, Paul. Well, I think we've had enough of this."

"What now?" Paul asked. "And what about Pat, why the hell did you have to bring her here?"

"From those touching little phone calls, it was obvious that you'd tell her anything. I assumed you had. I'm sorry about her, I really am. I have no reason to dislike her but how else will I be able to justify killing you, Paul, if it isn't to try and stop your harming her."

"What do you mean?" Pat gasped, in a tiny squeak. She was becoming more and more scared now—something she hadn't thought possible since she'd been terrified ever since she'd first seen the gun.

"Why to stop his stabbing you. It's awful how seeing something like a savage killing as a child would later return and make your husband reenact the event."

"You're crazy," shouted Paul, rising from the chair, and Pat tried again to move further away from their captor. Paul was right, the man was crazy and he was going to kill them. She could tell that Paul's body had tensed up and that he was going to do something. What could she do to help, she wondered as she again looked frantically for a weapon, anything. Then her eyes fell to a bright green ashtray of chunky glass sitting on the coffee table slightly to her left. Sliding, ever so slightly, she tried to get within reach of the hefty chunk of glass.

As if knowing her intentions, Beck grabbed hold of her right arm, brutally yanking her once more to his side, but this time she fought back and kicked his leg. Just then Paul started to move across the room. Beck, his attention partially diverted, aimed his gun at Paul and Pat grabbed the ashtray. The gun went off, an explosive noise, and she wondered how something that small could make such a thundering sound.

CHAPTER 13

As if in slow motion, Pat saw Paul, an amazed look on his face, fall, no slam back, hitting the chair and then landing in a sprawl on the floor. She realized she was screaming as she brought down the piece of heavy glass. She had been trying to hit Beck's head, but he suddenly turned and instead she struck him on the shoulder. It was enough to make him loosen his grip upon her arm but still he tried to seize her. Jerking away, she leapt to her feet, stumbling past the coffee table.

"Paul, Paul," she was half wailing, half moaning as she lurched towards her husband. He was lying there so still, so awkwardly. No one lies like that, she thought, he's dead. She bent to touch him when from the corner of her eye, she saw Beck, recovered, and getting up to come after her. Worse yet, he was blocking her exit to the bungalow door. Screaming again, she ran out the open glass doors onto the balcony, hoping she could escape from the man. Vicious, dangerous Beck, a Beck now holding a knife, was in close pursuit but the wet leaves caused him to slip and slide.

Somehow avoiding this, Pat dashed to the balcony's exterior edge where she looked down and saw to her horror that there was a drop of at least thirty feet. Oh shit, but what option did she have? Beck was getting closer, but for some reason, not shooting. Ah, she suddenly realized with horror, the gun for Paul and the knife for her! As fast as she could, she scrambled over the top railing of the protective enclosing, still shrieking wildly, "Paul, Paul!" But Paul couldn't save her. He was dead. "Help me. Someone help me!" She couldn't die. Not now, especially not now.

Pat balanced perilously on the balcony's exterior edge, on inches mere inches, her feet between the balusters and her hands tightly gripping the handrail. I'll work my way down, she thought, and then drop. That should make it a shorter fall but she was petrified. She hadn't been kidding when she'd told Paul she always hated heights. Even fully suspended, she'd still be plunging at least twenty feet and no doubt breaking bones and probably worse. And then what chance would she have? For that matter what chance did she have now? Beck had reached the balcony edge and stopped, a nasty smile on that nasty, smug, rounded pig-face, distastefully Orwellian. He stood quietly a moment watching her, clearly amused by her predicament. "Paul," she sobbed broken hearted, "oh, Paul."

"He can't help, my dear," the older man said in a quiet voice, which would have almost been soothing if the undertone weren't so sinister. "Why don't you stop now? I'm just going to hurt you more if you don't. Stop now and it will be easy, I promise. The slashing will be after you're dead. I'm not a sadist, dear child."

Pat shuttered. "Like hell you're not. Damn you, you old bastard, no! Oh, Paul," she wailed as she rapidly slide down until only her hands grasped the lower part of two of the balcony balusters. Her body was now hanging perilously and she knew she had to make the decision as to whether she'd jump or not. If only she were directly over the water, rushing current be damned. Beck had moved closer. Still smiling, he was looking down and regarding her obviously with amused interest as though she were some poor insect, trapped but still struggling in a spider's web—the same web that had ensnared and destroyed Paul. The man had pulled off flies wings. At this point Pat knew that for a fact.

"No place else to go, is there, my dear," Beck said softly, almost lovingly.

"My dear up yours!" she yelled back.

"Tut, tut, and I thought you were such a lady."

"And I thought you were a gentleman when I met you, you excrement, you!"

"You do have a mouth on you, don't you?"

"What do you expect, you miserable fuck?" Pat was now as furious as she was afraid and wished she had the heavy ashtray again. This time she wouldn't miss. She'd smash in the bastard's head gladly and maybe not stop there.

Lizzy Borden had had the right idea.

Beck continued in his reasonable, studied tone, almost as if he were giving a lecture or asking a question at a seminar. "What do you intend to do now? You're going to pulverize all those pretty little bones when you fall. You know that, don't you? You'll be crippled if you live, not that you're going to have to worry about that too long but just think about what it will feel like. Your body hitting the rocks down there, the bones fracturing, some probably protruding through your flesh. And then you'll have to lie there bleeding, waiting until I arrive and wondering, will it be in a few minutes or is he going to take his time? I think now probably the latter since you've been so discourteous."

Beck laughed suddenly, a wild, high pitched sound. "Dissing...disrespect...no wonder that seems to send young black men wild. I can really understand now. I don't like rudeness, young lady. That's something Claire discovered when I had to teach her a lesson too! And then when you fall, you'll try to drag yourself if you can, but to where? Visualize it, dear child, you're smart and no doubt imaginative. You'll think to yourself, is that the sound of him coming and then when I do, you'll wonder where I'll cut you, slash you, how many times, how long."

Pat listened in disbelief, a horrid death as punishment for discourtesy! Then she looked down again and, shuttering, prepared to take her chances when suddenly she heard a voice. Impossibly, it was Paul and she started sobbing at the sound. "Get away from her, you fucker." She could see him through the rails and Beck turned. Paul, blood on the side of his head and not overly steady, was standing in the doorway holding onto the frame.

As if to settle the matter, Beck bent over and suddenly slashed down at Pat's left arm and she let out a screech. It was as though she'd been burned, the sharp pain radiating up and down the lacerated limb while blood was spurting out. She felt herself weakening and her hand slip. She was afraid she couldn't hold on. The arm was throbbing and smarting and she was so afraid that Beck would stab again for then she knew, without doubt, that she'd fall all that distance to the rocky slope below and it would be just as he said. She's smash just like Humpty Dumpty with all the king's horses and all the king's men unable to put her back together again. Tears were streaming down her face and she was having difficulty breathing. She couldn't let go. Not now that Paul by some miracle was here.

Beck though had turned to face Paul, the bloody knife thrusting forth. Paul was trying to circle him, to get closer to Pat, but the man was beginning to make shrill, wailing sounds, inhuman and mad as he kept poking the blade at Paul, who'd jump back while the crazed Beck came closer and closer with his nasty weapon.

"Give it up, you bastard," Paul was shouting. Then suddenly Beck turned and raised the knife again to once more slash at Pat. She closed her eyes, trembling, waiting for the expected blow when there was another sound—that of a shot. Opening her eyes wide, she saw Beck lurching against the balcony and looking perplexed as blood started pouring from his chest. Feebly, he made one last effort to cut at her and just then Paul grabbed him from behind, pulling him away.

Still gripping the baluster with her uninjured hand, Pat stared below at the rocks and knew her hold was loosening. Nauseated physically, she also felt utter anguish. She was so close to salvation but she was slipping and just couldn't hold on any longer. Then she heard her husband's voice, calm and reassuring. "Hold on, Pix. Don't panic, sugar. Just another minute. Shut your eyes, that should help, and just reach one of your hands to me."

"I can't," she sobbed as she tried to bring up her injured arm but it wouldn't seem to work.

"Ok," Paul said quietly and she saw him through the balcony railings as he bent down and stretched a hand out, his strong grasp now tightening on her uninjured wrist. "Good," he sighed relieved. "Now listen to me. Try again to see if you can reach up your other hand too, but when you do, don't make any jerky movements. I've got you, understand. Just nice and easy."

She tried, she really did, but her left arm hurt so much. The weight of her body was straining and she felt so weak. She was gasping in a combination of pain and frustration now. "I can't, I can't."

"Ok, ok, darlin'. Don't worry. I'll come over the railing and get you then."

Suddenly Pat saw Beck, looming behind Paul. Covered with blood, he had somehow regained his feet and he was holding the knife again. "Paul," she shrieked and her husband turned just as the knife came slashing down. In horror, she shut her eyes, not wanting to see. Her precarious grasp was weakening rapidly. There was the sound of a struggle and then she heard her Paul again.

"It's ok, Pix. I'm all right."

She reopened her eyes and saw Beck lying on the balcony. The knife was nowhere in sight. "I'm slipping," she moaned piteously and once more Paul grabbed for her, catching her wrist just as her fingers loosened their shaky hold, and then tightening his grip. "Good girl, sweet girl. Now I'm going to pull you up as much as I can so you have your whole arm around this lower rail again, ok?"

"Ok," she murmured, but as he started to tug, she began to whimper. "It hurts, Paul, it hurts so much."

"I know it does, sugar, I'm so sorry. But you're going to have to support your own weight for a minute until I can get over the side and grab hold of you. Do you understand?" He looked down at her with concern and compassion. "Be brave, little darlin'. Be that tough little skater. I'm only going to let go of you for just seconds, I swear."

And suddenly he did. She looked up, terrified, to see him scrambling over the side of the balcony and sliding partially down. He had one of his long strong arms wrapped over the top of the railing and his feet caught to the edge while with the other arm he was again bracing her.

"Ok, I've got you, but you want to hold on with your good hand if you can." Pat groaned as she felt him pull her up. "Oh, Pix, I'm so sorry I'm hurting you. It'll just take a minute. Hang in there," he coaxed.

"What else can I do," she wailed weakly.

Paul laughed in sympathy, "Oh sugar." Slowly he began to haul her up, straightening himself as he did, keeping his feet and knees between the balusters. "You're almost there. Try to get your feet on the edge—no, don't kick, just do it slowly. Don't panic, Pix. I've got you, but we've just got to take it slow and easy."

Pat's eyes were tightly shut and she was biting her lip. All she wanted to do was to pass out but somehow, she controlled herself and gradually she felt him drawing her closer to the top. "Just a little farther, darlin'. Just pretend you're on that toboggan that was caught on the stream and I'm Lyle holding the ropes. We'll get you off the creek this time before the ice breaks."

"Funny," she murmured, trying to keep herself from throwing up.

"Right, funny. Fun like playing on the ice, right?"

"I'll kill you, Paul."

"No, no, just relax. Pretend we're home in bed."

"Pervert."

"Slow, darlin', we're almost there." And then Pat felt him pull her to him and to the balcony handrail. He positioned her leaning against it, her arms draped over. "Ok," he said, "I'm going over the top now and then I'll lift you over. Just hang on."

Apprehensively, she felt his body moving upward and then one of his legs press against her, pinning her against the side of the structure as he loosened his arm. Suddenly he was over the rail and bending back to grab her with both strong hands. Slowly, carefully he helped her over, trying not to punish her angry, aching arm. And then he had her clasped next to him and she was safe inside his sheltering embrace. "Good girl, little sugar, my good sweet girl," he whispered. "It's ok. You're safe now."

Pat was sobbing and shivering and her teeth were chattering. Then she heard another voice. "Better put this on her to stop the bleeding, mister, and get her inside as fast as you can. Find some towels or something."

A small, wiry man was standing on the balcony behind them. He was older, maybe in his late sixties, and dressed in heavy work clothes. In one hand was a rifle and in the other a large red bandanna which he was offering to Paul. "Heard the gun from my yard, called 911, and then came over to see what was happening. We're supposed to be posted down here but the damn kids still hunt and I was hoping to catch them. Then I heard the lady's screams."

"You're the one who shot Beck," stated Paul, who had been equally astonished at the unexpected but welcomed shot.

"Yup, saw the lady dangling and him brandishing the knife. Wasn't sure what was happening but he was the one with the knife so I figured I'd see if I still was a marksman."

"Thank God, you were," exhaled Paul.

"Is he still alive?" asked Pat shuttering.

"Good question," said their rescuer. "I'll check but you better attend to that bleeding. She looks like she's going into shock."

"Oh shit yes," agreed Paul, hoisting Pat up and carrying her into the bungalow.

"Your Armani," moaned Pat, "we'll never get the blood out."

"Oh, darlin', only you," said Paul as he gently laid her down on the very couch where Beck had made her sit, his terrified captive. Running over to the small kitchen, he started pulling open drawers and in a minute was back next to her with several hand towels. Forcefully but as tenderly as possible, he worked to stop the flow of blood.

"Bastard's still alive," called their rescuer from the porch. "I'll stay out here with him. The sheriff and someone should be here in a few minutes."

"You're dead," Pat was crying uncontrollably now. "You're dead and I ran away. Oh God, I ran away because I thought you were dead. I left you!"

"No, I'm not...dead. I thought I was going to be, and I would have run too, sugar," Paul soothed.

"No, no, you wouldn't. You didn't even as a little boy." He looked at her strangely and then nodded his head. "You were a hero then too, Paul." She looked back at him, but she was feeling disoriented. "What...how?"

As if in response, he reached into his breast pocket. From it he pulled a tarnished silver cigarette holder, dented, smashed.

"I thought you gave up smoking," she mumbled.

"Oh Pix," he laughed slightly. "No, it was my mother's. I recognized it immediately. It was here in the house and I found it while I was waiting for Beck to arrive. That's how I began to know. She'd had it the morning she was attacked. She'd usually pull it out after Dad left for work—a little secret, *très méchant*—naughty, she'd tell me. My father wanted her to stop smoking, even though they didn't know then how bad tobacco was during pregnancy. Hey, maybe that explains me," he quipped and Pat smiled faintly back.

"Anyhow, she'd still have one cigarette each morning— just one. She had tremendous will power according to Grandpa. When the case was missing, some of the police thought at first there might have been a thief after all but others believed it had just been mislaid since that was all that was gone. I remember now that Beck had given it to her, which is probably why he took it. Thank God, he did; it saved my life, but I hit and cut my head when I fell and was stunned for a minute or two."

Pat was sure she should be following what he was saying but she didn't seem to be thinking too straight. "Blood," she murmured, "blood, I'm getting it all over your expensive suit."

"You just said that, Pix. It's all right. I'll get a new one, darlin'." He was holding her arm tighter and had now pressed another towel over the first but she could see blood was soaking through that too and she realized she was shaking. Her stomach felt cramped and she was getting woozier.

"Sorry, but I had to run, he was going to kill us," she mumbled incoherently, wondering if she hadn't said that as well. She felt very tired now and wasn't sure if she was making any sense.

"Us?" Paul asked puzzled.

"The lines," she said, "test showed... two... lines. Hadn't paid attention last couple months... two lines, saw the doctor."

"I don't understand, darlin'." Paul clearly wasn't following what she was trying to tell him.

"Baby, the baby. Couldn't let him kill this baby too. Mysterious stranger...," and with that, she did what countless movie heroines on the late show have done and passed out.

Concerned but utterly bemused, Paul stared down at her. "Oh Pix...a baby," he whispered. He'd never believed he'd be a father. Leaning over he kissed her and then gently pressed his lips to her abdomen.

When Pat recovered consciousness, she was still lying on the couch in Beck's bungalow and for a moment she wondered if it were all a dream or worse yet it was going to happen all over again. Her left arm was neatly wrapped but still unneatly throbbing like mad and she felt hot and uncomfortable as well as nauseated. Paul was sitting by her, holding her other hand.

"What," she mumbled, her lips dry.

"The state trooper got the bleeding stopped and is talking to a doctor now to see what he can give you for pain. I told him you might be pregnant?" Paul's eyes were clear, lucid, the beautiful green eyes of the man she'd met almost a year before and they were also very puzzled.

She nodded, her teeth still chattering. "I am. With everything that was happening, I didn't realize at first and then somehow I couldn't discuss it with you."

"Oh, sugar. From what you were trying to tell me, I'm apparently the responsible party. When?"

"The first time you were the mysterious stranger."

"Oh... that's ok with you?"

She nodded her head. "And you? Are you angry?"

He turned her question, "Are you?"

"Oh, counselor," she smiled faintly. "No, it was on

my list."

"List?"

"Of things we forgot to talk about or you didn't want to."

"The latter I'm afraid. That's another reason I've avoided your hints about having a baby."

"I've been that obvious?" she asked surprised, and he nodded. "We didn't talk about it before we married. We didn't talk about much, did we? Was it because of your blackouts?"

"Yah and because I didn't know if my father had killed my mother."

"But he didn't."

"I think we've both figured that out now, the hard way," Paul commented wryly.

"Beck told or at least showed me another of the reasons when he came to pick me up. He thought your mother should have married him. He loved her, Paul. He met her first and your father took her away."

"Love," Paul choked out, "what a way to show it but all those years..."

"His career. Your father and grandfather were his ticket to success."

"Hell, he was good enough at what he did. He could have done it by himself. But you're right; that wasn't the only reason for today. I'm beginning to remember researching some of those records—ones not even pertaining to my dad's case. I think that was what had started me off on coming back to see all the old files. In one of the estate trusts I've been handling, there were some discrepancies I didn't understand. The rest of the missing time I think I spent in Georgetown, walking around my folk's old neighborhood though I'm not sure I could still face going by the house."

Pat nodded her head, that made sense, and then she murmured, "The Foshées."

"Right—it's a trust that was set up on behalf of a mentally ill son. The parents were French but they lived here and the boy—man now, the poor guy is in his forties, was born here. The family wanted him to stay in America if anything were to happen to them because of the special school he attended. Of course they never did expect that to happen, but their appointment in Samarra was a car wreck on the Beltway so Beck and Stringfellow assumed custody. I inherited the case from my predecessor, whose French was limited. It soon became apparent he obviously also wasn't as thorough as he should have been. Anyhow, probably because the family name was the same as my Swiss school, I became really interested, wondering if there was some connection. But when I started to review some of the information about the foreign assets, there were those irregularities. Then when I tried to get earlier material, I discovered it was locked away. Now that's not normal for an on-going trust and when I finally did get access to the older files, I had even more questions. For one thing, it was odd that it was Beck and not my father who'd originally handled setting up the trust and evaluating the French portion of the estate. I mean Beck didn't know much French whereas Dad did...better than just pillow talk," Paul added.

Then he placed his hand, warm and solid, on Pat's uninjured arm as much to assure himself as her. He knew he was more thankful than he could express that this tiny and perfect woman would be there to continue to share such intimacies when definitely he'd teach her that French. "I didn't want to think that there'd been some unethical hanky-panky by our firm, but..."

"But you did," mumbled Pat. "Why didn't he just get rid of those files?"

"Arrogance—just like *Grandpère's*. I doubt that he thought anyone would ever catch that, but at the same time, he was enough of a lawyer not to want to destroy his files. Maybe he thought if anyone ever did find out, which would no doubt be after he was dead and gone, that they'd just be full of admiration for his cleverness and audacity. Also, I realize now that Beck had wanted to work with Martin Internationale right from the start but that *Maman* was even more opposed than my father. It might have been more than jealousy or injured rage that made him kill her. We know now he was getting involved in all sorts of dubious things back then. It was only a matter of time until my father would find out. I'm afraid he was right though about Dad always being willing to give the benefit of the doubt as well as the fact that Stringfellow never would have had a clue."

A large man in a trooper's uniform was suddenly standing over Paul. "Just got off the phone with the doctor at the emergency ward. I'm going to give you a shot, Ma'am, and then we're going to drive you to the hospital so they can get those stitches in."

"I don't have to talk to anyone?" she asked feebly, afraid to face officialdom and the outside world.

"After," the big man said with a smile. "Besides, I don't think your lawyer here would let us now." Gently, the man reached over and took her right arm from Paul's protective grip. "Some alcohol first and just a prick. Won't hurt at all."

"I wouldn't know the difference," said Pat as she felt her left arm's continuous throb. "Wouldn't know," she sighed as slowly she sank back into thankful oblivion.

The next time she awoke, she was lying on a gurney in the emergency ward. Paul was still with her and she had new bandages wrapped around her arm—this time pristine and white. "Fifty stitches," he said, his face full of loving concern.

"Oh, dear. I'm going to look like a patch work doll. Will you still love me."

"As soon as you'll let me, *ma petite*," he whispered into her ear and she laughed weakly in spite of the dull, nagging ache. "Oh, sugar, I don't know what I would have done if I'd lost you. When I saw that bastard with the knife and then you bleeding... I knew I couldn't have lived without you, Pix. You're all I have."

"Don't Paul. It's over," she said putting her fingertips up to his lips. "I'm not your mother. We were luckier."

He nodded his head solemnly and gently grasped her free hand, so tiny, slender, and graceful. Then finally he said,

"Not quite all over. The county detectives have to talk to you, but I'm not going to let them until you feel up to it."

"I guess I do," she mumbled, still somewhat woozy.

"Are you sure? Don't worry. There was a witness." She looked puzzled. "The cavalry, remember? The rifle shot."

"Oh... I guess I forgot." God, maybe she'd eventually forget everything if she was lucky. Certainly Paul once had although maybe that wasn't so good after all.

"The neighbor who was outside chopping wood and heard the shot when Beck tried to dispatch me? He was so upset because the area's supposed to be posted that he went in to get his rifle and find out what was happening. Then he ended up hearing you screaming bloody murder."

"It was bloody murder."

"Well, you have good lungs. Anyhow, he came running around the house, saw you dangling, Beck with the knife, me jumping and sliding around on those damn leaves, and just did what a good retired military man is supposed to do and let Beck have it."

"Oh..."

"He was the one who came up and said he'd called 911. Do you remember now? You were fairly incoherent then. I'm not sure I was much better. You were bleeding all over me and worried about my suit much less trying to tell me about the baby. What, you're two months pregnant? Why didn't you tell me, Pix?"

"You know I'm irregular and of course you hadn't used a condom. Then I suddenly realized I'd missed another period but you'd been so strange again and I wasn't thinking and then I got one of those drugstore tests."

"Ah yes, red like the TV advertisements."

"No, this kind was blue—definitely blue so I called the doctor because I wanted to find out for certain before I told you."

"The day you were late coming home last week."

"Yes, I went to my gynecologist. She thought I was probably right but wanted to do some other tests. I'd just gotten the results over the phone when Beck showed up and then..." Pat started crying.

"Pix," Paul said concerned, suddenly afraid she didn't want the child after all.

"Oh, Boytoy, I thought he'd killed you and I thought he was going to kill me and I wouldn't have gotten to tell you about our baby and then it would have died." By now she was sobbing uncontrollably.

"Oh, little darlin', it didn't happen. I guess I was stunned when I hit the floor and cut my head after that bullet plowed into me but just bruises, honest. I'll probably also have a horrendous bruise from where the cigarette case pressed into me."

"Just as long as it's not humongous," she whispered through her tears.

"Never that, sweetheart, I promise," he smiled glad she could joke about the adjective she hated. "But, you're the one that got hurt and I'm so sorry. I would have killed the bastard myself if I could have. It was just like *déjà vu*..." he stopped a moment. "When I got my senses back, I heard you screaming and at first I thought it was my mother again and then I remembered. I mean I knew intellectually by then that he'd done it, but I remembered, really remembered. You were right. I had seen it, Pat, just as he said. I had gotten out of bed and seen him and he had the knife and it was covered with blood. And the bastard was cooing to her, 'Claire— bright and clear' and humming *Clair de lune*. My father used to whistle that all the time. But Beck was taunting her with the song although I was too little to realize it. I mean I couldn't understand why someone would be singing that when he was hurting her. My father did it to please her.

"Anyhow he'd looked at me and I guess I must have just gone into a catatonic stage or something after I ran off to hide. She told me to, you know. She was screaming to me in French to hide in the little toy house my dad had built for me. It was so cleverly constructed that she figured Beck wouldn't realize I was in it and she knew I loved to go in there anyhow and would feel safe. I was the Paul she was calling."

Paul stopped and stared vacantly, back in the past Pat was sure, to that long ago dreadful sight. Then, slowly, he began again. "After she stopped screaming, I heard him coming down the hall from her room. He had to pass by my room on the way to the next flight and the steps stopped. It's amazing he hadn't bothered to look in to see if I was there when he first went up to her. But this time, he looked into my room all right and just stood there. I don't know how long. I was afraid to reopen my eyes, but I knew he was there, waiting to find me. Then the steps started again and I heard him running down the next flight of stairs. There was a basement exit out back to the garden and alley, which is why apparently no one saw him. After I don't remember anything clearly until my father found me in my hiding place. I must have passed out or something. The police didn't even realize I was still in the house. I evidently never made a sound although vaguely I knew someone was there but *Maman* had told me to be quiet. Anyhow, it's all a haze until my father arrived back late that afternoon."

"Oh God," Pat moaned, feeling sick not from her injury but Paul's obvious pain and what he'd witnessed.

"They didn't arrest Dad right away, you know. We went to a hotel, I remember, and then back to the house maybe a week later after my grandmother arrived from Alabama to stay with me. There was press all over and they wouldn't let me return to school and my father was spending a lot of the time at the hospital the first few days because my brother was there. My mother hadn't died immediately although she never regained consciousness. I guess she was just a vegetable from all those injuries. That beautiful, vital woman, a mutilated..." He stopped, taking a deep breath, his face ashen. "They did a caesarian, some more cutting," he finally said bitterly, "but Jamie was too little and he'd been slashed too." Paul started crying again. "A little baby, not even born and Beck stabbed him. They performed some surgery on him but Jamie died within days and who knows what condition he'd have been in if he had lived. I think that hurt my father as much as losing my mother."

Paul looked at Pat. "I could never believe that Dad meant to kill the baby too when I was worried that he was the killer, even if it wasn't his child. That was something I was so afraid to learn. They weren't doing DNA testing then and the blood was my mother's type, A+ like mine so there really was no way of telling. When Dad got back from the hospital after Jamie died, he came into my room and held me and cried for what seemed hours. I was the only one left, he kept telling me. The only one left and how glad he was I'd been smart enough to hide in my little house."

"The little house, you keep talking about the little house."

"For my fourth birthday, Dad built me a small wooden box for my room about the size of a steamer trunk. To other people it probably looked like a big toy chest, but that was part of the charm since there really was a lid on top and a small storage area in the upper portion. I could open that and put some of my toys in it and it served as kind of an addition overhead porch when I was playing inside so I usually did keep it open. Then there was a slide attached to one side and a little ladder on the other when I wasn't using it as a house. I'd keep the lid shut then and climb all over, though thank God, I'd had it open that day so Beck thought it was full of toys. Anyhow, I absolutely adored it because I could do all sorts of things with it, but the best part was that the bottom section was actually a little crawl space or house for me. There were peep holes but they were concealed in the decoration—kind of like those portraits they use in horror films where someone is peering through a picture's eyes. It was open in the back so that I could get inside and pretend I was hiding from space invaders or wild animals or something."

"And so you did."

"Yah, I guess so, but it was a secret between my folks and me—my own private place. I remember asking my dad if the baby would know and he told me it was up to me to tell and that maybe when the baby was a big girl or boy like me, we—my dad and I—we could build him or her a secret place too."

"Is that why you liked to work on furniture so much?"

"Yes," Paul smiled gently. "That really was something my father did. I guess when he was in law school, he and my mother looked for second-hand stuff like we've been doing and he'd refinish it so it became a kind of hobby. He'd let me watch and 'help'—pound in a nail or something. I remember I had a little tool set. Real miniatures in wood and metal and he'd give me scrapes of wood for my projects and *Maman* would bring us ice tea and cheer us on."

Pat smiled, "Your ghastly iced tea?"

"No, you can blame that on Grandma and Alabama," Paul smiled back.

"Our furniture quests weren't too economical, were they?"

"No, there was no need. I was trying to recapture a memory and share it with you."

"Broken fingernails and all," she laughed feebly.

"Yes," he answered seriously.

Appraising his demeanor, she responded quietly, the levity gone, "Thank you."

"You're welcome. It was meant to be a compliment."

"I realized that."

"I know you did. You understand me well."

"Not as well as I should have."

"Oh Pat," he sighed. "How could you really. A background like mine is so out of the ordinary. No one normal would imagine it or want to have it. That's why I only tried to share the good parts. I never wanted you to have the bad and now you've had that too."

"For better or worse, Boytoy."

"Only better now, Pix, I swear. Why Beck didn't kill me right away today or then, I don't know."

"Because he was arrogant again today and wanted to learn what you knew as well as for us to know how smart he was."

"That and your being handy with that ashtray, Pix," Paul smiled, "but back then..."

"Because your parents had kept your secret about your hiding place and because you did obey your mother. Also, didn't Beck say that someone was pounding on the door just minutes after it happened?"

"Yah, I guess so and then there'd been the...the episode out here. I'd forgotten that too."

"But why did you come out here?"

"Beck called me at the office saying he felt our conversation was going to be so confidential that he thought it should take place here. I had no idea he was at our place and intending to bring you. I guess I was pretty dumb at that point. Maybe it was supposed to be a test, to see if I recognized his bungalow and remembered..."

"The rape," Pat stated bluntly and Paul nodded his head in dismal agreement. Hesitantly, she asked, "Was the baby really his?"

"I honestly don't know, Pix. I suppose it could have been. I told you my mother was despondent during the pregnancy. That was something that surprised my grandparents because she'd wanted another baby so much and had been disappointed that I was already four before she conceived again. I think now that she was worried that Beck might have been the father but didn't know what to do. Remember, *Maman* was practically raised by nuns after her mother died. She'd never have believed in abortion. I don't know if my parents even practiced birth control. Then too, she probably wouldn't have wanted to tell my father for fear of what he'd do." Pat bobbed her head in agreement, having seen Paul's reaction to her being harmed. "As close as they were, those were different times. I think she felt she had no options and just had to wait and see."

"How awful it had to have been for her, worrying about whether that awful man was the father." Paul looked at her soberly as both contemplated the months of anguish his mother must have suffered. Poor, poor woman, thought Pat, knowing the torment she would have felt if her own world were in such a quandary—uncertain whether to abort a baby that might really be the longed-for child of the man she loved.

"Yes," he agreed, "but tough like you. I guess the final straw was that she'd laughed at him when he insinuated it was his baby, much less the suggestion that she go off with him. He was crazy, sugar, crazy and he destroyed them all. Thank God, he didn't us."

Pat clasped his hand tightly, holding it to her face. "He tried."

"Yah, he certainly did."

Pat hesitated a moment and then asked, "Was it true? Had she had an affair with him before she met your father?"

"Oh Pix, we'll never know for sure, but I doubt it. It probably was just another of his crazed illusions. When *Maman* first got to Alabama, she stayed with my grandparents a couple of weeks before she married my dad. I know that could have been just for propriety back then but my Grandma told me so many things about her when I finally came home and more than once she said how sweet and innocent my mother had been—not at all what she expected from a Parisian, but much more like the girls she'd been brought up with. Grandma may have been a hellion in some ways but she was fairly conventional when it came to sexual morality."

Paul momentarily brushed his eye and Pat knew it had been a tear. "I can't tell you how wonderful those first months being back were, Pix. I didn't know Grandma was fighting cancer again and she wouldn't let Grandpa tell me. I was just so happy to have them, to be in America, to know I was going to Tulane like my dad that I guess I didn't realize she was so ill and she didn't want to spoil that time for me. She had so much she wanted to share about *Maman* and Dad and what I'd been like as a little boy. Losing them and me had been a prison sentence for her too. Grandpa told me after she died that she'd said talking to me was like having my parents back"

Pat nodded her head. "What's going to happen now? I mean after I talk to the detectives?"

"I get to take you home but you know it's not all over,"

Paul said sadly.

"A trial or something?"

"For him. It looks like he's going to live. But it's the press I'm thinking about."

"Oh, Paul," she sighed. "And what's going to happen to us—to you and me?"

"This is all going to come out. The whole story all over again." And that he knew from experience would be horrible but at least it would lead to the exoneration of his poor father. If only he could have remembered earlier, but *Grandpère* never would have revealed the truth so perhaps it was just as well and his grandparents had never considered hypnosis. And Pat…maybe he should send her back to Saint Paul, he thought. Maybe she'd be better off without him. She'd married Paul Martin, not Paul Wolfe. She didn't need this.

"Are they going to believe us? I mean about your parents."

"Undoubtedly. And then there's our witness to that bastard attacking you on the deck and I don't think they're going to believe I knocked myself out or slashed you with the knife. The knife, I'm fairly certain, is the same one Beck used on my mother—more of his arrogance like keeping the Foshée records. It was knocked off the balcony but they should find it. And, there's the fact we have the missing cigarette case too; that was in the trial transcript…and just everything. There's no way this will stay quiet. Beck's too prominent and my father's trial before was too big plus all the publicity about me when I disappeared and was taken to Europe, much less the legal battles after."

"Poor little rich boy."

"Right, but no longer little and not very rich."

"That's ok," she said, and then reached up to touch him on the cheek. "Your poor head."

"Not bad, honest, and hey, the danger's over. Now we just have to weather the trial. That," he sighed, "will be bad."

"But then everyone will know that your father wasn't guilty. That's what you always wanted, isn't it?"

"Yes, but it won't be the same for us after, Pix. Everyone is going to know who I am, what happened now, about us. Our privacy will be gone." He had to ask. "Do you want to stay with me? Maybe you should think about going home to Saint Paul. It's going to be a circus just the way it was before. That's one thing I never forgot."

Shocked, Pat looked at him. Home was supposed to be with him. "You don't want me?" she asked in a tiny voice, the hurt cutting.

"Oh God, Pix, of course I do!" Of course, more than anything! He hadn't meant to hurt her again—just the opposite. Why did he constantly say the wrong things at important times?

"That's ok then. We're going to be ok," she asserted stoutly. "Besides, now you know what really happened."

"Yes, that was what I needed."

"She must have loved you very much."

Paul had a sad little smile on his face, "You know that was something I never doubted. I'm not saying she wouldn't have kept fighting that bastard, but I'm sure she held on to him, was injured so much more grievously, just because she was trying to give me a chance." Pat nodded her head. It was something she could now well understand. A mother wolf protecting her cub, just as she would want to protect her own baby. Just as she had in her attempt to escape a mad man. Without knowledge of their child she was sure she would have stayed with Paul and then they all would have been dead.

"We can remain here after Beck's trial or we can go somewhere else if you'd rather. I don't imagine the firm will shut."

"To hell with the damn firm," she said, "but you don't mind?" Becoming a partner in his father's firm clearly had been a goal for years.

"Well, I have some ideas about that and what we should do. I'm going to look over all the incorporation papers for Beck, Stringfellow and Wolfe and find out where we—the family—stand legally. Who knows, maybe I'll end up owning the whole kit and caboodle by default. I guess maybe I'll even need a lawyer," he grinned. "But, no, I don't think I really want to continue there although I do want to investigate some things. Watching the shake-up should be fairly interesting, especially the dealings with *Grandpère* and what he did to my dad. I wouldn't be surprised if Louis was the one to bankroll Grandpa's opponent in his last senatorial race either. Beck probably was the conduit." Paul grimaced. "In any case, *Louis le Grand* caused me and the Wolfes years of anguish. They wanted me as much as I did them and he took me just for spite or otherwise he wouldn't have shipped me right off to school after the first few months. He hated me because I was stubborn and wouldn't do what he wanted and I hated him because he had taken me away. I really was a small, obnoxious kid by then, Pix. If I just couldn't stay where I wanted to, where I'd be loved, I was going to be as terrible as I could be and I guess I was."

"I don't believe that, Paul. You were just a fighter. The way you were today for me—the protector you told me you thought you should be the time I found your poem."

He looked at her lovingly and somewhat embarrassed although he knew he would have died if necessary to afford that protection. "Right, but what do you want, sweetheart?"

Pat shook her head, almost afraid to ask, afraid he might not want the baby.

Slowly Paul asked, "Do you want us to go back to Minnesota or would you consider Alabama? I really did live there and it was where I spent some of my happiest times. I've got enough money, regardless of what happens with the firm, that we can start somewhere else—maybe a small practice for me—lots of pro bono work." He placed his hand gently to her slightly enlarged midriff region. As tiny as she was, the whole world would know she was pregnant within weeks. Only his own self-absorption had kept him from realizing before now. "Some place nice to raise a family? A place where one could have a little home and yard, big enough to garden and plant a magnolia tree or two, close enough to a pond or creek to take a kid fishing?"

"Alabama sounds nice. I always wanted to go there," Pat sighed in relief, a small smile appearing on her face.

There was a responding one on his as he pulled her closer. "I didn't really answer your question about the baby back at the bungalow. Remember when you once told me you wished you had a beautiful way to tell me how much you loved me?"

"Like your poem," she said, indeed remembering.

"I told you you'd find a way and you did. A baby—that's true poetry. Epic in fact."

She huddled even closer. "I think we're collaborating on this one, counselor."

"Sounds good to me," he murmured, holding her tenderly, "but no junior, ok? Tom, Dick, Harry, I don't care, but no junior. We've had enough Pauls in the family."

Understanding, she agreed. It hadn't been a lucky name. "How about Donald then or what about Ann, Barbara or maybe even Claire?"

His face lit in appreciation. "Fine, any will do but no juniors. And Pix, later can we try for more than one verse?"

ABOUT THE AUTHOR

Glen Ellen Alderton is a former journalist, university instructor, and federal employee. She has lived and worked in Cuba, Jamaica, Greece and Jordan as well as the territory of Guam. Currently she resides in Montgomery, Alabama, where she is finishing her next novel, *Breakup!*